# Blue Co

MW00929552

## Martin L. Shoemaker

**Old-school science fiction
on the cutting edge!**

Published by Old Town Press

ISBN: 171705188X
ISBN-13: 978-1717051882

Published by Old Town Press, a sole proprietorship.
*http://OldTownPress.com*

# DEDICATION

To Mark "Buck" Buckowing, brother-in-law;
and to "Editor" Bill Emerson, brother-in-arms.
See what you started?

# CONTENTS

# PART I: OLD TOWN TALES

Memoirs, anecdotes, and tall tales from the customers and patrons of the best bar on Luna.

# SCRAMBLE

Audio-video record from Tycho Traffic Investigation, Incident Report from the crash of Lunar Transport *Reynolds*.

**LOGFILE:** REYNOLDS/PsgCbn/AVRec/2062:04:13:01:23:12

**LOCATION:** Passenger Cabin, Lunar Transport *Reynolds*, en route from Neper Crater to Tycho

"Everyone, please strap in!"

"Steward Abraham, the explosion, his head—"

"Mr. Zhou, he'll have to wait until Captain Hardigan has us safely on the regolith. Now please strap in so I can deploy the safety cushions."

"But why did the Captain seal the hatch?"

"Standard Lunar emergency protocol, Miss Drew. Seal the cabins to isolate leaks."

"Will we make it to Tycho?"

"I'm sorry. Captain Hardigan has already contacted Tycho Traffic Control and Tycho Rescue is on the way. They're the best Rescue service on Luna. Now, please, raise your arms to make room for the safety cushions."

"How long—"

"Martha, brace for impact. *Hard.*"

Crashes are the worst.

Not that there are any kind of good accidents. Sure, it's good when we can pull them all through, but that's still not *good*. You feel like a million L when you pull off a miracle save; but if some guy has to have one of the worst days of *his* life just so *you* can feel like a hero... No, you can keep your million L. Even the good days ain't so good, and the bad days... Well, the bad days make me wonder why I don't just quit.

Industrial accidents are bad, but they're usually quick and clean. Either a guy survives or he buys it in one shot. A crash means tension and stress for an extended stretch, too long for adrenaline to keep you going. You start with a rush, but you always end up exhausted, persisting on little more than the support of your squaddies and the knowledge that if you stop, somebody dies. I'll take a quiet Duty Watch any day.

Unfortunately, today wasn't a quiet Duty Watch. Doc, Liza, Adam, and I were in our couches in the *Jacob Evans*, playing cards on our suit comps. Cap and Mari were in the front, running diagnostics for the third time this Watch. Cap's a pain, running sims and drills to the point of obsession, but the Corporation of Tycho Under has given us top performance awards two years running, so he knows what he's doing.

Our routine day was interrupted in the worst way: by the sound of umbilicals snapping away and an alert on our suit comps and main consoles. "Scramble! All squads scramble! Transport *Reynolds* inbound from Neper is off Traffic, repeat, off Traffic. Nav beacon has cut out. Pilot reports mechanical failure, attempting soft landing. No further communications. Scramble! All squads..."

Cap's training and drills paid off: before the second "scramble," we had helmets snapped to. Mari had the engines from idle to warm-up before the second "off Traffic." Six green lights showed us all strapped in for launch before the alert repeated.

Cap cut off the alert. "Pad Control, Third. Clear?"

"Third, Pad. Clear. You're Go." Patty Hayes, our Pad Controller, drilled as much as Cap did. Between Patty's crew and ours, we had the ribbon for fastest launch three quarters running. They're aiming for one full year, and I'd bet we earned it today. Before Cap could say "Launch," Mari had already punched in the command and the *Jake* hopped. There was a quick jolt of G forces as we set off on a ballistic arc calculated by Traffic. Mari would take us out of ballistic when I told her where to go.

⊥

**LOGFILE:** REYNOLDS/PsgCbn/AVRec/2062:05:24:01:23:54

LOGFILE INTERRUPTED. UNEXPLAINED INTERFERENCE. ATTEMPTING RESYNCHRONIZATION.

⊥

Why would a squad *want* Outer Watch? Why would anyone want this job? It ain't the money, that's for sure. There are people getting rich in Tycho Under, but we ain't them. I'll bet their jobs are safer and less stressful than ours.

The stress starts with the flight out, and it's worse with a search. Even with nav beacons and sat recon, there's a lot of Lunar surface to cover out there. Sometimes, a nav beacon gets damaged in the crash. Other times, there's no recon eyes in good viewing position for as long as thirty minutes. Thirty minutes is a long time in Rescue. So, if we don't have a beacon or an eye in position when a crash is called in, they scramble every squad and send us in the right general direction.

As per drill, Cap depressurized as soon as all helmets had snapped to. Before long, the cabin was in vacuum. We didn't want to waste precious seconds depressurizing later.

"Ron, it's a search."

"Got it, Cap."

That's what "off Traffic" means: no nav beacon, no sat recon, start searching! Sometimes Cap is a little *too* pushy. I know my job, damn it. They call me "Scout" because the brass are too stuffy to say what we say: G3, General Gopher and Grunt. Everyone else in a squad is a specialist: Commander, Pilot, Doctor, Programmer, and Engineer. I'm the utility guy, the one who pitches in when someone else needs a hand. I like it—I learn a little of everything, and it might even set me up for a command of my own someday.

My one specialist duty is scouting for lost vessels and survivors, and I'm good at it. Even Cap admits that when quarterly review comes around… but in between, he pushes like I'm a green recruit who can't see a live drive flame in front of my nose. I had already pulled open a split screen on my couch comp, showing the radar signature and stats for Nashville-class transports, Tycho Traffic's track for the *Reynolds*, flight plots for the other hoppers, and maps of the likely landing zone.

The record track didn't make a lot of sense. I'll never be half the pilot Mari is, but I've logged enough flight hours to know how vessels usually behave. The *Reynolds* was off course and getting farther off *before* the nav beacon cut off. The last seconds of the record track made even less sense—the beacon diverted suddenly and veered sharply east-northeast of its course, fast enough to give me the shudders. With acceleration that severe, anyone not strapped in at that divert point was probably lost already. Even those strapped in would have restraint injuries, at a minimum. What was wrong with that ship?

I pushed my audio to the Scout Circuit. "Scout One, Scout Three. Check that track?"

"Three, One. Checked. Damnedest thing, Ron. Hope you packed extra splints. Breaks aplenty."

We didn't use actual splints, of course. Instant casts predated the Lunar Era. "One, Three. What's the search strategy, Mack?"

"Three, One. Two, Four, Five, and Six got off the Pad slow. We almost had you this time, Ron. Tell Mari Tim wants double or nothing on the next scramble. I'm having the slugs cover the near edges of the projected cone from that last track. Want to join us at the divert point and scout forward from there?"

"One, Three. Hold please." Mack made sense, but that cockeyed track still bothered me. "Liza, can you prep a Q&D?"

"Sure. Specs?"

Liza's a perfectionist by nature, and she hates Quick and Dirty sims. She wants to plan and prep and get everything exactly right before she tells it to run. But she's also the best Q&D artiste I've ever worked with, and no-nonsense on a scramble. Time is too scarce for perfection when a ship is off Traffic.

"Assume a mass—small, but larger than a Nashville nav beacon." I pushed the Nashville specs over to her couch comp. "Assume some system failure propelled that mass away from the *Reynolds* at the divert point. Can you get a sim that matches this track from there?" I pushed over the track data as well.

Liza went to work, talking to the comp and keying in code simultaneously.

"Three, One. What's the word, Ron?"

"One, Three. Trying to make sense of that track." I looked over at Liza. She had a frown on her face, but she looked at me and nodded. "One, Three. Mack, I think maybe somehow the *Reynolds* ejected her nav beacon. Believe the track record from the divert point forward is a bogie."

Cap looked at me in his overhead mirror. "You sure, Ron?"

Before I could answer, Liza jumped in. "Ninety-three percent, Cap. I'm pushing the sim to all channels now."

Cap opened the Command Circuit. "All Squads, Command Three. Please confirm receipt of sim. High probability track record is that of a separated nav beacon."

Confirmations came in, and then Mack returned in my ear. "Three, One. Nice eye, Ron. Liza have a projection for the rest of *Reynolds*?"

I looked at Liza. She was already waving for my attention, so I pulled her into the Scout Circuit.

"All Scouts, Prog Three. Revising sim with new projected zones based on how many pieces the *Reynolds* is in."

I was proud of her. Liza's good, but she's the most squeamish of the squad. Translated from cold jargon, she had just said "whether they might be alive or strewn dead across the surface," and with only a small tremor in her voice. I pushed her back out before she had the chance to say more. I didn't want to risk her voice cracking on an open circuit.

"All Scouts, Scout One. Cover projected zones indicated in the pop I'm pushing out now. Scout Three, you get the Good News Zone." That's Scout slang for the zone with the highest chance of survivors. I must've done well in Mack's eyes. He always gives the harshest peer reviews I've ever experienced, but today, I had his endorsement.

Matching orders were coming in to Cap on the Command Circuit as Liza turned us towards the Good News Zone. Good news? We could still hope.

⬇

**LOGFILE:** REYNOLDS/PsgCbn/AVRec/2062:05:24:01:24:26

*"Aaah... Aaah, owww..."*

"Everyone... please remain calm. Please... don't remove... your straps yet. We've tumbled and landed... upside down. If you fall, you could get... further injuries—"

"My arm!"

"I'll... help. Give me a second.... Now. Please... give me the safety cushions. Young lady, please... let go of the cushion. I need to put them down so... there's a soft landing if anyone... falls.

"Now, Mr. Zhou.... No, he's unconscious. Mr. Reed, you look okay. Do you think you can unstrap and lower yourself down? I can help you, and the cushions... can you make it?"

"I'll try, Steward. Let me... okay, I'm coming down now. Slowly..."

"I've got you.... *OWWWWWWWWWWW*... I'm sorry... dropped..."

"The cushions worked, I'm okay. Steward Abraham? Are you all right?"

"I'm... all right. Just need to... rest a second. My side. Can you unstrap the others... and lower them down?"

"Some of them are—"

"I know. We have... enough to deal with. Let's not discuss casualties yet. Just... lay them in the rear. You'll find blankets in the cupboard, so you can cover... cover.... Help me up, please. I need... to get the first aid kit."

⟂

Liza had simmed a large ellipse of high-probability landing sites. It's never a "crash site." We never, *ever* say "crash site," not if we don't have to. Not until we see a crash and we just can't avoid the words any longer. Until then, always assume a safe landing at a *landing* site. Superstition? Fine, then it's our superstition.

Now, to find the *Reynolds*. I could choose one of the obvious strategies: start from the center of the ellipse and spiral out, or start from the edge and spiral in. But both were time consuming, and seconds were precious. So while we flew, I tried to devise a better strategy.

*Pilot reports mechanical failure, attempting soft landing.* OK, go with that. Doc had taught me his strategy in card games: when your cards aren't obviously winning or obviously losing, play as if the other cards are *exactly* what you need to win. The thinking is, you're stuck with the cards you have. If you can't win, it doesn't matter how you play; but if you *can* win, you have to play a specific way to do it. That's how I'd approach a search: assume the best, and start from there.

So, assume the pilot maintained some control over the ship. What were his goals? Ground the *Reynolds* as close to Tycho Under, and to Rescue, as he possibly could.

Get her down as softly as he could.

8

Make her as easily discoverable as he could.

Bring her down someplace where the Second Quarter sunlight wouldn't cook the passengers if they had to evac.

The Sun helped in the visibility goal, but hurt the shelter goal. Sometimes there are no good answers, only the least bad options.

How would he—assuming a he, I hadn't checked the crew roster—prioritize these goals? Soft first? If they didn't survive the landing, the rest wouldn't matter. I cut out almost thirty percent of the ellipse, because it overlapped an ejecta ray from Tycho's formation. That ray would be full of rocks, large and small, that could tear a hull to shreds in even a soft crash.

Close, visible, or sheltered? If he's worried about close, he won't worry about sheltered. Or would he? If he's considering an evac, he might be worrying about how far his passengers and crew might have to walk mid-month. A shorter walk might be the way he'd bet.

"Ron, I need a course."

Mari had followed a general approach vector, and I could see from the main comp that we were nearing the ellipse. We needed a specific vector ASAP.

There was a choice that was close *and* sheltered, but risked not being soft. If he'd landed very near the ejecta ray, which was also near the closest edge of the ellipse, then the survivors could use the shadows of the large rocks for shelter. It was a classic trick from Lunar Survival School—manual thermal control. When your suit gets hot, duck behind rocks for a while and let it cool off. With practice, you can make maybe fifteen percent normal progress that way. That's better than zero, and could be the difference that keeps you alive.

A quick pull from the *Reynolds*'s records: Captain Neil Hardigan was a high-scoring graduate of Lunar Survival School and top-rated on Nashville class transports. He knew the tricks, and he had the skills.

"Mari, bring us in on the nearest edge, and skirt along the ejecta ray here." I traced out a rough course and pushed it to her nav comp. "Low and slow. All eyes, you know the drill."

All couch comps shifted to camera-eye view as Mari brought us in low.

ʇ

**LOGFILE:** REYNOLDS/PsgCbn/AVRec/2062:05:24:01:29:31

"They're all down. I've covered…. How are the injuries? I've had first aid training. Can I help?"

"Hmmm…. Air is holding. I don't hear leaks. But… you'll help more if you make sure we're sealed."

"But you—"

"I have a job to do. And I… need your help. I'm moving slow, and… we need to seal the cabin. Have you ever applied seal strips?"

"No."

"It's not hard. There's a roll in the cupboard. Our air seems to be holding, but there's no sense… no sense skimping on strips. Tape every joint, every corner. Anyplace plates meet the frame. Lay down a strip, touch it with… this activator, press the button, and you're done. If you hear a leak, strip it immediately… and call me over."

"Strip, activator, repeat. Got it."

"I'll be… I'll keep working on the injured."

ʇ

Adam spotted the *Reynolds*. "Camera five." We all pulled five into focus. "It's bad. She's on her top, half in the shadow of that big boulder. The tail's pointed toward Tycho, so the pilot cabin's near that smaller boulder."

From Adam's description, I found the *Reynolds*. There was a large, crumpled dent in the exposed underbelly of the pilot cabin, roughly the shape of the small boulder.

"All Scouts, Scout Three. Confirmed sighting. Converge Beacon

Three." Mari was already on course to the clearest spot, a little beyond the *Reynolds*.

A hopper's a rough ride. They're meant for speed and maneuverability, not comfort, and Mari knows how to make one dance. From spotting to contact lights in under 8 seconds—even Neil Armstrong and Buzz Aldrin might've balked at that approach. Mari cut the main engine, and the *Jacob Evans* was down.

"CTU Rescue, Command One. Supply drones converge Beacon Three."

A search often burned more fuel than a hopper could spare for the return flight, and sometimes we need more supplies than we can carry. The AI-piloted supply drones aren't built for search or first response, and they're uglier than sin… but when they home in with supplies just as you're running low on null plasma or jump juice, they're the prettiest things you've ever seen.

As we hit regolith, the big side doors cycled open and we unstrapped. We dropped out to the lith, closely followed by our swarm of scan bots.

This was the start of **A1: Assess**. Adam briefed us.

"Nashville class is an older transport—all function, no style. Flight frame's solid and reliable. Shell is standard civilian-grade hull tiles in the stock configuration: flight cabin, passenger cabin, pressurized cargo cabin, and unpressurized cargo deck."

Hull tiles have an ingenious design, stronger in their joins than in their middles. If there's going to be a hull stress break, it's far more likely to be in the middle than at a join—and the core within that middle contains vacuum resin. The epoxy bubbles up through cracks, then hardens to a rigid seal when it hits vacuum.

"Ron, I've found an attachment point for the Ear on the flight cabin. Let me know when the Pinger's attached."

I felt sorry for Adam—when he looked in through the port to the flight cabin, he said nothing. That crumple was where Hardigan would've been. If there were good news to report there, Adam would've been all over the circuits with it. The crumple was also where the nav beacon should've been, which provided the explanation for its ejection.

But that wasn't my concern now. I needed to get the Pinger to the other end, ASAP, so I could feed Adam some pings. I leaped up on top of the *Reynolds* and bounded across.

"Ron, be careful…"

"Yes, Cap." On a smaller vessel, I might've just leaped over it in one bounce, but Nashvilles are pretty long. Cap was right; I couldn't risk a spill. First rule of the Academy: "Don't add to the casualty list."

I was about to leap down when I heard something.

**⊥**

**LOGFILE:** REYNOLDS/PsgCbn/AVRec/2062:05:24:01:38:54

"All right, Miss Drew. Just a little needle prick… I know, it hurts, but it's in now. You've… lost some blood, so you need null plasma. I'll… just tape this down, so the needle will stay in."

"I need to get out of here!"

"Please, relax. We can't leave… we're waiting for Rescue."

"You have emergency suits, right? Where's, where… wh—"

"What happened?"

"She's fine, Mr. Reed. I added a sedative to her IV, so she doesn't… injure herself further."

"Steward Abraham, I've used up the seal strips. Are there more?"

"In the cupboard… but I think we're good for now. I checked the pressure gauge, we're holding."

"I can probably work the radio. Should I call for help?"

"No radio. Antenna's on the roof. Was on the roof. Gone… crushed now."

"Steward! I hear something on the roof."

"*Shh.* Everyone, quiet for a moment. Listen…"

*Thump... Thump...*

"Someone's up there. Everyone... strike the walls! Find something solid and hit the walls."

⊥

Newcomers to Luna have an understandable misconception that the surface is quiet because of the vacuum. Actually, you bring your noise with you: suit noises, comm chatter, comp feeds, your own breathing. And air isn't the only way to conduct sound. It'll conduct through any good rigid object, including parts of a suit—even the boots. Our boots are pretty rigid, both for pressure and for traction on the regolith. I heard, and also felt, a slight thumping beneath my feet.

"Cap, thumping inside. Someone heard me."

Cap relayed the good news as I leaped down. That meant I was likely wasting my time. The Pinger and the Ear form an acoustic hull integrity tester, and the hull was probably intact if there were survivors. Still, I attached and activated the Pinger.

⊥

**LOGFILE:** REYNOLDS/PsgCbn/AVRec/2062:05:24:01:40:17

*Weeoweoweee... Weeoweoweee...*

"Good news! Tycho Rescue is here."

*Weeoweoweee... Weeoweoweee...*

"What's that sound?"

"They call it a Pinger. It sends coded... acoustics through the hull. At the other end of the ship, they've attached an Ear."

*Weeoweoweee... Weeoweoweee...*

"The Ear receives pings and measures how they propagate... through the hull. Rescue compares the results against the acoustic signature from our last maintenance review. The Ear filters the echoes into a 3D model of our flight frame, hull... contents..."

*Weeoweoweee... Weeoweoweee...*

‡

The Ear pushed its model to Liza's suit comp. She integrated the acoustic model and the visual model from the darting scan bots into a sim of the crash site.

There, I'd thought it at last: *crash site*. Hardigan had done an admirable job, given what I could see. The *Reynolds* would never fly again, but the ship wasn't a total loss and there were survivors. I was sure Hardigan wasn't one of them. Liza pushed her model to our suit comps and confirmed my suspicions.

"Sim fit is ninety-seven percent. Some glitch in the cooling system blew a chunk right out of the flight cabin, took the nav beacon, long-range comm, and part of the guidance system with it. Captain Hardigan must've been suited, because he survived to seal the cabins. Then with crippled guidance, he brought the *Reynolds* down here. He would've made it, if he'd cleared that boulder. The sim says he could have, but that probably would've ripped the bottom out of the passenger cabin. He took it himself. Sim and acoustics say his lower half was crushed." She swallowed, a dry, painful sound. "Probably instant."

‡

**LOGFILE:** REYNOLDS/PsgCbn/AVRec/2062:05:24:01:41:58

"Where are they?"

"Working. Protocol for our safety... the Four As. Assess, Atmosphere, Access... Assist. If they don't follow protocol, we could... lose our air."

‡

"Cap, problem here." Adam pushed the structural model into the common view. "Flight frame is intact, but seriously twisted."

"Any join breaks?"

"Weak spots, no breaks."

I was already ahead of Adam and working my way around the hull, applying seal strips from my roll wherever the model showed a weakness. The scan bots helped, lasers pinpointing the weakest areas. Apply a strip, then apply the activator to dissolve the seal granules, little carbon bubbles with vacuum resin in them. You wouldn't want to fly in a vessel patched together with seal strips, but you wouldn't have to worry about losing air. This was **A2: Atmosphere**. "If they can't breathe, you can't save 'em" is the second rule at Rescue Academy.

"But that's not the problem," he continued. "It's the airlocks. This ship has three. In the nose, the side, and the roof."

"And the nose is gone, and she's flat on her roof. Let me guess... the frame is too twisted to open the side lock?"

"You got it, Cap. Impact with the boulder and then the tumble stressed it too much. We *might* get it open. We'd never close it again."

"Where's the best access?"

"Bottom—well, topside now. Least chance we'll injure someone."

"Ron, how's the stripping?"

"Still about a dozen joins to hit. One or two could use a second strip."

"Keep on that. We'll unship the lock. But take a moment to establish comm, if you can. Tell 'em we're coming in through the top, and to stand clear. Don't want to drop anything on them."

Cap, Doc, and Adam went back to the *Jake* to unship the rear airlock. Rescue hoppers are modified so the rear lock is removable. We can fix it to a hull, seal strip it good and tight, and *voila*. Instant airlock. It's massive, but nothing three strong men can't handle in Lunar G.

Meanwhile, I checked the broadband comm scanner. No signals other than us and our data bands. I pulled the Pinger from my belt again and hooked it to my comm line. The Pinger's a multiuse device: it can ping, and it can also serve as a conduction speaker to project into a vessel. It could also give me at least a muffled listen into the interior. I affixed it to a join where the model showed good hull contact.

**LOGFILE:** REYNOLDS/PsgCbn/AVRec/2062:05:24:01:43:26

"Anyone inside *Reynolds*, this is CTU Rescue Three. If you can hear my voice, strike something solid three times."

"Everyone... quiet."

*Clang, clang, clang.*

"*Reynolds*, we're beginning rescue efforts. More squads are en route. Do you need medical assistance? Strike once for yes, twice for no."

*Clang!*

"How many injured?"

*Clang, clang, clang, clang.*

"How many able?"

*Clang. Clang.*

Six survivors, four injured. We never ask the last question: How many dead? It only depresses or even panics the survivors. Their departure log told the tale: Captain Hardigan, one steward, fourteen passengers. Ten dead already.

"Have you begun first aid?" *Clang.* This person was good. I checked the log again. "Is this Abraham?" *Clang.*

Martha Abraham, ship's steward. The odds for the survivors just went up. Abraham was fully rated on emergency protocols, first aid, and Lunar survival.

"Martha, I'm Ron Ward. Have you sealed your joins?" *Clang.* I could stop stripping. Her internal seals would hold far better than mine. "Fantastic. Martha, we're rigging a lock in the deck center, aft of the thruster assembly. You read?" *Clang!* "OK, get your passengers clear so we don't drop anything on them." *Clang.* "Martha, I've gotta help with the lock. You're going to be all right." *Clang.* I hoped she believed it. I was starting to.

⚓

**LOGFILE:** REYNOLDS/PsgCbn/AVRec/2062:05:24:01:45:18

"All right... Rescue is here. Mr. Reed, please help... keep everyone in the front."

⚓

"Cap, ship's steward has stripped the seals internally and started first aid. I can help with the lock."

"Negative. We've got it. Bounce topside, help us lift from there."

As I returned topside, I saw the *Alex Evans* landing a safe distance away. Rescue One had arrived. In the distance, I saw nose jets from the other hoppers. It was about to get crowded here, but nothing wrong with that. Six Doctors for four injured is much better odds than just Doc and me. I'm a fair field medic, but not even close to an MD. We Scouts could run null plasma to the docs, carry wounded, and otherwise play G3s, but the Doctors did the critical work.

I looked down and the lock was hullside, waiting for me. I crouched and grabbed hold. "Got it." Then, just like a drill, my squaddies took turns bouncing up to join me while the others held the lock up. As soon as we were more up than down, we hoisted the lock up and over.

Cap and Doc bounced up as Adam directed us on where to place the lock. Again, just like drill, Adam and Doc crouched down and we placed it over them. That way, they could start work inside as it pressurized.

We fixed the lock to the flight frame with mag clamps as Adam directed, then I spread a liberal helping of seal strips all around the joins. Before I got halfway around, I ran into Mack laying strips from the other side, under the guidance of his Engineer, Matt Winter.

"Howdy, Mack."

"Howdy, Ron. Seals look good. I'm pressurizing."

As soon as there was enough air pressure to confirm the seals, Adam set to work on the hull plates. This was **A3: Access**, sometimes the trickiest part.

⊥

**LOGFILE:** REYNOLDS/PsgCbn/AVRec/2062:05:24:01:47:50

"What's that noise?"

"They're grinding the hull plates. Plates are attached with... molecular adhesive, don't want to let go."

"So they're cutting through the plates?"

"No. Vacuum resin in the plates is a sticky mess. Worse when you hit vacuum... whole suit goes rigid. So they'll remove plates at joins. Just takes time...."

⊥

Adam and Doc were hard at work on the joins. I watched them using the lock's cam. Adam picked out and ground cuts into the joins, and then Doc applied solvent. Working their way around, they soon had one plate free, enough for a slim hand to snake through and shake Doc's gloved hand. No, they weren't shaking...

⊥

**LOGFILE:** REYNOLDS/PsgCbn/AVRec/2062:05:24:01:48:37

"Steward Abraham, I'm Doctor Jones."

"Good to… see you, Doctor. We need more null plasma…"

"Martha, you sound weak."

"Doctor, please… null plasma. Still have passengers in shock."

"All right, here's my aid pack. We'll have more when the lock is working."

⸸

"God blessed—"

Adam had been working on the third plate, which would give them enough room for Access in suits, but he held up his grinder. On camera, I could see that the grind shaft had snapped clear off.

"Adam, we've got Matt's kit here. You need another grind wheel?"

Doc cut in as he started shedding his suit. "Negative. I don't want to waste time on a pressure cycle. People are in bad shape down there. Adam, unsuit. We can squeeze in through the gap."

I was sure Doc's lanky frame would fit, but Adam would have a tight squeeze. Adam's a moose. I've never been Downside, so I've never seen an actual moose… but if they're as large as Adam, they must be impressive.

"Once we're in, we pull in our gear, then Ron can fold down the lock doors and let Matt and the other Doctors in."

The pressure doors on portable locks are panels that fold up against the side walls, then down to seal the lock. They're not fancy like a modern passenger lock, just functional and reliable.

"Good call, Doc." Adam pulled off his helmet and started stripping off his suit.

⸸

**LOGFILE:** REYNOLDS/PsgCbn/AVRec/2062:05:24:01:48:37

"I've got you, Doctor."

"Thank you, Mr...?"

"Reed, Johann Reed."

"Adam, hand down my pack and then join us. Johann, my backpack unfolds into a stretcher capsule, which we'll likely need. Can you help Adam assemble it?"

"Doctor... here."

"Martha?"

"Mr. Zhou is the worst. Compound... fracture and..."

"Martha, let me—"

"COMPOUND FRACTURE and multiple lacerations from flying debris. Also suspect internal injuries from... restraining harness. I've given three... four units of null plasma. Pressure's up, but sinking again. Shock..."

"Yes, I expect he is in shock. I'll take care of him, and you should lie down."

"Other passengers need me. I'll be over here. Be fine..."

"Okay.... Adam, Johann, if you're done with the stretcher, Martha could use some help with the other passengers. Don't let her exert herself."

⊥

The other Doctors queued up with Matt to enter the lock. Doc was already deep into **A4: Assist**. He was pushing reports out on the Doctor Circuit for opinions: compound fracture, lacerations, restraint-induced internal injuries, shock; concussion, multiple fractures, possible internal injuries, shock; concussion, possible hematoma; multiple lacerations, sedated to prevent further injuries; internal injuries, likely severe, shock.

"Pressure zero. Let's go!"

Matt opened the outer lock door and he and the Doctors climbed in. It would be a tight fit—he could remove more plates in there, but all I could see on the lock's cam was Doctors' legs. Some of them unsuited to crawl through while Matt worked.

I hate these strange, idle moments we get at odd times in a rescue. There's literally nothing I can do for a while, even though every impulse in me is screaming at me to do *something*. Third rule of the Academy: "Hurry kills." Those idle-tense moments are when I most wonder why I took this job. Just when my adrenaline is pumping hardest, I have to sit and wonder and plan for the unforeseen, because I can't do anything. The fight-or-flight response kicks in hard, and I hate it.

Matt pulled up the third tile, and the remaining Doctors dropped inside. He dropped in their packs as we Scouts queued up to help our Docs.

⚓

**LOGFILE:** REYNOLDS/PsgCbn/AVRec/2062:05:24:01:52:34

"Jones, where we at?"

"Compound fracture and lacerations are bandaged up, and I've stabilized BPs. The steward did a fantastic job."

"The steward? Really?"

"Uh-huh. Ultrasound confirms concussions and hematoma, so I've started fluids, null plasma, and analgesics."

"And the internal case?"

"Now that you're here, I'll take care of her."

⚓

Doc came across the all-hands circuit. "Scouts, hold back. Matt, can you help us lift? Stretcher capsule coming out."

If Doc had a patient, *I* had a patient. My chief duty on the lith is as the Doc's corpsman. I shouldered aside Mack and the other Scouts, leaped up on top of the lock, and checked the indicators. "Cap, depressurizing at fifteen percent." I looked at Cap, and he nodded— we could spare that much air. I keyed the override, and the lock opened with a brief white puff as moisture in the air sublimated.

Matt and Doc were ready when I reached down. They had the stretcher poles right where I expected them. Hand-over-hand, I hauled out the stretcher capsule, a large plastic bubble stretched between two poles. A comp on the side hooked to cables and hoses that snaked in to the form strapped to the base. I tried not to look too closely; too much red, and I would get a closer look all too soon.

Mack helped me steady the stretcher as Doc bounced out and began issuing more orders. "Cap, emergency evac here. Spleen, liver, maybe more. Can you spare the *Jake*?"

"Plenty of rides home here. Go!"

Doc nodded and gave one last instruction. "Mari, prep the table."

We dropped down to the regolith, and the Scouts passed us the stretcher. Then we set off in a long lope designed to cover ground quickly without losing control or jolting the patient too much.

"Operate here, or do we evac?"

"Both, I fear... but let's plan on evac."

The spleen was pretty serious for a field operation. Doc wouldn't consider it if the patient had good odds of reaching CTU. I didn't look forward to this trip.

The big doors of the *Jake* were already sealed except for port aft, the door where we bring in patients. Mari had stayed on board, keeping the hopper ready for a quick departure. Too often, we need every spare second in getting the injured to the hospital.

We reached the big door in a hurry and lifted the stretcher through. Mari closed and sealed the door, and we clamped the stretcher capsule to the table. The umbilicals hooked in automatically, and the med comp lit up with a body scan and readings. As the cabin pressurized, we strapped into our couches. Mari didn't wait for us to let her know—she hit launch as soon as the board showed three greens.

As soon as the initial thrust ended, she called back, "Quick or smooth, Doc?"

"Let me check." He pulled up the table diagnostics. "Damn. Smooth, Mari. Ron, masks and gloves. She can't wait."

For the first time, I looked closely at our patient, and all I could do was mutter "Liar" under my breath. Martha Abraham wasn't on the able list—not even close.

I pulled up Doc's log. She had to have known she had internal injuries—maybe not the spleen specifically, but she must have been in a hellish amount of pain. Yet she had struggled to stay conscious, treat the injured, comfort them, and assure them that Tycho Rescue would find them soon. Then she communicated with me, took supplies from Doc, and applied more treatment. Not until all the Doctors were inside would she let Doc look at her.

*You're one hell of a strong woman, Martha.*

Now Doc was saying without saying that she wouldn't survive the trip without emergency surgery. The ride settled enough for us to unstrap. We stripped off our gloves and helmets; then, as Doc popped the stretcher and looked over Martha, I got out the sterile packs. I opened a set of bath gloves and offered them to Doc. He thrust his hands in, then yanked them out, as sterile as modern science could manage. Then I put his sterile op gloves on, careful to only touch the removable grips. Same with his mask. When I pulled the grips off, Doc was clean.

Before I could ask, Mari hit the autopilot long enough to help me with my gloves and mask. If Madhu weren't such a good friend and Helen weren't my wife, I could go for Mari. She can practically read my mind.

The autoclave and the supply locker were both open and ready. I started handing Doc whatever he needed: scalpels, clamps, scissors, sponges, and far too much null plasma. Three times I had to adjust the anesthetic on the stretcher. Whether from pain or the ride, or just pure stubbornness, Martha kept struggling up from sleep.

Finally, Doc adjusted it. Not that he didn't trust me, but this was delicate: too much would kill her, and not enough would let her keep struggling and kill herself. While I held an incision open for him, he tweaked some levels up and others down, until Martha settled down. Then he picked the scalpel back up and resumed work.

And so we passed the trip back. It seemed to take a Lunar day or more, but the ship's clock read twenty-three minutes when Mari said, "Approach, Doc. Do we circle, or do we land? I have clearance for Watson Pad."

Watson Medical Labs was the finest hospital on Luna, and also the top-rated ER.

"Two minutes, then land." He didn't tell her to have a team ready. They all knew their jobs. "Another plasma, then let's start packing this. Surgical tape. No sense in sutures, they'll have to open her right up again."

I slapped another unit of plasma into the stretcher as Doc pumped some drugs into her IV. Then we closed her up as best we could, and strapped in.

Right on schedule, Mari took us down. Not many pilots outside of Rescue are certified to land at Watson. The Pad is right next to the emergency room, with a dome that can be extended over a ship for fast evac. One slip in landing could be a disaster *and* shut down a big part of the disaster relief mechanism. Mari made no slips.

We landed and didn't wait for pressure—we had Martha's stretcher sealed and mobile again, ready to go. The big doors opened, and the suited emergency team lifted her onto a gurney. They left at a run, Doc keeping pace and filling them in on her latest stats.

That left Mari to taxi the *Jake* back out, and me with nothing to do. The adrenaline rush was over, the stress was gone, and the exhaustion wasted no time settling in. I hustled to get inside the lock so they could clear the dome, but that was the last hustle I had left for the day.

I shuffled down Under and took the tram to the Rescue offices. On automatic pilot, I found my desk and started my incident report. That's boring work, but after a crash, boring is about all I can do.

I'd started reviewing the model, trying to make sense of how the nav beacon and comm unit were lost (T.I. will probably ground all the Nashvilles for a cooling system overhaul, because that was the likely cause), when the *Reynolds* AV record logs came in on the Rescue net. Reviewing logs takes even less energy than paperwork does, so I switched on the log player. After scrolling to the beginning, I watched the camera-eye view from inside the *Reynolds*.

⚖

**LOGFILE:** REYNOLDS/PsgCbn/AVRec/2062:05:24:01:54:10

"Can you believe that steward?"

"Not sure I could've held up like she did. Transport Academy can take pride in their first aid classes. I don't think any of these patients would've lived if she hadn't been here."

"And the pain she must've been in—the shock."

"Uh-huh. Jones has his work cut out for him."

"Do you think she'll make it?"

"..."

⚖

And there's my why, always the same why. I could walk away from this whole business, but Martha Abraham's out there because her passengers need her. And Martha needs me... they all need me. What choice do I have?

I was reopening the paperwork files when a pop announced the news of the successful rescue of the *Reynolds*. The squads were inbound with survivors.

About the time I realized I'd reread the same hull specs for the fourth time and still didn't know what they said, there was another pop: the announcement of the Lovell Medal for Command in Service to Crew, Vessel, and Mission, awarded to Captain Neil Hardigan, Pilot

*Reynolds*; and to Lieutenant Martha Abraham, First Steward.

Both awards were posthumous.

I shut down my desk comp and set course for the Old Town Tavern and the largest whiskey they would serve me. Needed or not, I'm done.

At least for tonight. Tomorrow is another day in Rescue.

# THE NIGHT WE FLUSHED THE OLD TOWN

No, we can't do anything about "that smell". I knew you'd ask—everybody does. But you haven't thought it through. Take a barstool and I'll explain.

And no, I'm no candy-ass for calling it "that smell". You heard me down in City Engineering: I don't exactly watch my language. But here in the Old Town, I try to be more circumspect. If you want to keep drinking in the best bar on Luna, you'll do the same. Eliza—she's the former drill sergeant behind the bar—kindly asked us in Eco Services to be a bit euphemistic when we talk about our work. She'd rather we not ruin any appetites. So, we talk about "that smell" and "liquid waste" and "sludge", not... well, you know.

Eliza, this is Wanda Meyers, my new Intern. Can you pour the rookie a drink? I need to teach her a bit about Eco, stuff that's not in the Doctor of Ecological Engineering curriculum. Kid, let me tell you what *really* happened the last time someone tried to get rid of "that smell", and why I drank free for a month here at the Old Town Tavern.

We start straight from the textbook: there's no such thing as a closed ecology. No control system is perfect. The limits of sealing technology, the inevitable last whiff of air out an airlock... Hell, even nonlinear dynamics and entropy play a part. Nothing is ever perfect. And past a certain point, the cost of near-perfection is higher than the cost of replenishment. Your professors will teach you lots of examples of "perfect" control systems and where they fail.

We get as close to perfect as we can here within the limits of time and budget and technology. The Corporation of Tycho Under isn't a closed ecology, but it's as closed as we can make it. Our replenishment budget's as low as any city's on Luna. The Ecology Service's unofficial motto is: "Nothing is wasted. Not even waste."

On Earth, many cities just vent their wastes in lagoons as part of the treatment cycle. Imagine that—Downside, with open sky and weather and everything—imagine just walking down your street, the wind turns the wrong way, and... there's "that smell". And they think *we're* provincial!

But every so often, some brass—usually some brass from Downside, who never grew up on Luna and just doesn't get it—decides to do something about "that smell" and then we have to educate them. They usually hit on the same "brilliant" idea: put the treatment plant on the surface, in vacuum, so the smell can simply vent into space.

They just don't get vacuum, not deep down where it counts. The difference between "venting" and vacuum sublimation eludes them. They don't realize that we'd lose a lot more than "that smell". Just imagine all the water and other liquids and volatiles boiling out into space, and then we'd have to mine for more or fly it up. And they also don't realize what havoc pure vacuum would play with the treatment units. Lunar equipment comes in "vacuum rated" and "not". Waste treatment units fall under "not". We'd have treatment vessels bursting from pressure differential, spattering the regolith with wastes.

But what they *really* don't understand is how "that smell" is an incredibly valuable resource and we'd be ecologically negligent to vent it into space. "That smell" is nearly 100% volatile organics—methane and hydrogen sulfide plus a stew of trace compounds. Do you know how much hydrogen sulfide Bader Reactor goes through in heavy water production? Do you know how much they pay per tonne for $H_2S$? It's also valuable in fuel cells. Plus, we can break it down to hydrogen and sulfur, and there are plenty of markets for both. Nothing is wasted.

So, we don't get rid of "that smell"—we use it. Every Lunar chamber has air recirculators with scrubbers, but we use super scrubbers in the treatment plant—the best in the industry. They're energy intensive, but far more effective than consumer-grade scrubbers: nanofluidic hydrodesulfurization, molecular methane extractors, and a lot of other trace compound nanofilters. What's left over is some of the purest oxygen and nitrogen you could ask for, and we pipe that right back into municipal air. In fact, since the Old Town's right over City Engineering on Second Level, that air hits here first. Yeah, you're breathing "that smell" right now, it's just post-scrubber.

Oh, now you gag? You breathed "that smell" half the day on your intro tour today. Now you gag at air purified out of it? It's amazing to me how so many loonies never understand how closely we recycle materials here. We're all taught in grade school that what we eat is grown in what we excrete, but somehow it never really sinks in. Then Interns see it up close and personal for the first time, and they gag.

Get over it, Wanda, or you'll wash out. With my twenty years' experience, I can promise you this: someday, somehow, this job will have you standing shin-deep in liquid wastes and sludge, breathing in "that smell" as you try to fix a treatment unit or patch a leak. Keep your head about you. Keep your *feet* about you, if you don't want to find out how it tastes! That story will have to wait, though, or Eliza will kick us out for sure.

When that day does come, do your job—because Tycho needs you—and be glad Eco Services pays for full-spectrum immunobooster treatments at Watson Medical when that happens. The job may get filthy, but it won't make you sick. Well, except for hydrogen sulfide itself. You get enough of it and it's toxic.

What you smelled today was probably less than 2 parts per million. Your body can process that easily. But if you ever see the yellow strobes go off, put your mask on *immediately* and then call in a leak. Those alarms will trip at around 5 ppm. Ten ppm is considered risky, and 20 is the outer limit per our safety guidelines. Fifty ppm is tolerable for short bursts, but we'll send you to Medical afterwards.

So the brass gets dumb ideas, but some brass has more say than others and Jack Brockway had a lot of say. He had just enough engineering knowledge to come up with an ingenious dumb idea, and when he decided to do something about "that smell" he had the clout to sell it to Admin.

I was just an Eco Intern then, like you today, working days in CitEng and taking classes at McAuliffe at night. I was still two years from my Eco.D. You'll find that Interns get two kinds of assignments: dirty or boring. Unless you screw up, and then I'll make sure you get dirty *and* boring. But normally, you'll either get to clean out scrubbers and treatment units or you'll get gopher duty for someone in Eco Admin. The day I met Jack Brockway, I was on gopher duty, assigned as "Assistant to the Executive Assistant to the Director of Ecology Services", and Jack Brockway was the newly-assigned Director, fresh up from Downside and looking to teach us "modern methods of waste management".

Look, Jack ends up looking like a fool in this story, and I don't think that's a fair picture even if there's some truth to it. So I want you to know some things up front. First, Jack always treated me right. As an Intern, you'll be lucky if I'm as good of a boss as Jack was. He was a know-it-all, but he never treated anyone as his inferior.

Second, Jack really was a smart engineer and he won awards for his work on Earth. He just never realized that Earth experience loses a lot in translation when you bring it to Luna. Even something as fundamental as fluid flow rates is different because you can't count as much on gravity helping to pull the fluid through the pipes. At least he was bright enough not to suggest treatment units on the surface. That alone makes him smarter than most brass.

And third, you probably don't realize just how messed up Eco Services was back then. Brockway had a lot to fix in a short time. This was just after the Archer administration—I'm sure you read about them in Lunar history class—and all of Tycho was a mess. That was the worst blend of patronage, corruption, and incompetence Tycho has seen since its founding, and Director Teller was the worst of a bad lot. He skimped on repairs and skimmed off the maintenance and replenishment budgets to line his own pockets. Tycho's ecology wasn't just compromised: it was *failing*. There are some who argue that Teller's life sentence for mismanagement was too severe; but if Eco had been his jury, he might've gotten the death penalty. He could've killed everyone in Tycho Under.

So Jack was fair, smart, honest, and earnest. That made us Interns a bit starry-eyed. He was restoring respect for our chosen profession. Heck, even a few Doctors of Ecology were star-struck. He was just what we needed after that crook Teller. He gave us back the pride we'd lost. We wore our uniforms out in public again, spit and polish, our tools and comps on our belts, as a way of saying, "We're Jack's crew. We're here to clean up."

The Exec, Murkowski, had her hands full untangling Teller's crooked books so it fell to me to accompany Jack on his Grand Inspection, as the journos called it. We looked at every single piece of Eco Services equipment in the city. It was "Photo here, Wayne" this and "Take a memo, Wayne" that. Before he was done, it was "Take a memo, Scott." We knew each other pretty well by then. It took so long, it set me back a term in my degree program—but it was an education in itself. No book covers Eco Services in that kind of detail.

And in my own small way, I educated Jack too. I showed him around Tycho, showed it to him as a native sees it. So naturally, one of the places I showed him was the Old Town Tavern. He took quite a liking to this place. "Scott," he said, "look at this: mirror, fans, lights, stools, even an antique cash register. It's like they picked up a neighborhood bar from back home, put it on a rocket, and launched it to the Moon. Except for the pressure doors, of course. Oh, and the beer: it pains my Earth pride to say it, but this is better and stronger than any I had at home."

"Thank Eliza and Paul for that, Jack. They brew their own, except for some imports. And most of those are strictly for tourists."

"Then raise a glass!" Jack raised his, but gently: I had finally coached him to remember how liquids can slop in Lunar gravity. "To Eliza!"

"And to Paul!" We drained our brews. This became our regular stop whenever the Grand Inspection brought us nearby, and Eliza always treated us like honored guests. I suspect that's why Jack did right by her and the Old Town in the end.

The Grand Inspection lasted nearly four months and true to his promise of transparency, Jack pushed a daily report out on the nets for anyone who cared to pull it. For a while, the journos hung stories on that hook: a dozen variations on the theme "Brockway cleans up." They made Jack something of a momentary celebrity. He's not sim-star handsome, mind you, but he's got your basic healthy good looks. So, they kept him near the top of their pops for a while. Eventually, the repetitive sameness of the daily reports turned them away. Another inspection report from Jack, another repair status report from Murkowski, ho hum. They found another story to leech, and Jack faded into the background. There he stayed until the Eco Summit, and again until—well, I'm getting ahead of my story here.

Meanwhile, the news pops also made *me* something of a celebrity, at least around here. I was often in the background of Jack's reports. As he relied on me more, sometimes he even had me make the reports when he was tied up in meetings with Admin. So I got a fair amount of pop time for an Intern, and my buddies here in the Old Town didn't let me live it down.

They recorded my pops, and then one of them applied morph and sim transforms to the feeds. Sometimes they drew thought balloons with obscene thoughts. Sometimes they shrunk me. Sometimes they gave me an extra 20 kilos of flab, like I needed that. But their favorite trick was to morph me into a character they called "Scotty the Skunk". They said that when I came off work, I had "that smell"; and I believed them, until I realized they said that even on days where I'd spent all day in the office. But you *will* have to watch for that: when you're around "that smell" long enough, your nose gets desensitized and you might never realize it's still on you. Another unofficial motto of Eco Services: "Bathe early, bathe often."

And then, when the Grand Inspection was done, Jack held his Eco Summit: a week-long series of meetings with Jack and his department heads, plus field team leads, expert contractors, community liaisons,

CTU administrators, parts suppliers, and anyone else who Jack thought could contribute. An old engineer once told me, "'Meeting' rhymes with 'beating'." But as week-long meetings go, it was astonishingly not painful.

Jack was smart: he let Murkowski organize the agenda and chair the sessions while he sat back and listened and probed—and cut through the bull when needed. He recognized that Murkowski's a natural talent for Admin, as her later career proved. By then, I was Jack's permanent Intern, having learned his work methods over the months, and I got to watch the whole thing up close. Now, I hate meetings as much as the next engineer—but if Administrator Murkowski's chairing a meeting, I know it won't be a waste of time.

I'll never forget Jack's closing address. Simple and brief: "Citizens of Tycho, you are rich. You can't see it right now because your government has treated you shabbily. But you've kicked the varmints out, and it's time you saw some changes. Since you hired me for this job, I've been *inspecting* machines, but I've been *meeting* people—as many as I could. And I tell you, Tycho is rich in people: hardworking, smart, and dedicated. No, I'm not trying to sell you something—I'm just telling you straight: you're a great people, and the previous administration held you back. With a government as hard-working as you, there'll be no stopping us. And today, we're taking steps to become the Eco Services you deserve."

And then Jack submitted his overhaul plans. Eco had made emergency repairs since Jack came on board plus running double shifts to catch up on maintenance, but that was all miniscule compared to Jack's new plans. Modernization, reinforcement, redundant backups, monitoring systems, transparency, efficiency... Really, all of our current quality metrics were all there in Jack's plans. It wasn't just recovering from the Teller years: it was a complete rethinking of the role of Eco Services in Tycho Under. For once, the journos were incapable of hyperbole: when they called it brilliant, that was simply a fact.

And like something out of Sophocles—what, you don't think a big bum like me can read the classics?—buried deep in Jack's ambitious plans were the seeds of Jack's downfall: the CR Program. Containment and Reclamation: Jack's plan to do something about "that smell".

Like so many others, Jack fixated on "that smell". He knew we couldn't waste the volatiles. He accepted the basic soundness of our super scrubber designs. But he just wouldn't accept that we had to let "that smell" vent before scrubbing it. He was convinced to his core that there had to be a way to filter out the volatiles and let out purified air, all without venting into the treatment chambers.

It's not like he was the first to have this idea, but Jack was sure there was an angle no one had considered yet. "Scott," he told me, "it's inefficient: let the gases disperse and *then* run them through scrubbers to reclaim them? We should be able to run them straight to the scrubbers." I pointed out that dispersing helped the gases to separate naturally, so we could concentrate the scrubber energy where it was most effective, but he waved that off: "That just takes engineering savvy. We'll find another way to separate them." Jack started sketching out his vision for the Containment and Reclamation Units; and the final units looked a lot like those early sketches with a small mountain of engineering savvy added in.

But then, Jack made his one *really* big error: he did the detailed design and prototyping of the CR Units himself, trusting only himself to get his vision right. That's a classic engineering error: the Two Hats Pattern. You can work on the project or you can manage the project, but you can't do both. You can only fail at both.

The best engineering managers will tell you how the Two Hats Pattern leads to failure. They know that it always applies—except to them. Deep in their hearts, where they won't admit it to anyone, they're sure that *they* are different, or that *this project* is different. Maybe they'll rationalize it: *yeah, this is a bad idea, but I've got no one else to spare.* Or *yeah, this is a bad idea, but this part is so important that I can't trust it to anyone else.* They convince themselves that *this time* it won't be a mistake. We always know better when it's the other guy, but never when it's us.

When Jack finished his CR design, he tried to explain it to me. It was only later that I understood it—far too late. "See, Scott, the trick is in the separation. With the old approach, we let 'that smell' vent into the chamber, eventually passing through multiple series of filters. Venting lets the gases separate; but we still have all kinds of gases passing through all kinds of filters and scrubbers, even when those filters and scrubbers won't apply to those particular gases.

"But if we could separate the gases more effectively, then we could guide each gas *only* to the filters or scrubbers that apply to it. The reduced scrubber energy will provide almost all the energy we need for separation."

"But how will we separate more effectively?"

"I've licensed some new tech: nano-ionizers. They're little molecular machines that can ionize a gas—well, except inert gases, of course—in a way that falls somewhere between mechanics and electronics and chemistry. It's a real breakthrough and highly efficient. Once they're ionized, we can use mag fields sort of like a mass spectrometer to guide them on separate paths based on molecular density. Each CR shell then has a number of outlets positioned to release different gases into different scrubbing ducts. The components that make up cleansed air can just be piped back into the ventilation system."

"Wow. I can see that. I think. But… I can't see how it could possibly use *less* energy than our scrubbers."

"Not *less* energy; but not excessively *more*. And then here's the *really* sneaky part: by confining the gases close to the treatment units—basically wrapping the treatment units in CR shells—we maintain those gases at their original, non-dispersed pressure. That's a weak but measurable positive pressure, and we can use that to help drive the separation. It's still a slight increase in energy usage, but it's well within our budget. And it's a small price to pay to get rid of 'that smell'."

I was still new—still somewhat sensitive to "that smell" myself. And if Jack thought it was important, then *I* thought it was important. So I studied Jack's designs until I had the basics down cold. Every CR unit is unique, a shell fitted around some existing equipment, but I became an expert at fitting and installing the ionic separators.

I received a *de facto* promotion. Oh, Jack couldn't *really* promote an Intern, but after the initial pilot test, he made me his field rep for CR installations. There was plenty for him and Murkowski to do in bringing his vision to Eco, too much to let him spend much time on CR.

So, title or no, I was effectively in charge of CR installations throughout Tycho. And I tell you, the real engineers resented me! One in particular, Irina Stewart, called me names behind Jack's back: "Jack's Boy" being the least offensive. Oh, I hated her too. She wrote me up for the smallest infractions, and she was brutal on my review boards. Looking back, I think she was more right than I was—more right than Jack was. That was too much responsibility—too high a placement for an Intern. A real engineer might've caught Jack's mistake in time.

In a way, I got even better than a promotion: Jack attached my ID as a rider on his comp credentials, giving me almost Director-level powers on the nets. That was a sacred trust that Jack placed in me, and I was determined not to disappoint him. I told no one about the comp credentials. Well, until the night came when I had to.

So I got *real* familiar with the Treatment sectors, including sector 7, one level down from here. When I could, I ended my day in sector 7 so I could clean up and come here to unwind. Without Jack here as a buffer, my buddies stepped up their humor at my expense. My pop career was over, but not Scotty the Skunk's! He frequently inserted himself into the sports and news feeds over the bar. I left myself a recurring pop to make sure I *always* bathed before coming up here.

The pilot went pretty smoothly: all gases conformed to the expected profiles within margins of error. After that, it was a regular procedure: use scan bots to build 3D models of the equipment to be contained; run the models through fitting algorithms to design the CR shell; order the shells from local fabricators; install the ionic separators; and hook them into the ducting system. Oh, and one more thing: for pressure-balancing reasons, Jack decided to bring the whole CR system up at once rather than phasing it in. Sound engineering decisions are sometimes counterintuitive and Jack made this seem like one of those, but I fear he wanted to show his brilliance off in a "grand opening".

But, Jack knew that sometimes when you schedule a dog and pony show, the dog dies and the pony runs away. Things go wrong and you need a dry run to work out the bugs. So we were going to unofficially power up the CR system, let it run overnight, and check the gas readings in the morning. Then we'd fix the bugs and try again the next night. Jack scheduled three nights of dry runs and then the grand opening.

Even though the CR units were 100% automated, you'd think we'd all be camped out in treatment, waiting for the dry run results. Jack wouldn't have any of that. "They're automated. What kind of confidence are we showing if we have to watch them?" Jack's confidence was infectious; and frankly, watching the test results was boring. So after monitoring the meters for an hour, Jack ordered everybody except the night crew to go home.

Naturally, I cleaned up to head to the Old Town. Jack went off to a party. His success had made him quite a star with Tycho's elite, and he got invited to all the major events. All the movers and shakers wanted his ear. He was flying high... like Icarus. See? Again with the classics! Don't underestimate this old man, kid—I have depths you'll never guess at.

There were maybe two dozen diners and drinkers scattered around the tables and seated at the bar that night. I swung up onto a bar stool between two old drinking buddies—Adam Stone from CTU Rescue and Al Grant from Bader—and called out, "Eliza, a weiss when you can." Eliza nodded as she hustled into the back room.

"Evening, Skunky." Adam tilted his glass a bit in my direction.

"Evening, Moose. Al." Adam may be the largest, strongest looney I've ever met. When he's coming down a tube, he looks to fill his lane and half the cross lane as well. And though he looks like nothing but muscle from ear to ear, he's one hell of a mechanical engineer. Al, on the other hand, is a wire-thin guy and all nervous energy. They make an odd pair, with a partying reputation in half the bars in Tycho.

"You hit the cycler tonight, Scott? I ordered a steak. I'd hate to have you ruin my appetite."

"Clean as a brand new air bottle, Al. Smell!" I shoved my arm right up under his nose.

"Careful, Scott. You know he likes his meat rare. He may mistake you for his entree."

I yanked my arm back as Al reached for his steak knife. It's a close call which Al enjoys most, a good steak or a good beer, but it's not safe to stand between him and either one.

Eliza showed up with my beer, and I ordered a sandwich. We drank and ate and talked, sometimes trading jibes with Eliza as she passed. They asked me how the CR Project was going, and I asked Al how the crops looked at Bader Farms. Adam never talked about Rescue work, and we knew better than to ask.

At our third round, Adam whistled. "Man, Skunky, are you sure you hit the cycler? You've got quite a whiff about you tonight."

"Very funny, Adam. Want to see my cycler receipt? Over fifty-eight mils down the drain, enough water to get even your carcass clean."

Al sniffed. "Sure, but did they run out of soap?"

"You, too, Al? This 'Scotty the Skunk' stuff's getting pretty old."

Al put his beer down, a sure sign that he really was serious. "I hate to be rude, but you smell a bit rank tonight."

Whatever they smelled wasn't strong enough to reach my desensitized nose. Assuming they really smelled anything—both of them could play deadpan if they wanted to. I decided to play along. "Fine! I can see where I'm not welcome!" I turned on my stool...

And then I saw it: here and there in the room, people had their noses crinkled up and faces twisted in disgust. Most were clustered near our end of the bar or over at a table in the far corner near the latrines. I got up and walked to that corner. I didn't have time to be inconspicuous—I just crouched down and looked under their table. There between their legs, I saw a municipal air duct.

I went back to our end of the bar where it curved around and joined the wall. "Adam, can you stand up, please?" Adam caught the tone in my voice. He didn't joke, didn't question—just stood. Behind his beefy legs was another municipal air duct.

I pulled out my gas scanner and held it to the vent. Mostly it was standard municipal air, but there was a trace of hydrogen sulfide: 4.7 parts per million. Not dangerous, but certainly not safe. I stepped back a pace and took another reading: 3.8 ppm. Another step back: 3.0 ppm. "That smell" was definitely coming from the vent.

Just then, a woman from the far table came up to the bar. "Eliza, it smells like something died over there. Can we open the tube door and let some of the smell out?"

As Eliza was putting down her bar rag, connections formed in my brain. I could see what *might* be wrong. I jumped in. "No. Eliza, turn on the Closed sign and seal the door."

The look in Eliza's eyes should've knocked me dead right there. "Scotty, are you telling me how to run my bar?"

"Sorry, yes." I pushed my comp credentials into Eliza's console. "I'm acting for Jack now. There's some kind of Eco malfunction here. Until we know how widespread it is, we don't know if it's safer here or out there. I have to assume we need to contain it."

"Safer? Contain it? Are we in danger?"

"I don't know. Probably. Maybe. But we're not guessing—we're analyzing. If I find it's more dangerous in here, you'll all be out in the tube with me pushing you along. Adam, Al, get those people up. Don't panic them, but get some distance between them and those vents." Adam went into Rescue mode, assessing the situation and taking action. Once she realized I was serious, Eliza also took charge, sealing the doors and herding and cajoling the bar crowd.

I got on my comm and contacted Treatment. "Sector 7, Treatment, Engineer Stewart speaking."

Ah, hell. "Engineer Stewart, this is Mr. Wayne up in the Old Town tavern. We have a sulfide leak. You need to shut down the CR Units."

"Hmph. Jack's Boy, that's lousy form for a report. You're sure you're not just drunk? Stinking drunk, maybe?" She laughed at her own joke, doing nothing for my mood.

"Stewart, check your meters. Mine shows sulfide at—5.0 ppm. It's climbing."

"All right, *Intern*, I'll check." There was a pause. "Sulfide duct shows 0.003 ppm post-scrubber. I'm going to trust my industrial meter over your belt unit. I'd say you haven't calibrated yours lately, rookie."

"Damn it, Stewart, I can *smell* the sulfide!"

"Then take a bath, Intern!" She laughed again and disconnected.

But she was right: her meters were hundreds of times better than mine. Why was she reading purified air post-scrubber?

I looked again at *all* of the gas readings. And there was something… I pulled some of the numbers into a calculation. And suddenly, it *almost* made sense. I pulled up a diagram of an ionic separator, and the last piece fell into place. "Oh, shit."

"Scotty!"

"Sorry, Eliza, but this time it's warranted." I hit Jack's comm circuit, but got his machine. He was at that damned party so I had to leave a message. "Jack, Scott. I'm in the Old Town. We're getting hydrogen sulfide in the air ducts at 5 ppm. Repeat: H-TWO-S at 5 P-P-M and climbing. Stewart's not seeing this in treatment, but I think that's because the sensors are after the scrubbers, and we're testing in the wrong ducts. Jack, there's a flaw in the ionic separators, and I never saw it. You based the calculations on Earth normal atmosphere, which is slightly heavier than sulfide. The sulfide floats in the air but never really rises. When you ionize it, it separates lower. The gas mix in our air isn't the same as Earth's; it's slightly *lighter* than sulfide. The sulfide still floats but it floats lower. The ionic separator doesn't send it to the sulfide ducts, not all of it. Some slips into carbon dioxide ducts and eventually into the cleaned air ducts. Jack, it's pumping the stuff straight into the Old Town. Probably other chambers in the neighborhood, too, but this looks like the epicenter. You have to shut it down, Jack. You have to shut it down!"

I disconnected. Eliza, Adam, Al, and Paul were all looking at me. "So how bad is it? And what can we do?" Adam asked.

"Bad. And we have to shut the CR Units down, which I can't do from here even with Jack's credentials. We have to shut them down or... or starve them, create a negative pressure. They run on pent-up gas pressure. If they can't reach operating pressure, the separators won't kick in."

"So we need to cut off the flow?"

"Can't do that, Al. Way too much flow in the city; it's constant. But maybe we can go the other way: *increase* the flow, and get the wastes moving through so fast there's no chance for pressure to build up. What I'd *really* like to do is move so much material through that it creates a negative pressure, not just neutral."

"What, so we have to flush the johns?"

"Paul, that won't be enough but it can't hurt. Go ahead: turn on all the taps and start flushing all the johns. Get some help. Adam, how are you on fluid dynamics?"

"Not much fluid flow on the regolith. I haven't looked at those equations in a decade."

"Well, dredge them up. You've just been drafted into Eco. I need you to pair with me on these calculations." I checked the meter: 5.6 ppm. "And we'd better hurry."

I started running through duct diagrams and scenarios, while Adam ran numbers and checked my work. Al's a hydroponicist, so he knows something about fluid flow. He looked over both our shoulders. "You're dreaming. No way."

Adam spoke up from his comp. "The numbers work out, Al. If we get enough flow in a short time, it *will* create a negative pressure large enough to cut out the ionics. Maybe even kick them into shutdown mode."

"Yeah, but you're going to need so much flow... "

"How much?" Eliza was getting nervous. She finally smelled the sulfide too.

Adam checked his comp. "Thousands of flushes in minutes. More like tens of thousands. More would be better."

I checked another spec. "Yeah, that will do it. It may burst a treatment pipe somewhere, but that will drain the system even more. It'll be a hell of a mess, but not as bad as..."

"As bad as what? And how do you plan to get tens of thousands of flushes?"

"Bad, Eliza." The meter was at 6.6. "Really bad. But I have a plan to get those flushes."

I held out my comp so Eliza could look at my plan. "No way." The look on her face was the one you'll see when she cuts you off after one too many: the pleasant hostess becomes the drill sergeant. "No way you're pushing that. That'll kill my profits for the quarter."

I pointed at Adam: he was starting to look nauseous. The sulfide hugged the floor in the Lunar air, but was slowly pushing up. "And that won't? We need the negative pressure and fast. Hydrogen sulfide doesn't just smell—if you get enough of it, it's toxic. And it burns or explodes if you give it an excuse. Very soon, we won't just have a stink: we'll have explosions all over this quarter if we don't cut it off now."

Eliza looked at her antique cash register, the symbol of her bottom line, and winced. "OK, push it."

I clicked PUSH, and I started to hear pops on comps all around the room. And if Jack's Admin code was doing its job, the same pop was showing up on every active comp in Tycho:

*08/26 15:31:00 FREE BEER!*

*What happens when we flush every john in Tycho at the same time? Let's find out! Flush your toilet in the next 10 minutes and get a free beer at the Old Town Tavern. Just bring your monthly cycler receipt showing a full flush cycle before 15:41, and we'll give you a beer. Help us give Eco Services a real test! (Flush test approved by Ecology Services Director Jack Brockway.)*

*FREE BEER AT THE OLD TOWN!*

"Will Jack have a fit when he sees you used his code and his name?"

"If this doesn't work, it won't matter."

"Eliza, can I have a beer while we wait?" We used to say Al would stop for a cold one on the way to his own funeral. That day, I learned how true that was.

Then I remembered a chem lecture from the previous term, and I pulled my notes. "Wait! No beer."

"Huh?"

"H2S will react with the alcohol. Not easily without an acid catalyst, but possible. That'll make ethanethiol, and that will *really* stink."

"Worse than 'that smell'?"

"Like rotten onions stewed in foot fungus. It's officially the smelliest substance in existence."

"Ewww!"

"Yeah, but...," I read further. "But it's less toxic and less flammable. And it'll settle as a liquid at room temperature, not hang in the air. This may buy us some time."

"So pour the beer?"

"No, we need a way to mix it with the airborne sulfide. Usually, you make thiols by bubbling sulfide through alcohol. Since the sulfide's airborne, we need to mix them sort of the opposite way. We'll want some sort of acidic catalyst..."

"We've got lemons, limes, pineapple juice, vinegar..."

"...then we need to maximize the surface interface between the beer and the air. It may not work—this ain't exactly a reaction chamber—but if we can spread the beer to expose it to the air, spread it fine and spray it through the sulfide layer, it might work."

"You mean like this?" Eliza uncapped a bottle and poured in some lemon juice. Then she stuck her thumb in and shook the bottle until she couldn't hold back the pressure. Her thumb popped out, and foamy beer spewed into the air, soaking me, Adam, and the tables around us.

"Oh, yeah?" Adam grabbed another bottle, added juice, shook, and aimed straight for Eliza's big mop of hair. It's hard to aim beer foam, though, so he sprayed half the table next to us.

"Adam! Aim higher! Give it some distance!" Would it work? I couldn't guess, but I couldn't see we had anything else to try. I poured some juice in a bottle and started shaking it. In one-sixth G and with our lower air pressure... well, Downsiders have never seen how high and how far beer suds can fly. Maybe it would be enough.

And thus was launched the First Annual Great Old Town Beer Brawl. Eliza armed everyone with bottles and citrus, and they filled the air with suds. Adam had the idea—ingenious? flawed? who could tell?—of spraying the beer taps through lemon slices. I don't know how effective that was, but it sure made the beer foam! And soon, along with the aroma of Tycho's finest beers, we smelled the pungent odor of the most sickeningly rotten onions you've ever imagined. Foaming and spraying makes an excellent dispersal mechanism, and we were actually gaining ground on the hydrogen sulfide in the air. All the while, Paul was back in the latrines, flushing repeatedly.

And somewhere during the Beer Brawl, I heard the sound of water rushing through pipes under the floor plates. Lots of water. "They're flushing! God damn, they're *flushing!*" Eliza and Al both celebrated by spraying me with some of Eliza's best weiss beer. "Wait! Let me at the vent."

I knelt by the vent. Foamy beer ran down the wall and drained in. The smell that emerged was almost too much even for my desensitized nose, but it was drifting out... not gusting. The positive pressure had slowed, almost stopped. The meter read 5.7. The promise of FREE BEER! was working. Toilets were flushing all over Tycho. For good measure, I pushed the pop again, hoping for maximum flushage.

And then through the vent, I heard a soft, low *whump!* Somewhere deep in CitEng, a seal had finally breached. Wastewater and sludge were draining at high velocity—I didn't dare think about where, but it would be an ugly mess—and creating a big negative pressure behind them. Instead of ethanethiol odor rising from the vent, I felt a slight but unmistakable air current flow *into* the vent. The meter actually dropped while I was watching, from 5.4 to 5.3.

"Everyone!" I stood on the bar for attention, and Eliza glared at me. Then I almost lost my footing in the beer foam. "Everyone, keep spraying! We're settling 'that smell' out. Adam, Al, get mops. Push the foam down the kitchen and bathroom drains. Eliza! We can open the door now. Pressure in the tube should be higher than in here. Let's set up fans and get the sulfide moving in. And *keep flushing those toilets!*"

And so the Beer Brawl continued in earnest. We call it the First Annual Great Old Town Beer Brawl because every year since, we've celebrated the day the Old Town didn't blow up. When you're here for Beer Brawl, don't drink the beer. Paul saves up his failed batches all year long, keeps them in a storage locker for the Brawl. You'll think you're drinking liquid wastes.

When CTU Security showed up, they didn't know what to make of the place. A pair of floor fans blocked the doors open, blowing fresh tube air in. When Security got past the fans, they found bar patrons and staff spraying the place and each other with beer—the citrus had long since run out, but the Beer Brawl had become a purpose unto itself—while Al and Adam and Eliza mopped around them. And in the far corner, leaning over a vent, I alternated between calling out readings from my meter and trying to raise Jack on his comm.

They would've arrested the lot of us on drunk and disorderly. Wouldn't you? But I flashed my Eco credentials and hoped they were convincing. Plus, Eliza offered them whiskey, beer being in short supply at that point. I don't know what persuaded them, the whiskey or the creds, but they postponed arresting us long enough to hear the story. Then they contacted Security Central and told them we had an explanation for the Third Level Flush. I abused Jack's code some more, ordering up overtime for Eco Services cleanup crews to clean out the

Old Town. Adam had already called in Rescue medical teams. I doubt anyone there had had a serious exposure, but sulfide poisoning is nasty stuff so we took no chances.

The Flush could've been much worse. Not through any planning on my part—as luck would have it, the breach was directly over the Bader Farms Co-op plots. Yeah, a lot of crops were washed away and the Baders filed for damages, but for the most part, the Farms were exactly where that sludge was headed anyway. At that stage of treatment, what was left was destined to be fertilizer once most of the liquids were filtered and baked out. So the Farms were a mess, and the sludge was wetter than usual. The clean-up took weeks. But if the breach had been 100 feet further east and north, the Flush would've been in an entertainment or a restaurant district. That would've been a much larger PR disaster.

Not that the incident wasn't a PR disaster as it stood, you understand. The Old Town got the worst of "that smell", being closest to the refresh pumping system, and a lot of residences had to be cleaned. The CR Program was written off as an unmitigated failure and Jack was written off with it, naturally, since CR was his baby.

He received a brief burst of sympathy: when he got my message, he rushed to City Services, assembled a crew, and tried to dismantle the CR units. They were still on duty when the Flush hit. There he was, in a tuxedo, standing his ground in the face of a river of raw sewage, trying to save the city. It briefly made him a hero; but, once the journos learned that his miscalculation was at the root of it all, the story changed. "A looney wouldn't have made that mistake," the story went, even though I never noticed the mistake myself. And eventually, someone coined the name "Jack Blockage". Once that name stuck, it was only a matter of time before Jack was asked to resign.

Jack's last official communiqués were a letter of commendation in my file, which also retroactively approved everything I'd done with his code, and an invoice to Eliza for 20,000 liters of beer. He didn't figure she should save Tycho Under *and* pay for the privilege. That invoice covered everything we used in the Beer Brawl and all the free beers she had to give out for my pop, and there was plenty left over. And that, rookie, is how me and the rest of the Beer Brawl Brigade drank free for the next month. Eliza said we deserved it. After all, with enough beer and a few thousand flushes, we saved Tycho Under.

# FATHER-DAUGHTER OUTING

"We're doing okay, Daddy. Doing okay... Nine-seven, Nine-eight, nine-nine, *twelve* hundred!

"Okay, Daddy... Gotta catch my breath... And check your stretcher pressure —

"No, that's wrong. Lunar Survival Manual says check my pressure and oh-two first, *then* look to the injured. I know, Daddy, I know: follow the manual.

"Pressure is point-eight standard. LSM says keep pressure light, conserve air. Oh-two is nominal. I'm not breathing hard from carrying you, not too much. I wish I had my LSM. Maybe I should turn up the oh-two to compensate for the work, but maybe I should turn it *down*. I don't remember, so I'll leave it alone.

"Temperature is a little high from exertion. Turning up the radiator a bit, but I want to save the batteries. Sun might catch us if I stay here too long.

"Okay, Daddy. Stretcher pressure is high. I turned it down but the med comp overrode me. I think it's trying to keep you well oxygenated. You lost a lot of blood, so it's compensating. I think.

"I just need to sit a little. Sorry for sitting on the stretcher. That regolith is neg one-forty, and my suit butt's not insulated enough for that.

"No joke about my butt? I guess you're really out cold, huh?

"I'm up, I'm up. Sun's coming.

"Twelve-one, twelve-two, twe'-three, twe'-four, five, six, seven, eight..."

"Looking for Moon Men, Ellie?"

"Daaaaad!" I turned from the port and scowled at him. "I haven't believed in Moon Men for five yeeeeeears!"

Okay, it was really only two years, but Daddy didn't have to know. A girl's entitled to some secrets, Mom always says, so Dad didn't need to know I still looked for Moon Men back when I was twelve. He forgets I'm practically grown up. Why give him another excuse to forget?

Daddy thinks I want to become an explorer because I'm still looking for Moon Men. Mom thinks I want to find a diamond mine and get rich. But they both think exploring is just a phase I'll grow out of. They don't say that to me, but it's in their eyes, and in the way they smile at me when I study Dad's old Lunar Survival Manual.

Well, I may be a kid — *legally* — but I'm serious about this. I *will* be a Lunar explorer, and that's all there is to it! Why else are people living here if not to explore? Our cities cover half a million hectares, maybe two million if you count space ports and mines and other Outside facilities. Ninety-nine-point-nine-five percent of our world is still begging for explorers. I know I won't find Moon Men, no matter how Daddy teases. I don't know *what* I'll find, that's the point! But with that much unexplored surface, I'll find *something*!

As for Mom... Well, *maybe* I'll find something valuable, you never know. Shoes aren't cheap, and a famous discovery could buy me lots of shoes...

"Five years, huh? I guess you've lost interest, then. I guess you wouldn't want to go Outside tomorrow..."

"Outside?"

"Oh, I had a father-daughter outing in mind. But since you're bored with Outside... "

"DADDY!!!"

"Jim, don't tease her." Mom came into the viewing room, Jimmy bouncing on her hip. "Eliza, we got your grade report today. You've brought your grades up. *Way* up."

"Well, Mr. Huynh says explorers have to know math and science. And I see what he means! My LSM makes a lot more sense now. There are still some equations I can't understand, though. Mom, can you show me —"

Mom cut me off. "Math later, dear. You *can* take a break, you know."

"There's plenty of time. We're not sending you to Lunar Survival School. Maybe when you're sixteen, if you're still interested."

"But Daaaaaad!"

Again Mom took control. "*But* we're going to set up some more Outside expeditions for you, and for us as a family when I can find a sitter for Jimmy. You're growing up — you've earned it."

"And as for tomorrow..." Daddy tapped his comp, pushing a message to the wall screen.

> *ISSUED BY: Kirk Hanson, Supervisor,*
> *Merrick Lunar Mining Co.*
>
> *ISSUED TO: James Wall, Mining Technician.*
>
> *SUBJECT: One Career Observer Pass,*
> *registered to Eliza Wall.*
>
> *ATTACHED: E. Wall's certifications for*
> *Spacesuit Operations, Orienteering,*
> *Communications, and First Aid.*

"I talked to my supervisor. He checked your certifications and approved it. I've arranged it with Mr. Huynh. You're excused from school tomorrow for the Career Observer program. We'll spend all day out checking the prospecting stations. You'll have to write a report, of course, and —"

"DaddyDaddyDaddyDaddy!"

"Whoa! Feet on the ground! No launching in the house!"

⚓

"Nine-eight... nine-nine... Damn it!

"Oops! I didn't mean to swear... honest, Daddy!

"Oh, you're still unconscious. Whew!

"But I wish you *were* conscious! I'm just upset. I don't remember if I'm at twenty-eight hundred or twenty-nine.

"The count really doesn't matter, I know; I just have to keep walking until I hit Tycho. But I have to keep up the pace. The sun is getting closer! When it hits, the temperature will start to climb. The lith'll get up to 75C eventually. Suits have a higher albedo so they won't get *that* hot, but I don't know how long our radiators can keep our temps down.

"I did like you taught me: a count helps you keep up your pace. A song, a chant. Anything rhythmic... just to keep me trudging along.

"Hmmm... Remember the way you taught me the constellations and the stars?

> "*Crux, Centaurus,*
> *Lupus, Ara,*
> *Telescop'yum,*
> *And Corona*
> *Aust-a-ralis,*
> *Sagittar'yus,*
> *Scorp'yus, Libra,*
> *Hydra, Corvus,*

*Virgo, Serpens,*
*Ophiuch'us,*
*Scutum, 'quila,*
*Cygnus, Lyra,*
*Herc'les, C'rona*
*Bor'lis, Bootes,*
*Co' Ber'nices..."*

Daddy had six prospecting stations to inspect that day. They're big robot platforms that creep over the lith: scraping up samples, running analyses, and storing away anything really unusual. They follow some sort of search pattern; I can't explain it.

I didn't want to get Daddy in trouble with Mr. Hanson, so I didn't say my *real* opinion of the prospectors. But even though they're Daddy's job, they're a poor substitute for real explorers! Would an AI have recognized the Genesis Rock that Irwin and Scott found on Apollo 15? I don't think so!

Daddy stopped at the first station, nearly two hours from Tycho. We sealed our suits and buddy-checked them. Daddy had taught me to buddy-check a suit as soon as I could understand a pressure gauge. I can't wait for when it's my turn to teach Jimmy!

When both suits were green, Daddy evacuated the crawler. Pumps sucked all the air into air bottles. Then he opened the hatch. I stood patiently, following protocol as he lowered the ramp, climbed down, and did a quick visual inspection. When he came on the radio — "Observer Wall, clear to disembark" — I carefully stepped down the ramp. I wanted to leap. Heck, we leap longer ramps in gym class and we're *graded* on that. But again, with the recorders running, I did things by the book.

And then Daddy threw the book out at the second station: he let *me* go out and do the arrival inspection! If we weren't suited, I would've kissed him.

At each station, Daddy used his remote to stop the drive and put the whole unit on standby. Then he inspected the treads, the tread drives, and the electronics. Meanwhile, his comp talked to the station AI, the two of them *blip-bleep-blipping* back and forth until each of them agreed that the other was healthy. At the second station, I asked: "Dad, what happens if each one thinks the other is malfunctioning?"

"Well, Ellie, you remember what I taught you about calibration?"

"Uh-huh." I thought a bit. "*Ohhh!* You calibrated *your* computer this morning, so you *know* it's healthy!"

"Well, tech support calibrated it, and even a calibration can be wrong. But you're close enough. Mark yourself down for a cookie."

After the inspection, Daddy removed the station logs and replaced them with new storage blocks from the crawler. The stations upload their logs any time they detect a satellite overhead, but the company wants the physical logs as well. I asked why, and I got a twenty-minute lesson on redundant systems, error checking, and data consistency tests. Sometimes Daddy's the most irritating man on Luna! He can *never* answer a simple question. He always answers with a question, or a story, or even a *homework assignment!* He says I'll learn more if I figure the answers out for myself. I guess he's right. But just *once*, I'd like him to give me a simple, direct answer. Does *everything* have to be a test?

↓

"The terminator's really close now, Daddy. The LSM says it moves about sixteen klicks an hour at the equator; I'm guessing ten to twelve here at Tycho's latitude. I should be able to move faster than that in Lunar G. But I've been walking a long time now. And besides, I'm dragging your stretcher. And we both know I didn't inherit my big butt from Mom.

"Again with the butt jokes. Sorry, I'm nervous. Gotta rest a minute, but I can't rest too long.

"I need something with a faster beat. Something simpler. I get thinking about the star names, and it slows me down. Hmmm...

> *"Two little looney birds sittin' on the pad*
> *One named Lou and one named Chad.*
> *Blast off, Chad; blast off, Lou!*
> *Space is calling, and it's calling for you!*
> *Ten, Nine, Eight, Seven, Six, Five, Four, Three,*
> *Two, One, BLAST OFF!*
> *Now off to Earth! Off to Mars! Off that pad!*

"Don't worry, Daddy, I know hundreds of rhymes!"

At the fourth station, the accident struck. I don't know what happened. I was bored with Daddy's routine after the second station, so I was watching the stars, naming off constellations and looking for spaceships or satellites, when Daddy suddenly yelled like I'd never heard before.

I turned and looked, and I screamed. Some sort of fluid was jetting out of the drive unit.

I don't know what could remain liquid at that temperature and pressure, but I never thought to wonder when I saw that the jet had sliced into Daddy's left calf. The thin, pressurized stream had cut the suit like a knife. The suit absorbed the worst of it — but as I pulled Daddy away from the stream, I saw blood boiling into the vacuum. And his yelling was now screaming. A girl should *never* hear her daddy scream. That's just wrong.

Before I even got him out of the stream, the suit's auto-tourniquet activated. The AT would stop the bleeding and also prevent any further air loss, but I knew from first aid class that an AT is only for short-term emergency treatment. It can starve the limb of blood and kill the tissue.

I had to get Daddy into the crawler and then apply pressure.

I pulled him in and slapped the switch to seal and pressurize the cabin, and then I lifted Daddy onto the stretcher from the rear storage locker. I didn't want to waste any time getting him out of the suit when the pressure reached normal. As soon as the light was green, I pulled off my helmet and gloves, then Daddy's. He was mumbling half-coherent instructions. I remembered the first aid he taught me, so I knew what he meant to say; but it was a good thing the stretcher's AI prompted me what to do. I was — I —

I couldn't help shouting: "I trained on a simulator. This is *Daddy!*" It actually calmed me down. I said it, it was done, and I could move on.

I stuck diagnostic patches to Daddy's neck and temple, feeding data to the stretcher. Then I went to work on his suit. You have to be able to remove spacesuits piecemeal for emergencies like this, so there are seals and buckles you can undo to separate the sections. They're not easy to work, because you don't want them releasing accidentally. It took me nearly five minutes to get the sleeves and vest off: three minutes of fidgeting with seals mixed with two minutes where I just gave up and cried until I got control of myself.

When I had his upper body free, I stuck another diagnostic patch on his chest. The stretcher extended a transdermal IV, and I slid the cuff around his left wrist and up to his elbow. When the sensors detected good venous access, the stretcher chimed and the cuff constricted, making a complete seal. Medicine started pumping in. I don't know what it was, but Daddy stopped mumbling, relaxed, and was soon unconscious. His color was still good, so I was sure it was a sedative that put him to sleep and not the blood loss. Pretty sure.

The stretcher confirmed my diagnosis: the auto-tourney had to go. Following its instructions, I unsealed the left leg of Daddy's suit but didn't deactivate the AT yet. Not 'til the stretcher told me to. I removed the left boot, and attached another transdermal IV. I bet this one contained null plasma to keep the tissue oxygenated below the AT.

The stretcher popped open a drawer. Inside was a pressure bandage. I read the instructions, just in case I had forgotten how to apply it. Then I turned off the AT. Immediately, blood started oozing from Daddy's calf. I don't *think* I fainted, but I got mighty dizzy for a few seconds. Then as fast as I could, I removed the rest of the suit leg, and I applied and taped down the pressure bandage. The red seemed to stop.

And that was all I could do, except look at the stretcher readouts. They have a doctor mode, but I couldn't understand all those numbers. I pushed it to simple mode, and I watched the bars bounce around and the colors shift. Eventually, all of the bars settled into normal ranges — low, but normal — and the indicator lights all went green. I wasn't in charge of Daddy anymore — the stretcher was.

We had air; we had immediate medical care. Next item according to LSM was communications. I went to Daddy's control console and tried to work the communicator. Everything should've worked. I wasn't trained on a system this complex, but it had all the features of a basic comm unit with fairly standard controls. And I feared there would be a security lockout that would need Daddy's passcode, but I think the ship somehow tied the controls into the stretcher system. There *were* lockouts but they all seemed to have disengaged. The comm system was active.

Everything *should've* worked... but it didn't. I couldn't pick up anything, either on local or satellite. The local channels were very low power, intended for communications between the crawler and personnel outside. They wouldn't pick up anything else. And the satellite channels... Well, I got nothing there. Maybe I did something wrong. Maybe there were no satellites in view. I waited a half hour and tried again. Still nothing. Again, I let my frustration out by yelling: "I'm only fourteen! I never called a satellite!"

And again, yelling put my frustration out where I could handle it. Mom never likes it when we kids yell, but sometimes I just can't keep stuff in — almost like a sneeze I have to let out. And after a sneeze, you can get back to work.

So just like one of Daddy's damned tests, I started to work the problem. The prospecting station had a communications channel...

but if I couldn't figure out the crawler's, no way I could figure out *that*.

I needed to get Daddy to a real doctor. I didn't know how much medicine and null plasma the stretcher had, and I didn't know how much oxygen we had or how long the recirculators were good for. A clock was running, but I didn't know how much time was on it.

I hadn't paid attention to where we had driven. Daddy drove and I was enjoying the sights too much. Now I pulled up the nav record. We were maybe seventy kilometers out from Tycho Crater. That was a short distance for the crawler; but try as I might, I couldn't figure out how to start the crawler engine. If I rode in a crawler twice a year, that was a lot; I never saw anyone start one.

I couldn't call for help, and we couldn't drive to help. What was left? Walking?

Well, it was still pre-dawn. It would be cold out there, but it would soon get hot when the terminator crossed. The Lunar Survival Manual teaches a technique called Manual Thermal Control. When you're caught out on the surface for an extended period, you can extend your radiator battery by using light and shadow to regulate your temperature. In basic MTC, you use available shadows from boulders and ejecta to cool you down when you get too hot. In advanced MTC — and I studied this a lot because it seemed like a quintessential explorer skill — you use the terminator itself for regulation. Move into the dark side when you're too warm, back into the light when you're too cold. It's simple in theory, as long as you can keep up the pace; but they don't even teach advanced MTC until the second year of Lunar Survival School. You really have to understand Luna and your equipment to do it right.

But I couldn't see another choice. Maybe a real LSS grad would, but I couldn't. So I sealed Daddy's stretcher cover, loaded it up with all the meds and null plasma from storage, and put my suit back on. Then I vacuumed up the compartment air, strapped those bottles and all the spares to the stretcher, and opened the hatch.

I tugged the stretcher down the ramp and onto the lith. The foot of the stretcher folded out into a sled to slide over regolith. The head of the stretcher folded out into hooks that clamped onto the rear of a suit belt. I hooked up to the stretcher, and with the constellations to guide me, I started the long walk to Tycho.

"One, two, three, four... "

⟂

"Daddy, we need to talk. I wish you could answer. If ever a girl needed her daddy's advice, I need yours now.

"Ah, who'm I kidding? You wouldn't tell me what to do; you'd make me figure it out for myself. Well, I have.

"Daddy, we won't make it with me dragging you. I thought I could, but this is *hard!* I can't *believe* how hard! The terminator caught us. It's getting warmer, fast.

"But I *think* I can make it on my own. I can catch the terminator, stay ahead. Stay ahead all the way to Tycho. And then, Daddy, then I'll send help back for you. You hear me? I'm gonna send a doctor back for you.

"I'll use basic MTC here. I'll leave you in the shadow of this big boulder, Daddy. The stretcher will keep you warm, and the shadow will keep you cool. The sun won't hit this shadow for days. And by then — by then —

"Oh, Daddy, I don't wanna leave you! But I don't know what else to do. I wish —

"That terminator's not standing still, Daddy. I've gotta go catch it.

"Goodbye, Daddy.

"Goodbye... "

⟂

I caught the terminator without completely exhausting myself and without my radiator burning out as it bled off my waste heat. And after that, staying ahead of it wasn't hard. Leaving Daddy behind was the hardest thing I'd ever done, but it made the difference. I was still tired but I wasn't losing ground.

Eventually, I could see the walls of Tycho in the shadowy distance: not really the walls themselves, but the crater rim lights. I didn't expect my suit radio could reach yet, but I called anyway, as much as breath permitted.

Soon, I saw a blinking light. I couldn't see Tycho's central uplift, but that had to be Tycho Traffic Control on the peak. If I had visual contact, I *had to* be in radio distance. I sat down and started continuous distress messages.

Soon I heard an answer. I explained where I was, where Daddy was.

I fell asleep before the hopper landed near me.

When I woke up, I was staring at knees. Looking up from there, I saw bending over me the tallest looney I've ever seen — and we grow 'em tall! He was unsuited, so we were in pressure. For that matter, I was unsuited too and under a thermal blanket. It was warm, the bed was warm; I was wonderfully warm.

"Ah, Miss Wall, you're awake! Don't move, please, young lady; I need you to stay in the warming bed. I'm Dr. Benjamin Jones, by the way, very pleased to meet you." He had a great smile and a soothing voice, just what you imagine a doctor should be. But tall! "You don't really have frostbite from sleeping on frozen regolith, but you came close. I want to keep you warm."

With that, I suddenly remembered everything. "My Daddy! You have to —"

"Shhh. We picked him up before we found you. He's still pretty weak, but he's fine. From the stretcher records, I'd say you saved his leg."

And then I cried, really cried in relief. When I was done, Dr. Jones handed me a tissue. Then he asked, "And *why* were you walking to

Tycho?"

And so I told him everything, mixing up my story as I went: time on the lith, time back in Tycho, time in the crawler, all jumbled together. And when I told him how I learned MTC from the Lunar Survival Manual, he nodded.

"Yes, that *does* work. It worked this time, and that's what really counts. But do you know what *else* we would've taught you at LSS?"

I shook my head. I had made a mistake... I just knew it.

"We would've taught you to *stay with your vehicle unless you're low on consumables.* Most Lunar traffic has a schedule on file, including your father's crawler. When he failed to check in on schedule, we waited a reasonable time and tried to contact him. Then Tycho Rescue sent our squad out looking for him, following his planned route. Imagine our surprise when we found an empty crawler!"

Now I was sobbing again. He softened his tone further. "But then we saw your tracks and his stretcher tracks. And they were headed straight for Tycho — you're a pretty good navigator! And so we swung back. We found him first. Before we could find you, Traffic Control sent us your location."

"But then I —"

"You did the best you could do under the circumstances, and that's what it will say in my report. More than that: since you're so interested in Lunar Survival School, I'll write you a letter of recommendation. After all, you just passed your second year practical exam."

And with that, he left to do something on his computer. With him out of the way, I could see that Daddy was in the berth next to mine, still in the stretcher but with the cover open. He was haggard, but he was awake and looking at me.

"Daddy!"

"You heard the doc: stay right there in that bed, Ellie."

"Daddy —"

"Hush, we'll talk about it later. Everything's okay."

I settled back. I felt warm, not just from the blanket and the bed.

*Daddy was safe!*

"Hey, Ellie!" I looked at him again. "You sat on my stretcher! Put a dent in it with your big bottom, I'll bet! No cookies for you, young lady."

"Daaaaad…"

"Oh, all right. One cookie. You can work it off in Lunar Survival School. You start next month."

*"Daddy!"*

# NOT ∧NOTHER V∧CUUM STORY

Look, what you *don't* want to hear is another vacuum story.

Oh, we've got plenty of them here in the Old Town. They're older than this bar, older than Tycho Under, older even than space travel. They're our *essential folklore*, as my old lit prof called it: tales that teach you how to survive in your culture. The most important lesson on Luna is: keep your vacuum on one side, and you and your air on the other. So our essential folklore includes lots of variations of *How I Almost Breathed Vacuum* or *They Screwed Up, and So They Breathed Vacuum.*

But you've heard them all before. *You* could tell *me* all the same stories. So while I may spin you a tale now and then, the one thing I promise I'm *not* gonna tell you is another vacuum story. Ever.

But sit down, order a drink, and I'll give you something different. Let me tell you how a young smart ass—OK, it was me, back when I was younger and more of a smart ass than I am today—got in trouble from *too much* air.

⊥

The story begins when I was hanging in the door of a short haul flyer, looking for a soft place to land without breaking my neck when I jumped.

Well, no, I think it's important that I be honest here, because I don't want you to miss my point. The story *really* begins a couple days before that, when I snagged myself extra homework by mouthing off to Fontes. Again.

Sergeant Armand Fontes, Lunar Defense Reserves, Lead Instructor at Lunar Survivor School, Tycho Under Campus. I always figured he hated me because I was an extension student from McAuliffe University, and all my classmates were from Defense or Rescue or the other services. I figured he saw me as a college punk, wasting his time. Now I know he just loves to mess with vac-heads, and I was the king of the vac-heads.

It was time for the solo practical exam in prefab shelters. I had two hot dates lined up for that weekend—*one* woman is more than I can handle these days, but I was young and stupid—and I was more interested in them than any exam. Plus it sounded like a cakewalk, and I wasn't shy about saying so. "This is such a waste, Sarge. We should test manual thermal control, or something even more challenging. Who uses prefab shelters these days? They're as safe as a home cycler."

Fontes looked at me with distaste. "Mister Morgan, how many injuries were reported in home cyclers last year? How many fatalities?"

"I don't know, Sarge."

"Well, you just earned yourself a homework assignment. And I've pushed a restriction to the AI Net, so they won't help you with your research. I want a full summary, cross categorized by root cause, severity of injury, and how each might've been avoided. By Monday.

"Now for those of you who aren't the daredevils that Mister Morgan is... Prefab shelters date from the earliest days of the Lunar Era. The modern versions can be found in the cargo decks of half the shuttles and freighters operating in Lunar space, maybe more. They're also common at mine excavations and other sites with no permanent structures. They'll keep one person alive for a full Lunar without resupply; and they're simple to set up, just follow a checklist. *But you have to follow that checklist!* And then you have to monitor your gauges—not just your idiot lights!—keep on top of your controls, and be alert for variances. Don't assume that 'basic' equipment works as promised. Here's your cheat sheet for this exam, ladies and gentlemen: *this exam is all about following directions and taking care of the details, even when you're bored.* Those are your two most important survival skills; and you don't graduate to 'challenging' until you learn 'em. Got that, Kenneth?" When Fontes switches to first names, it means you aren't respectable enough to be "Mister" or "Miss".

I had no intention of a long homework assignment interfering with my dates, so I planned to get the exam out of the way quickly. When Fontes opened the list for testing slots, I practically sprained a thumb pushing my name into the first slot. The tests were staggered in groups of five, starting every four hours. If I got the exam out of the way, I could be watching Earthset with Mary Sue Reilly before the last group started.

The goal of the solo practical is to survive for two days under simulated emergency isolation conditions. You can't rush it, except by failing. If for any reason you don't last the full two days, you fail, and you get to repeat that whole unit. So the test starts when the timer starts, and you're done when it elapses.

Two days is barely a shakedown cruise; but knowing Fontes and the rest of the instructors, I was sure it was plenty of time for trouble. We'd all heard the scuttlebutt: every practical exam has a bit of instructor sabotage thrown in, some zinger in the equipment or the scenario that would force you to improvise. If you flubbed that zinger, you shortened the exam the only way possible: hitting the panic button and flunking the exam.

I was sure Fontes wanted to see me flunk; so I buried myself in research on prefabs and prefab accidents. Those case studies.... Man, talk about your vacuum stories! I studied them all, and all the common causes. A hard ass like Fontes is the best teacher for someone like me, I guess. I'd even *study* if it would wipe that grin off his face.

And I studied that checklist. No, smart ass that I was, I *memorized* that checklist. I could recite the list, forwards or backwards, by

Wednesday morning when Fontes called my name. "Mister Morgan, front and center. You're with me and Schultz, flyer 3. Suit up, and head down tube J to the flyer. Miss King, flyer 4, also tube J." Sarah King and I went to the suit room and suited up, checking each other's suits and seals. Then we headed down tube J to our respective locks. We wished each other luck, and we boarded.

I strapped in, and was soon joined by Fontes. Rita Schultz strapped into the pilot's chair and requested a launch window. The tug clamped onto our nose hook and pulled us out onto the launch pad. As Schultz went through her prelaunch checklist and Fontes made notes on his comp, I reviewed my lessons. Soon enough, we launched; and once we were off primary boost, Fontes pushed a map to my comp.

"OK, Mister Morgan, take a look at that map. You trainees get it easy for this test. Later on, your testing ground will be a large crater or more; but your prefab is somewhere in that square." Yow. Some restriction: that square was half a klick on a side. "But not too easy. To make it more challenging, we're going to simulate crash conditions."

"You're going to crash land the flyer?"

"No, rookie, we're going to crash land you. You'll pick an approach vector, Schultz will fly low over the testing ground, and you'll jump out."

"What? We haven't covered free jumps yet."

"Oh, don't piss your suit. We won't be high enough up for any serious damage or injury, just enough to dust you up and make you nervous—I'll bet you are already! This way, the test is completely unbiased: you can't claim we set you down far away from the prefab, because you're picking the drop point."

So that brings us back to me hanging out the door of the flyer, boulders and regolith passing by beneath me. Oh, I was nervous, all right; but no way would I let Fontes see.

Part of the test is simply *finding* the prefab. Since Fontes wouldn't let me use my emergency locator while I was in the flyer, I was eyeballing as best I could. The testing ground was a semi-rugged section of one of Tycho's ejecta rays. It was late First Quarter, so the sun would be low in the west, casting shadows east over the ejecta debris.

Schultz interrupted my analysis. "Sergeant, we're at drop altitude on Morgan's vector. The flyer's depressurized, and he can drop any time."

"Thank you, Schultz. OK, Mister Morgan, your clock starts when you jump. Pick your spot. Take your time; but if Schultz exceeds our fuel budget while you're working up the balls to jump, I'm charging you for the extra."

We were over the debris field, moving slowly for a flyer, but still with enough forward momentum for my plan. I figured I would have time to run the locator as I fell, and that forward momentum meant I would pass over a lot of prime hiding spaces. I might just ping the prefab's beacon before I hit the lith, as long as I had the presence of mind to run the locator. As we approached the right spot, I breathed slowly: *trust Fontes, don't worry about the jump, focus on the test.* And then I jumped.

My relaxation trick worked: I was free falling, but I wasn't panicking. I turned on the locator in recording mode, and then I concentrated on where I would fall. By the time the regolith was rushing up toward me and I braced for a roll, a beep told me the locator had found the prefab beacon.

Modern suits are almost as sturdy as a prefab, relying largely on thinner layers of the same material and without the hard helmets common in the early Lunar Era. Fontes was right, LSS trained us in falling and tumbling in our Physical Training classes, and this fall wasn't that much faster than those. So I rolled three times and into a face dive, absorbing the last of the impact on my forearms. Then I used that momentum to bounce backwards to my feet. One simple pivot, and I was loping back to the beacon. That move could've gotten me into the Tycho Under Ballet.

It was another smart ass move, really, but that move made me feel ready for anything. As I ran, I started mentally working my checklist, and thinking on possible zingers.

*Step 1: Search.* I didn't even try a visual search: with the sun in my eyes, even max polarization left me plenty of glare, so the beacon was my guide. When I was practically on top of it, a hill-sized boulder gave me enough shade to see the prefab package, wedged into a cleft between two boulders. I had to wiggle it back and forth to work it out. When packed, a prefab is nearly as large as me, and in all directions— a mass of fabriglass and plastic and consumables that would be impossible for me to budge on Earth. On Luna, I could lift it, sure; but moving it is a matter of mass, not weight, and it's massive. Once it was unwedged, I rolled it onto its cage base, a smooth sled that would allow me to push it over regolith as long as I didn't hit any really large rocks.

*Step 2: Site Selection.* Fontes was almost kind to me in this step: Big Bertha (my new nickname for the hill-sized boulder) gave me plenty of shade. Out in exposed sunlight at Full, the prefab's cooling system would have more work. The fabriglass is largely reflective (and also photovoltaic for power), but far from a perfect reflector. It could get hot in there.

*Step 3: Unpacking.* The prefab has a thick floor disk and a thinner dome top. You pack it by collapsing the dome onto the floor and stacking the consumables package in the center. Then you fold the sides of the disk in, left then right then back, until it's all in a long, thick strip. And then you roll the strip into a massive roll, and assemble the plastic cage around it. I just had to reverse that process.

The cagework disassembles and telescopes to become support struts, which go into sleeves on the dome, a ground ring and a top ring and support struts between them. You lock these all together to make a skeleton for the dome. In case of a catastrophic leak, the skeleton holds the dome up so it doesn't collapse on you while you patch. I opened and disassembled the cage and laid the struts out in rays around the fabriglass.

One easy zinger comes in Unpacking: missing parts. Or you can create your own zinger by losing parts. I had memorized the parts list, too, and I confirmed they were all there. I put all the fasteners into my utility pockets on my thighs.

*Step 4: Unrolling and Unfolding.* I dealt with less and less fabriglass with each round, so unrolling got progressively easier. Then I unfolded the roll to either side and stretched it out. At the innermost center for maximum protection is the consumables package: air bottles, water bottles, liquid nutrients, and vacuum resin for seals. I set them aside.

Unrolling and Unfolding is an unlikely step for zingers. As long as the fabriglass was properly collapsed and folded, these steps should be trouble free. I looked for any tangles or creases, but found none.

*Step 5: Strut Assembly.* I put the upper strut ring in the sleeves around the upper dome, and attached the vertical struts. The verticals would also snap into the lower ring once the dome was sufficiently inflated. Next I assembled the lower strut ring in the sleeves around the flooring. I saw no cracks in the struts, nor any other sort of zingers.

*Step 6: Environment Prep.* I unpacked the environment package from the sled. This was a single-module unit, air pump and water pump and recycler and solar power storage all in one. I opened the lid, visually inspected every component, and ran through the diagnostic circuits. No zinger there.

*Step 7: Initial Inflation.* I unzipped the outer and inner doors of the airlock, so the vacuum wouldn't stick the dome and the flooring together. Then I propped up the struts nearest the airlock, creating just enough of a tent to let me crawl inside and close the lock behind me. I installed the air bottles and water bottles into the environment package, hooked up the feed lines, and hooked the whole package into the solar power line. I opened the first air valve, and prepared to start the inflation cycle.

Wait. The lack of any zinger so far nagged at me and made me expect the worst. What would be the most difficult thing to repair? That would be where Fontes would hide my zinger.

The snuff box. Those prefabs are made from the best fabriglass Corning makes, but even fabriglass will tear if it gets pierced by a shard of metal in a crash. Worse than a tear is a pinhole, large enough for a slow leak but too small to eyeball. Someone who's tired and maybe injured might fall asleep thinking he has good pressure, sleep through the pressure alarms, and asphyxiate. So LSS protocol recommends both an eyeball inspection and a dispersal density test—only we call it the "snuff test", not because it could snuff you out, but because of the dust or snuff involved. When the dome is inflated, you turn off the air recirc, get everybody out of the dome, and start the test. A little snuff box in the top center of the dome fires out a fine spray of reflective dust in all directions inside the dome. Then a camera matrix tracks the falling dust, and the AI in the snuff box looks for signs of air currents. It'll pick up even the tiniest pinhole leaks and then laser spot them so you can apply patches. You don't *have to* leave the dome for the snuff test, but still air gives you the most accurate patches. I'd hate to fail over a shoddy patch, so I would leave for the test.

When the dome was fully inflated, the snuff box would be at the top of the dome, more than twice my height. If something went wrong there... Sure, I could jump up there, but I couldn't *stay* up there. I'd have to let out a lot of air, waste a lot of time, just so I could fix the box. I knew of only a handful of snuff box failures; but a handful is more than zero.

I needed to check the snuff box, which at the time was buried between the two layers of fabriglass, so I needed to inflate enough to reach the box. I started the inflation cycle, and five minutes later I could just squeeze between the dome and the flooring to get to the snuff box. I opened it up for inspection.

"Gotcha, Fontes." Snuff boxes have six charges, so you can run the test multiple times if needed. The first charge had fired prematurely while wrapped deep inside the fabriglass. It hadn't damaged anything outside the box, but the box was a mess. If I ran a test like that, it would fire askew, wasting a *second* charge. Plus the snuff jammed in the box unit would foul up the camera matrix, so that when I ran the third test, the results would be useless. It would take four of my six charges just to get one valid test. If that test showed leaks, I would need to use the fifth charge. That would cut it close. Here was my zinger.

So while the inflation continued, I disassembled the snuff box and carefully cleaned it with supplies from the sled. Some of the snuff was caked into the screen, and I couldn't get it clean with a utility brush. If there were enough pressure to take off my helmet, I could've just blown through the screen to clean it out. But no, that was probably a bad idea anyway. Spittle could stick to the screen, gum it up, and invalidate the test.

But I had another source of air pressure: two full banks of air bottles, each full of clean, dry air. I pulled an air bottle from the second bank, cracked open the valve, and manually tripped the regulator to send out blasts of air and clean the screen.

When the screen was clean, I closed the valve, inspected everything under the magnifying glass, and ran all the diagnostic circuits. One charge was lost, yeah, but they couldn't mark me down for a precondition of the test. I reassembled the box and snapped it back in place on the dome top. *Take that, Fontes!*

But I was behind schedule! I was trying to shave time for that homework assignment. I had planned to assemble the remaining strut work as the dome inflated. Now the dome was more than half inflated, and my struts weren't assembled yet.

Still, I had mentally budgeted two hours for a zinger, and the snuff box took less than half that, so I was still good. I patted the snuff box like a good luck charm, hooked the spare air bottle back into its rack, and cycled through the airlock.

*Step 8: Strut Assembly.* It's hard to insert the struts in the sleeves at full assembly, and the dome had inflated quickly while I worked. Still, I refused to rush and maybe make a mistake. I checked each strut for a solid attachment to the upper ring and then snapped it into the lower ring. Once all the struts were elevated, I fastened down the lock rings.

*Step 9: Dispersal Density Test.* By the time the struts were done, it was time for the snuff test. I picked up the consumables pack, unzipped the outer airlock door and zipped it behind me, and waited for the pressure light to go green. My impatience was growing, and it seemed to take a long time. Finally, I zipped in, dropped off the consumables, hit the master cutoff on the environment pack, and zipped back out. After another impatient wait, I was back on the lith. I turned to my suit comp and pushed the command for the snuff test.

Poof! I watched the burst of snuff, silent of course, and then waited as it settled. Soon the results popped to my comp: seventeen pinhole leaks.

*Seventeen?* That was more pinhole leaks than in any case study. Usually before that, there's an obvious tear. A zinger is one thing, but Fontes was being a jerk here.

*Step 10: Shelter Integrity.* I zipped back in, waited to pressurize, entered, hit the master power, grabbed the vacuum resin, and headed to the laser spot identifying the first leak. There next to the leak, very small and practically transparent, was a little smiley face drawn in marker. If the laser hadn't pointed me in the right direction, I would never have seen it. Yeah, Fontes, screw you too.

I dabbed the leak with vacuum resin. In under a second, a small dot in the center turned light gray, indicating that vacuum had caused a state change and sealed the resin. I scraped most of the remaining resin off the fabriglass and back into the jar, and then smoothed down the last bit so no rough edge could get bumped and break the seal. Just like a lab exercise.

Sixteen more dabs of resin (and sixteen more smiley faces), and I was done. I sealed the jar and went outside to run the snuff test again. My impatience was mounting further (seventeen damned smiley faces!), but I wasn't going to let Fontes goad me into rushing. I climbed out, pushed the snuff test again, and smiled. No leaks.

*Step 11: External Reinspection.* You don't *have to* reinspect, if there's some reason you need to get into pressure quickly; but even as impatient as I was, I was determined to work the whole checklist. I carefully circled the dome, checking the struts, checking the lock rings, tugging and twisting and looking for unexpected movement. I found none. And then I checked the fabriglass as high as I could. Aside from seventeen tiny dots of hardened gray resin, I saw no flaws at all. Then I checked the airlock and its attachment to the dome and all the zippers and gaskets and seals. No flaws, all clean and functioning properly.

And then I had one more tiresome wait for the repressurization. And when that was done, I inspected the inner airlock. All clear.

*Step 12: Internal Reinspection.* Once I was fully inside, I was tired and hungry; but aside from a quick gulp of water (dehydration is a serious survival risk), I put biology aside. If I postponed reinspection for food, well, liquid nutrients make a lousy last meal. So I checked the environment pack, and all lights were green. I checked the solar power cable and the lighting (LED lights woven into the fabriglass). And last I reinspected the fabriglass itself, particularly the seventeen pinholes. All clear. I doubt Fontes himself could find anything to report.

And finally, I sucked down some nutrient compound and some more water. Then I lay back on the raised mat molded into the floor near the airlock. I tried to work on my homework assignment, but I was more tired than I realized. I was asleep in under ten minutes. Every two hours, my suit comp woke me for a spot inspection: all lights green, check the temperature, check the sealed leaks. Then back to sleep.

In the morning, I woke ahead of the alarm, and grabbed an early breakfast. After relieving myself, I hooked my suit's waste disposal tubes to the recyclers. I had plenty of food and water for more than two days (barring yet another zinger), so there would be no need for recycled water and nutrients. Still, I didn't want to carry the wastes in my suit, so into the recycler they went.

I was almost through my morning inspection when my suit radio spoke. "Mister Morgan."

"Sarge, what's up? I didn't hit the panic button."

"Oh, I know. This is merely an unofficial 'good morning, how ya doing?'"

"I'm doing fine. Just settling in to wait for my 'rescue'."

"Nothing unusual to report?"

"Oh, just routine stuff. My snuff box lost a charge, and I had to clean it. Oh, and I had to patch a few leaks, seventeen or so. Just routine." The smile on my face said: *I beat you, you bastard.*

"You're a clever one, ain't ya, Kenneth? Got it all covered. Well, then, I'll just leave you to your waiting. Fontes out."

I was so pleased with myself, I could barely finish my inspection; but

I wasn't going to slip up now, and give Fontes the last laugh. After I was done, I settled in, and started seriously attacking that homework assignment. It's not like I had anything else to do: outside of the two hour spot inspections, I had time to kill.

And so my day went, and my night like the night before: boring homework mixed with boring inspections. Boring squared. But I remembered Fontes's lessons: boredom kills. So I broke up the monotony with some game sims, some music, and a few comic book files.

When I woke on the second morning, though, something was different. It took me a while to realize what it was: the air recirculator was barely running. In an emergency, it manufactures air from electrolysis and reclamation of volatiles from waste storage; but even in non-emergencies, it's supposed to run in low-energy $CO_2$ scrubbing mode. This was low energy, all right, but it seemed too low. Was this a *second* zinger?

I checked the recirculator, took it apart, checked every part and sensor and circuit. It was operating correctly based on its sensor readings. It read a very low ambient carbon dioxide level, so it was running accordingly.

Why would carbon dioxide concentration be low? I knew I was breathing. But just as I was pondering this, my suit radio sounded again. "Good morning, Mister Morgan."

"I'm a little busy, Sarge, no time to chat."

"$CO_2$ levels a little puzzling?"

"Huh? How do you know that?"

"Tell me, boy genius, when you so brilliantly diagnosed the snuff box yesterday and cleaned it up, did you use an air bottle to clean the filter?"

I'm not *completely* clueless. "You have spy eyes in here."

"We have spy eyes in there, cameras woven all through the fabriglass. Other sensors, too, and I doubt you'll ever notice them. You think we want rookies dying on their first practical? Besides, we have to watch you to grade you."

"But now you're interrupting my test *again,* just when I've got an equipment anomaly. That tells me I've got a problem—not an immediate danger, or you'd flunk me now."

"I can't comment."

"And these calls come suspiciously close to being a hint."

"Oh, now what sort of test would it be if I gave you a hint? In fact, to be sure I *don't* give you a hint, I'm signing off. But Morgan, one thing, and this is *very important:* you call me before you try to leave the prefab. *That is an order.* Got me?"

"Got it, Sarge." He disconnected.

So the calls *were* a hint. He wanted me to know he could see me. And what he asked about: did I use an air bottle to clean the filter? Yes, I did. And then I put it back in the rack.

I checked that bottle and immediately I saw my error. I had forgotten to close the regulator when I racked it and clamped it into the feed system, so the bottle fed into the air system, right along with the bottle I had already opened. And since it was the first bottle in its bank, when it emptied, the next bottle in that bank fed right out through the regulator, too. For nearly two days, I had been pumping twice as much air as I expected.

And that would explain the $CO_2$ concentration: there was twice as much air, but I wasn't exhaling twice as much carbon dioxide. If the $CO_2$ level gets *too* low, you can hyperventilate; so the scrubbers cut back to keep $CO_2$ within a livable range.

But if the air pumps were putting out double air, shouldn't the pressure reflect that? I checked the console: all green lights. But then I looked at the pressure gauge. It was reading 1.96 standard; and the red zone where the light would change was at 2.0. I'm not sure why twice the air didn't make for twice the pressure. Maybe the dome expands under pressure just enough to keep below the limit. But whatever the reason, the light stayed green. Oh, Fontes was going to mark me down for that! He *hates* "idiot lights".

And I hadn't noticed the air pressure. Oh, my ears had popped a couple of times; but when you're in and out of suits enough times, you get so you hardly notice your ears popping. Other than that, the human body mostly equalizes internal and external pressure if the change is gradual, so it's hard to detect. After all, if it were easy to detect, we wouldn't need pressure gauges.

Or even idiot lights.

I turned off the second regulator and checked the air bottles. Well, I was going to get marked down more for all the wasted air, but I still had air to last more than a week, plus the air plant in a pinch. I could breathe through the end of this test.

So why had Fontes warned me to call before I left? I would lose a lot more air during my exit, get marked down some more. But he made it sound more serious than that.

So since I had time to spare, I tied into my suit comp. To simulate isolation, my comp was locked out of all Lunar nets for the duration of the test; but I had an encyclopedia chip in storage for my homework. I looked up pressure. And what did I find?

Well, I've saved this bottle of beer for just this point in the story. Let me open it, and... See those bubbles appear inside? See that head when I pour? That's carbon dioxide, dissolved into the liquid under pressure. When I released the pressure, it bubbled out of solution. When that happens in beer, we call it the best part of the beverage. When that happens in your body, especially nitrogen bubbles in your joints, we call it *the bends*, horribly painful and sometimes fatal. Caisson workers and scuba divers first discovered it, and died from it, until people learned how to gradually depressurize. It takes a long time, based on how much pressure and how long you were in it. The US Navy put a lot of work into dive and depressurization charts; but none in the encyclopedia covered my case.

I called Fontes. "How long?"

He chuckled, and I cringed. "We don't quite know, Mister Morgan. There aren't many cases where someone spent two days in double standard. The docs are sure you'll live, but you're going to stay there a while. We don't have a lot of scuba divers here on Luna, so they're consulting with experts Downside. Best guess is you'll be depressurizing much of the weekend. And then you'll have one long incident report to fill out. And *then*... Well, this doesn't get you out of your assignment for Monday. That'll take up the rest of your weekend, I expect."

"And you didn't call and warn me."

"And make you flunk your test, Kenneth? Never. Your suit comp told us your vitals were good. Our dome sensors and the environment pack readings said you were in no danger, as long as you decompress before you leave the dome. And you could've saved yourself the trouble if you'd ever wondered why the airlock cycles were getting so long. Or if *even once* in your inspections you had *read the gauges instead of relying on your goddamn idiot lights!*"

And with that, he laughed again, and disconnected.

Later, I received a program for the environment pack to manage the decompression in gradual stages over the next twenty hours. That was longer than anyone had ever heard of for decompression from double standard; but with such a long exposure, the experts didn't want to take any chances. And I think Fontes tacked on extra hours "just in case". So I was locked in the dome right through my date with Mary Sue Reilly. But at least I finished my homework during decompression, so I made Sunday brunch with Janelle Brooks. Not a total loss for the weekend, then.

And as for my incident report? Well, I wanted to make up some points from my exam, so I was extra thorough there; and when it was done, Fontes grudgingly acknowledged that it was a good case study and a good set of lessons learned. He even helped me submit it to the Lunar Survival Journal, and it's required reading today. So I guess that's my own contribution to our essential folklore: *Being a smart ass is hazardous to your health.*

# SENSE OF WONDER

"Hey, guys! Guess what time it is?" Oh, no. I just got in from the Lunar surface, digging samples most of the night. I'm too tired for this today. I just want a beer and a bite.

"It's time for the Captain Jayna show!" "Yeah, we want Captain Jayna!" Here it comes.

"OK, that sounds like a winner. Let me tune the channel, and here we go!" Eliza tunes in the big screen over the bar; and the first thing I see is my face in that blasted green makeup.

"I'm sensing something strange, Captain Jayna. I sense music, and exciting adventure and… I think my antennae are detecting… laughter."

"I see, Alpha. Music, adventure, and laughter. Do you know what that means?"

"No, Captain. As you know, we do not laugh on Centaurus Prime."

"Let's tell him, kids. That means it's time for a cartoon with Tex Tyler and the Star Circus! Let's watch… Escape from Planet Z!"

Oh, man, why does Eliza do this to me every Saturday morning? I come into the Old Town Tavern for an early lunch; and she *insists* on putting the Jayna of Space Command show on the big screen. She says it's to draw in families for the lunch crowd; but how often do you see a kid in here? No, I'm convinced she's torturing me through my alter ego, Alpha Centaurus.

Do you know how long it takes me to put on that makeup? Two hours! Two hours, and that's with practice. Putting on the stupid antennae takes up a lot of that time. And the green color: I swear I never completely get that out of my hairline. I put a cap on my water budget because I want to save my money for my Tycho Crater digs; and I swear there's never enough water in my budget to get *completely* clean.

Oh, I really don't mind Alpha that much. He pays my bills, and Lunar geology isn't a cheap field of study. And I really enjoy working with the kids. I think the personal appearances are even better than our studio shows, because then Jane and I get to improvise. For a geologist, I like to think I'm a decent actor, at least decent for kids' shows. The kids just get such big smiles when they meet a friendly "alien", even when they're old enough to know I'm just a guy in a costume. For a little while, they can imagine that they're great explorers meeting new life forms and discovering new secrets, and then wonder what will happen. Sense of wonder, that's what we're selling. Even the older ones love the idea of meeting an alien, the Downside tourist kids especially. They don't want Luna to be just a place where people live and work: they want it to be someplace where an Alpha Centaurus might wait in the next crater over. It's a mystery. It's exciting!

No, my only beef with Alpha is the laughs I get from my so-called adult friends around here. You know how it is with a group of friends who hang out together a lot. It's like a rock tumbler: we bash into each other repeatedly, through jokes and jibes and friendly insults, until we knock off all the rough edges. I guess sociologically that's a good thing, the way a community forms and bonds like all the rock fragments that cement together to make a breccia; but it's never smart to make yourself an easy target. Your friends *will* pounce. It's hard enough getting their respect as a geologist. Most of them are practical, hard-working types who can't see how I can spend so much of my own time and my own money studying rocks. If I were a mine engineer, they'd get that; but they don't see the point of geology for its own sake. So then add Alpha, and, well, I've learned it's best to just laugh at myself, because they all will.

"Gee, Captain Jayna, that really was a funny cartoon. Ha. Ha. Ha. I am practicing laughing. Is that right?"

"That's very good, Alpha. What was your favorite part?"

"The elephants. We don't have elephants on Centaurus Prime."

"What sort of animals do you have?"

"We have sundogs. They are like your dogs, but they glow in the dark. We use them as nightlights. And we have fleeps. They are like rabbits, but their ears are bigger. They use them to fly."

"Glowing dogs and flying rabbits. That sounds exciting! Boys and girls, would you like to see the sundogs and the fleeps?"

"YAAAAAAAAAAAAAAAAAAAAAAAAY!!!"

"OK, then let's climb aboard the Comet 3, and take another trip to Centaurus Prime!"

Fleeps! Oh, I'm gonna hear that one for weeks. It's a tossup which the guys find funnier: Alpha's dopey accent, or the made up language. Nah, neither, now that I think of it: it's the antennae.

And yet... And yet sometimes, when the vids get going, they stop laughing, and get interested. Oh, not in Captain Jayna and Alpha... Well, OK, some of them have a very adult interest in Captain Jayna, but that's not what I mean. Those Star Circus episodes, for kids' cartoons, they're really well done. The visuals are solid, and some of the jokes are aimed over the heads of the kids and straight at their parents. But more than that, the stories are rip-roaring adventures. Despite themselves, the guys get hooked. Life on Luna contains so much structure, so much work and routine, that we easily get jaded. We can forget that we live in an exotic city on a world so far from our species' birthplace that Earth just hangs in the sky like a baseball. The native-born looneys especially just have trouble seeing life here as anything but mundane. But scratch the surface, and you find they get hooked on that same old sense of wonder as the kids. What would it be like to travel to the stars with a circus, especially one that included alien performers and mysterious ambassadors and clever secret agents? What sort of worlds might they find? What sort of aliens might they meet? What sort of wonders might they see? It's a mystery. It's exciting!

And I know when I say this, sometimes it comes across as bitter, that they're so interested in fiction – scientifically implausible or even impossible fiction, really – and have no interest in my *real* work. And I'm sorry, I don't mean it to sound that way. I understand how they feel, really I do. I mean, just like them, I grew up with the classics: Kirk, Skywalker, Adama, Hutchens. And I loved the classic Outsiders, too: Spock, Chewbacca, E.T. I remember wanting to meet an alien. Heh, ironically, I remember imagining that I *was* an alien, hidden on Earth to await rescue. No green skin or antennae, though.

So I've got nothing against that sense of wonder. If anything, I think maybe I had a little *more* of it than the other kids when I was young. While the other kids had lots of interests, I was pretty much space happy. And so I hung out with other space happy kids. And we shared our knowledge, and encouraged each other. And so we learned more, learned real science. I could explain precession of the equinoxes, phases of Luna, continental drift, and even relativity (sorta) while still in grade school. It wasn't that I was smarter than my classmates: it was just that the time they devoted to learning their favorite sports teams or musical groups, I devoted to learning more about the universe. That exaggerated sense of wonder led, step by logical step, to my passion for science; and then the right instructor and the right books and a dozen other factors I couldn't name made geology my calling.

"Look at that, kids! We're approaching Centaurus Prime. Look at the floating cities! Alpha, is that where we'll land?"

"Yes, Captain Jayna. You have your gravitor to give us normal gravity on the Comet 3. On Centaurus Prime, we use antigravitors to hold our cities in the sky. Once we invented the antigravitors, we turned Centaurus Prime into a giant park, where all the animals can live. Except our sundogs and our fleeps, of course. Those are our pets. The fleeps like to fly around the cities."

"Are there dangerous animals on the surface?"

"A few. We'll go on a safari, and we can look for the clawbeast and the lionbird. So we'll have to be careful to stay inside our safari shield for protection."

Generally I think our scriptwriters are pretty good; but honestly, that's some clumsy foreshadowing. Even the kids in the audience may guess that the safari shield is going to break down, and brave Captain Jayna and loyal Alpha Centaurus will have to protect the kids. The adults certainly ought to figure that out. But look at them, they're hooked. It's like they're happy to accept an implausible script, because they can fill in the holes with their imaginations. As long as there are enough explosions and gunfights and chases and last minute escapes, it's all good. What danger lies around that next turn in the path? It's a mystery. It's exciting!

I think maybe that's where *I* got jaded, in my own way. I started to see the plot holes, and I lost some of my ability to suspend disbelief. Part of it, I'd like to think, is my scientific training. We scientists like to imagine we're a bit more logical and rational than most. But we're also supposed to strive to be objective; and objectively, I think that's largely conceit. We probably fall at or near the average for normal distributions of these traits. A little above average, maybe, but not as far as we'd like to think.

No, I think honestly what changed things for me was that I was a reader, not just a viewer, and a voracious one. In text, there's room and time for the author to explain more, provide more logic and reasoning; so the reader gets accustomed to seeing a more complete chain of cause and effect and choice and consequence. You learn to look for that, and notice when it's not there. Oh, a taut action vid can make me forget logic and just enjoy the ride; but if it's weak, or if it slows down, I have time to think and question. It's a natural consequence of the scientific view. And no amount of explosions or blaster fire will help me to overlook a story that doesn't hang together.

I guess that's kind of odd. When I was a kid, I was an eager consumer of these vids, had to be the first to see them. Now, I can take them or leave them unless they're really good – and good by my standards, not just popularity. My buddies here see me as a kinda dull guy, a mere catalogue guy who takes pictures and samples of rocks and writes for boring journals nobody reads. They tell me I have rocks in my head, and then laugh at my expense. I've never told them how many times geologists hear that joke. Why spoil their fun?

Of course, it's a little easier to dismiss the vid adventures when I'm actually *living* one. My parents were ready to disown me when I passed up a scholarship to go into freight handling, of all things; but I had a plan. I knew I'd never be able to afford both the tuition cost at McAuliffe University *and* the cost of a ticket up here to attend. So instead, I went into freight, and I worked my ass off. There was no sense of wonder in that job, lemme tell ya, but a hard worker could work his way up. Eventually, I worked my way up to freight handler on an orbital run; and from there, I finagled my way to a Lunar run.

Meanwhile, I kept my geology studies up. Besides my reading, I spent my vacations in field studies. And I took McAuliffe teleclasses, and I got to know my instructors there really well. So when I finally managed to work my passage to Tycho, I had connections and referral letters and the cost of tuition. After years of almost forgetting my sense of wonder, *I was going to school on the Moon!* I know that doesn't measure up well against a safari on Centaurus Prime. To the native looneys, it's no big deal; but to this little kid who read the classics every night in bed when he was supposed to be asleep, it was like Christmas.

But then reality asserted itself again. I was on Luna, and I had my tuition paid; but I still had to eat, and I still needed tube space, and I still had to pay for air and water. And there's not really as much demand for freight handlers here, with the lower gravity and ubiquitous automation. So I haunted the public boards, looking for Help Wanted pops. And one day, there was a pop from Jane Paulson, a young actress and vid producer with a lot of ambition. She was assembling a cast and crew for a new kids' vid program she hoped to pitch. The initial pay was barely life support. Maybe that's why competition was so light at the auditions, and I got the part based on whatever I had learned in my meager high school theater experience.

If I've become a better actor since then, it's all because of Jane. I hitched my wagon to a star there, and she'll be an even bigger star someday. Back then, she did all the writing, produced all the episodes, and even arranged all the marketing for Jayna of Space Command. Today, she has staff for much of that, but she still keeps a close eye on the details. My buddies who want me to introduce them to her don't realize: she's more woman than they can handle. She's a geyser of ambition and drive and goals, and they're just a bunch of guys who do their work and then hang out at a bar. I'm not saying she's better than them: they're just not ready for her level of energy. When you're on a Jane Paulson Production, you'll have an exciting experience; but you won't often have time for wonder, unless you're determined to make time.

"Captain Jayna! Behind you!"

"Look out, kids!" Zeowww! Zeowzeowww! "There! That lionbird is stunned. He won't wake up soon, and the noise scared the others back for a while. But my stunray charge is gone. How's that safari shield coming, Alpha?"

"I still need several minutes to finish the repairs, Captain Jayna. But you are right! The lionbirds are afraid of loud noises. That's what drove them back!"

"Loud noise, huh? Then I have a plan. All you kids, whenever I raise my hand, I want you to yell and laugh and sing as loud as you can. I'll let my hand down when you can rest. And since we need a really **loud** noise, we need all you kids at home to yell, too! OK, everybody ready? Here comes a lionbird. Yell!"

Oh, the yelling. Jane loves the audience participation. I guess the bar crowd is really into this episode: some of them are yelling, too. Or maybe they just want to give me a headache. And oh, my head aches. I was up way too late out exploring the central uplift, and I'm short on sleep.

You see that rock sample? I found that one last month, late one night. Or early one morning. Or whatever you call it. I'm still getting used to a 29-day "day", even though I've been reading about it all my life. I tend to work Outside way too long, because it takes two weeks to get dark.

That sample is tagged and coded. I found it on the central uplift, over on Aldrin peak. As large as that is, you couldn't lift it on Earth. It's an igneous sample comprised of very high concentrates of lead and bismuth, of all things. That's a pretty unique alloy, one we don't see that often.

For a long time, Lunar geologists have known that Tycho Crater's unusual in a lot of ways. Sure, it's big, but more than that. The local regolith is unusually high in lead and bismuth. It's nothing *too* far outside the Lunar norm, but far enough that it's noted in most area surveys. Digs in the melt sheet around the central uplift show the same thing. And the old mining tunnels were the same: the miners piled up a lot of their tailings around the uplift, and we find a high level of lead and bismuth among the breccias there.

In most of the books I've read, there are two competing theories to explain this. First, there's the local variation theory. This one says that this area's just naturally high in lead and bismuth. The second theory, the lead-bismuth core theory, says that there's a higher level of both deep beneath the surface, maybe down into the core; and that Tycho being such a large, deep crater, it exposed more of that subsurface material when the impact melted some of the rock and fractured a lot more into breccias. The proponents of these two theories all have some facts and some reasons on their side; but no one has a complete, persuasive picture that everyone will buy.

Now both of these theories have certain implications, and from those we can make certain predictions; and then being scientists, we try to falsify those predictions. If we can knock some of those predictions down, and knock them down good, then we can eliminate the theory that goes with those predictions. That's how we learn in the sciences, by proving ourselves wrong until we can't. It's hard work, and you have to be careful not to mislead yourself.

So that's the sort of research our teams have been doing Outside. I've been gathering samples and comparing to predictions: first for my profs; and now, finally, I'm leading my own teams on occasion. And I do some solo digs now and then. That's where I found and catalogued that sample.

See, what I started to see from all of these studies was that *neither* theory fit the data. Every time a prediction failed, the proponents of the corresponding theory would revise the theory to try to fit the new studies. That's what they're supposed to do, fit the theory to the data, not the other way around; but at some point, the theory gets so twisted out of shape that it fails Occam's Razor. It may explain the data, but it's not the simplest explanation. In fact, it's the most complex explanation.

Because what was the simplest explanation, in my mind, was that these lead and bismuth traces and samples were allogenic. Oh, sorry, that's geologist speak for "not from around here". You get a lot of allogenic samples on Luna, and on Mars, and anywhere with a lot of impact craters. The impact can throw a lot of material a very long way, so two rocks next to each other might've formed thousands of miles apart. You have to learn to read the lay of the land, the patterns of dispersion, to decide where a rock really came from. It's like a giant puzzle; and it can be frustrating, but it's also a fun challenge.

So I had a very crude hypothesis: the lead and bismuth were allogenic; and then I formed some crude predictions of where I might find more. If this was ejecta from some distant crater, then there should be a ray dispersal pattern that would point in the direction of the source. But my predictions fell pretty flat. I couldn't find a ray pattern. Finally I relaxed, took some time off, let Jayna and Alpha occupy my time. And then, right in the middle of filming a scene, I realized: the distribution pattern only made sense if it were more of a sheet than rays, and if that sheet were roughly centered on the central uplift itself.

And from there, I had some concrete predictions. I expected – I *knew*, which is an unhealthy attitude for a scientist, but hard to resist – that as I searched closer to the uplift, I would find higher concentrations, maybe even whole rocks of mostly lead and bismuth. I've been cataloguing larger and larger glass beads and molten lumps for the past month. But this baby... Oh, this baby is the prize.

See, this one is large enough that we could do more detailed analysis of it back in the lab: detailed spectrography, various chemical tests, and X-ray crystallography. I expected we'd find it a remnant of a large asteroid, mostly lead and bismuth, that was the actual projectile that created Tycho Crater. That projectile would've mostly or completely vaporized upon impact; and that vapor would settle down as a mist or precipitate out into bits and beads and lumps.

But what we found is more of a surprise than that. The crystalline structure of this rock isn't *natural* for lead and bismuth.

Oh, I'm not saying it's an alien artifact. What I'm saying is that crystalline structure is determined mostly by chemistry, which is based on the number of protons in the component atoms; but once those atoms are locked into the structure, the structure tends to hold fast, *even if the number of protons changes.* And the number of protons can change in only one way: if the atoms are radioactive, and they break down into their decay products.

So after doing lots of modeling and number crunching, we're pretty confident that when that rock formed, it was a crystal structure of various radioactive isotopes, starting almost certainly with isotopes of californium. I won't bore you with all of the deep analysis; but it's almost certain that this rock and the rest are remnants of a large radioactive chunk of californium – isotope two-fifty-one seems most likely, given that it has the longest half-life – that was the projectile that created Tycho Crater 108 million years ago. And then radioactive decay turned all those isotopic atoms to lead, bismuth, and less common decay products.

That by itself was enough to get me a paper in *Lunar Geology Journal*; but there's more. Now that we've got what seems like a working impact model, we're starting to get a picture of the size and composition of the projectile. And it just doesn't fit the composition of any other impact fragments we've found, *anywhere.* In fact, spectrographic studies and mining expeditions have found nothing that fits it in the belt. It left us all wondering: where did this projectile come from?

And I'll admit, the math for this is next part is over my head, but the AI's confirm it. The impact model doesn't make sense if the projectile was *huge*, like we always assumed for a crater as large as Tycho. But it makes sense if the projectile was only average size, maybe a little larger – but moving very *fast*, faster than Solar escape velocity.

And californium, theory says, is created in the stellar explosions we call supernovae.

And that makes me wonder: was Tycho Crater, home to our city, formed by a large californium projectile, birthed in the explosive death of a distant star and then fired like a bullet in our direction, with the unlucky Moon right in its path hundreds of years later? It's possible; but right now, we just can't be sure. There could be some other explanation, so we just can't be sure.

It's a mystery. It's exciting!

# PART II: THE PLANET NEXT DOOR

Stories from the exploration of Mars.

# NOT CLOSE ENOUGH

"Aw, hell, no!" That had been Bennie's reaction when he had first heard about the Tele Orbit Rendezvous plan. Others in the Corps had expressed less printable reactions.

But forty months later, TOR was the official NASA plan for Mars exploration; and so Commander Benjamin Cooper hung in his spaceship orbiting Mars, strapped in a harness in Control Bay 1 so the force feedback controls wouldn't push him away, while a damned *robot* made its way through the thin Martian atmosphere to the surface.

"*It makes perfect sense,*" Lee Klein *had explained in the Mission Planning auditorium. He had been forced to shout over the jeers from the Astronaut Corps, and then had to wait for the noise to settle.* "*It makes perfect sense. Getting you to Mars is the easy part. With what the transport companies have learned, it's safe. It's almost routine.*"

"*Da,*" Masha Desny *had called from the rear, where the Roscosmos contingent had clustered.* "*So easy monkey could do it. Klein, if monkey could do it, maybe you should go.*"

*Everyone had laughed. Even Ishiro Hitara, the shy young engineer from JAXA, had grinned.*

Bennie stretched out his arm as the micromotors pushed against him, mirroring the force on the robot lander. He could feel the wind as he pushed, and he adjusted the lander's angle in response. The atmosphere was thin, but the winds were fast and tricky. Still, Bennie and his team were trickier. They had lost only three landers since they had arrived at Mars. They had even managed some precision landings. Their success rate was an order of magnitude better than the robots had done on their own before TOR. But that wasn't enough to persuade Mission Planning to man-rate the landers.

And so Bennie and Masha and their international crew hung in orbit: two dozen brilliant, ambitious, enthusiastic explorers from Russia, Europe, Japan, India, Australia, China, and the US, all taking their shifts piloting landers, driving crawlers, running tele-experiments, and operating construction bots. The time lag from the *Bradbury* to the surface was negligible, well within the limits of teleoperation systems. To the limits of the engineering specs, it was as close as being there.

"But not close enough," Bennie muttered.

"*Nyet,*" Masha agreed from her station across the chamber. "Like Grandfather Oleg's flight, not close enough." Her English had improved in thirty months of training, seven months of travel, and three months in orbit. Bennie's Russian hadn't improved as much, but he kept studying. It was valuable for his relationship with the Russian contingent, and it was a way to pass the time when he wasn't teleoperating or riding herd over the international crew.

Masha was also an incorrigible tale spinner. Unless history had it wrong, her Grandfather Oleg had never gotten near the Moon. But though Bennie might banter with her at another time just for distraction, he needed focus right then. The cross shear on the lander suddenly dropped to zero, and Bennie corrected with a microburst of the pulse reaction jets. The trick was to milk whatever lift you could out of the thin Martian atmosphere and only use the jets as needed. If you relied on the jets too much, you could exhaust the fuel and leave the lander at the mercy of gravity and the winds. It took experience and instinct and human judgment. Despite the best efforts of programmers over the decades, no software had ever matched a top pilot at this job.

TOR had sucked the spirit of exploration right out of the program. The morale in the Corps hit a low point unmatched since Enos the chimp became the first American in orbit. Three veterans grew too loud and too public in their complaints, and they were quietly transferred to non-flight status.

That was how Bennie had ended up as Commander on this particular mission: he was the most senior astronaut who had been willing to swallow his pride and endorse TOR. And Flight Director had trusted Bennie to ride herd over a bunch of eager young explorers who would continue to argue against TOR. Or do more than argue.

Bennie eyeballed the landing strip, cleared and graded by the earliest robot landers in order to make the later missions easier. "Radar assess landing fourteen degrees starboard," Bennie commanded. The forward radar swept the area as Bennie nudged the engines for a slight turn. The deep radar showed firm ground, and the surface radar showed no unmapped obstacles. "SAFE FOR LANDING" flashed twice on Bennie's display, and he pushed down on the stick to drop down for approach. He had to make two last-second correction bursts, and then the lander touched ground and coasted to a stop. Another safe landing for the robots of Mars.

Just as Director Crane had predicted, Bennie had spent much of the past forty months playing wet blanket, squashing wild landing schemes both overt and covert. Safety be damned: these eager young explorers would never be happy driving robots from orbit. Ishiro was especially bad: he was a rabid fan of anime space stories, with posters all over his walls and collectible paper volumes under his bunk. He spoke of Mars landing with wide-eyed awe. But Dan Thorbjornsen was the worst: the big Swede from the European Space Agency had the boundless energy of a puppy coupled with more engineering savvy than most professional spacecraft designers. He never came right out and criticized the TOR plan, but he was always asking *what if?* "What if we landed life support and return fuel in separate landers?" "What if we constructed a landing strip to give us wider safety margins?" "What if we modified the profile with adaptive glide surfaces?" And the kid didn't just have wild schemes: he had intricate engineering diagrams and pages of calculations for every scheme.

And damn it, he had a point! Oh, none of his plans were sure-fire; and no astronaut deliberately tried to increase mission risk. But his plans were no riskier than the Apollo missions or Mercury.

But it was Bennie's job to rein Dan in and redirect his efforts back to the mission. As second in command, Masha ably assisted him in that. Her favorite tactic was to take the "good idea" upstairs…

"Is very good plan, young Daniel. I like adaptive glide surfaces especially." Dan was a real genius when it came to nano-materials, and the AGSes were one of his best ideas yet: a surface that dynamically redesigned itself on the molecular level. "I think will revolutionize lander design. I will take to Klein."

…and there it would be absorbed and yet also diminished, emerging days or weeks later as a less ambitious plan.

"But is good news, Daniel! Planners have approved AGS for new lander designs."

"Yes." Dan's face didn't reflect good news at all. "For unmanned landers only. They still refuse to allow manned landers."

"Today, Daniel. Today. Is like commander told Grandfather Oleg during LOK Lunar program—"

Bennie couldn't resist the bait. "Masha, you're too young to have had a grandfather in LOK."

"Hush, Benjamin, is my story, I tell my way. Commander told Grandfather, 'First succeed in this Mission, then ask for Moon. Everybody likes victor.' That is what you can do, Daniel. You succeed with AGS landers, mission is success, you are victor, and then you ask for Mars."

And he bought it: a line that Bennie could never have sold in a million years, Dan bought from Masha. She was attractive and charming and persuasive, and she knew how to find and push buttons. She was, Bennie thought (but only to himself), his perfect fifth columnist: ingratiating herself with all the different contingents and subtly coaxing them always back to the mission objectives. When she saw a need, she quietly informed Bennie where a commander's heavy hand was called for. But they seldom had to play good cop/bad cop. Mostly Masha just offered sympathy and subtle redirection. Bennie had worked with some good seconds before, but none with Masha's touch. She could play the iron maiden when discipline demanded it, but she had a positive gift for connecting with the crew.

Masha tapped Bennie on the shoulder. She had donned her control harness, the sensors and force feedback systems that tied into the control loops and gave the teleoperator a wide range of tactile inputs and controls. "Commander Cooper, I stand ready to relieve you." That was another great thing about Masha: off duty she knew how to relax; but on duty, Russian discipline governed her every move. She knew how to keep just enough order and routine so the crew didn't get sloppy, but also how to let them blow off steam as needed.

Bennie checked his indicators. Every one of his landers was docked or down. Every one of his ground crawlers was idle, waiting for instructions. He hit the safety switch on his control harness. "Officer Desney, I am powering down." All indicators switched to standby, and Bennie disconnected his harness from the control bay. He reached a hand out, and Masha grabbed it and helped him into the corridor. "Officer Desney, I stand relieved. Control is yours." And then he helped Masha into the bay, and she tied in and powered up.

"Anything to report, Benjamin?"

"Nah, fairly routine shift here. Ishiro?" Ishiro was just getting out of Bay 2, having been relieved by Karthik from the ISRA team.

"All quiet, Commander. Air and fuel distillation plants are at optimum outputs." Ishiro was also big on discipline, perhaps even more so than Masha. Bennie had taken months to break through the young man's shell; but he felt it was important to bond with the crew. Discipline was all well and good, but a mission like this needed stronger bonds of trust that came from a personal connection. Eventually Bennie had reached Ishiro by discussing anime. Masha had tipped

Bennie off about what a fan Ishiro was, and so Bennie had hastily studied up in his off hours. Once Bennie asked some questions about the classics, Ishiro went from reticent to talking to gushing. Bennie was proud of reaching Ishiro that way, and he saw him almost as an earnest little brother; but Ishiro was still very formal except off duty.

"All right, then. Masha, Karthik, the deck is yours." Masha looked quickly at Bennie, and Bennie slightly nodded. Then he and Ishiro left the control deck, pulling themselves along the corridor in the microgravity.

"Anything special planned, Ishiro?" Bennie had once tried calling him "Ishi", but the young man seemed troubled by that degree of informality. "Any new anime?"

"No, Commander. Something better, and more special to me. My parents have sent videos from home on the back channel." The *Bradbury* recorded personal messages and entertainment programs on the back channels and then routed them to the library or to the crew.

"That's great!" Family was one of Ishiro's favorite topics, right up there with anime and software. "Has that nephew of yours arrived yet?"

"I hope. In the last message, Niina looked like she would burst. She says little Ishiro oversleeps like his uncle."

Bennie laughed and clapped Ishiro on the shoulder, which was as much casual contact as the engineer could tolerate. Ishiro turned port at the first branch, heading for his quarters. Bennie continued deeper into the *Bradbury*, heading for the mactory deck. Ishiro's family news had distracted him, but he hadn't forgotten Masha's intel. He hoped she was wrong, but she hadn't been yet.

Bennie reached the mactory deck airlock. The stereolithography and laser sintering macro factories required partial gravity to control the flow of the resins and powders, but the *Bradbury's* scopes and other instruments required a stable platform. So the designers had made the M.D. detachable from the rest of the ship: the crew could deploy it on a long radial axis and spin it up while the rest of the ship remained stationary. The axis tube also served as an airlock. Like all ship's locks, it had an announcement chime to let you know when it was cycling; but Bennie keyed in his command override to disable the chime before entering.

At the other end of the lock, Bennie emerged into a deck full of noise. The ring-shaped deck spun slowly around the axis, raising a steady hum. Several SL/LS machines were at work, laser heads zipping back and forth over the work surfaces as the material elevators slowly descended. Even under the work hoods, that created a constant ratcheting noise in the background. Air circulators and filters added to the din; so Rick and Linda never heard Bennie as he approached.

The two Australians huddled over the frame of Lander 14. The wing panels had been removed, revealing an inner frame the size of a compact car, but thin and elongated. They were working with a laser removal tool, sort of the opposite of a laser sintering machine: laser pulses sliced material into powdery granules, and a vacuum tube hooked to a mass spectrometer ionized and sorted the particles. It was a reasonably efficient way to reclaim raw materials which could then be reused in SL/LS machines.

After watching them work for a while, Bennie cleared his throat. Rick and Linda both visibly started. "So, guys, got a private project going? A little redesign?"

"Ahhh... Yeah, Bennie. Just an idea Linda had to... ahhh..."

Linda nodded. "To reduce lander weight without compromising strength or stress resistance. I analyzed the frame structure and found a configuration that reduced weight nearly eight percent."

"Yeah," Rick continued. "And that will save fuel *and* give us better mass distribution, better overall control."

"Uh-huh." Bennie nodded and looked thoughtful. "That would be a nice improvement." He pointed at the interior of the frame. "And these new fittings here?"

Linda blanched. "Oh, that's just... something we were sort of playing around with."

"Funny," Bennie said, "they look like fittings for oxygen tanks. And a control harness. Planning a little trip?"

Rick threw the LRT to the floor. "Aw, hell, Bennie. We just had to try."

"Like hell you did! You know what sort of trouble this makes for me?"

Linda looked defiant. "How'd you catch us? Somebody dob us in?"

No need to reveal Masha's investigation. "Fourteen has been out of service a long while. I set a trace for that. Come on, it's an obvious sign that somebody's trying to mod a lander."

"Heh. I guess it is. We thought we had time." Rick sat on a wing strut of the lander. "So what happens now? You turn us in to Mission Control?"

Bennie scratched his chin. He tried to stay clean-shaven so he could look like a proper commander, but he sported his usual end-of-shift stubble. "No. No, I can't do that. That would make this an official incident, and then it would become a news item. Next thing you know, it would cause problems between ASA and NASA, and we'd all be tied up in meetings for a month. You see the spot you've put me in?"

Linda still had fire in her eyes, but Rick looked a little sheepish. "Sorry, Bennie. We just expected... Well... "

"You expected to finish the mods and make your move before the stupid old American caught on. Well this stupid old American has seen more crews pull more stunts than you'll ever know, and he still has a few tricks of his own."

"So what *will* you do now?"

"Now? Now... We'll talk about this later. Right now, I'm going to watch as you two get this lander reassembled and back into service *without* your special add-ons. And then you're both confined to general quarters for two days. And you're barred from this deck until I stop being pissed off. And let me tell you, that is going to be a *long* time."

1

Bennie had bought himself a little breathing room, but not a lot. Rick had appreciated his leniency, and even Linda had accepted their failure with reluctant grace; but the *Bradbury* crew was too small for secrets to remain buried very deeply. Rumors were spreading, and the teams were restless.

Bennie was tempted to begin regular inspections; but he knew that would aggravate morale, so he nixed that plan. Instead he asked Masha to work her magic and report what she could learn. The results were dismaying, but they could've been worse: although many in the crew speculated with ideas for a landing, only the Australians had carried their plans so far. Dan was a never-ending fount of ideas, still, but he had learned to route them through ESA. Karthik did the same, with regular briefings to ISRO headquarters in Bangalore. Masha seemed to have good rein over the Roscosmos team, and the Chinese from CNSA also were quiet.

"So worst is over, Benjamin," Masha assured him. They met mostly in virtual conferences so that she could maintain distance in public. "If you give it time, let Rick and Linda get over hurt feelings, crew will calm down."

Bennie frowned. "I wish I were as sure as you."

Masha smiled. "You demonstrated who is in command, and you showed no secret gets by you. Then you demonstrated mercy, and you supported crew when could have made example of them. They cannot fool you, but they can trust you. Is good combination."

"But all these plans... All these rogue efforts... We're not working together any more. For thirty months we trained together. I thought we were a unit, a *team*. Was that all just a lie?"

"Not lie, Commander. Just not whole truth. We will always be

Russians and Americans and Chinese and Indians and others. We will always be individuals, explorers. But you made us team, and you will keep us team. Worst is over, wait and see."

Masha's talent with people extended to her commander. Even knowing that she was playing him, Bennie found it hard to resist. Eventually he conceded.

＊

So Masha was more surprised than anyone when Ishiro made his move three days later.

The first Bennie knew about it was the comm call from Masha. "Commander, please patch into control interface."

Bennie was in his cabin, relaxing after a long day in the bay; but his command console duplicated most of the bay displays on demand. He glided over and flipped it on.

"What is this?" The displays showed Lander 6 on an unscheduled descent. "Masha, who launched that?"

"Ishiro. Benjamin, I think he's on board."

"Oh, shit! On my way. Door!" Bennie flipped off the display and pushed himself through the cabin door as it cycled open. He caught himself on the far wall of the corridor, absorbed the momentum with his arms, and then sprung off down the corridor to the control deck.

Karthik was in Bay 2, Masha in Bay 1. Control deck protocol didn't allow anyone in the bay with the controller, but Bennie hovered just on the edge, looking over Masha's shoulder. "What's the situation?" Bennie asked.

"Have transferred all landers and crawlers to Karthik," Masha replied. "He clears air space and landing strips. I try to reach Lander 6, but have no control."

"And Ishiro? What do we know?"

"Launch control overridden by software. Cannot be sure, but I recognize Ishiro's code. I call him to confirm, but no answer. I call JAXA lead Machida, but she cannot find him. Computer also cannot find him. I reach logical conclusion."

"But no answer on the radio?"

"Not yet. I still try to get control."

"Look at that!" Bennie pointed at the flight trace. "It's a smooth ride. Look at those corrections. He's doing pretty good."

"Da. But as you say, not close enough. Bigger turbulence, storm coming."

"Damn." Bennie patched into a comm panel outside the bay. "You keep at it, I'm going to try to get an answer. Ishiro!" Bennie paused, listening. "Ishiro Hitara, this is Commander Cooper. Answer me, Ishiro."

And then Ishiro's voice came through. There was some static, also some stress. "Mission Engineer Hitara reporting, Commander. I am very busy."

"Ishiro, get back here! What the hell do you think you're doing?"

It was a dumb question, but Ishiro answered it anyway. "I am doing what we should all be doing, Commander: going to Mars. It is why we are here."

"Ishiro, no! This is insubordination!"

Bennie had hoped that duty would motivate Ishiro, but the hope was immediately dashed. "I am sorry, Commander. This is something I must do. We are meant to explore, not play safe."

Bennie noticed Masha waving for his attention, so he cut his circuit. "What?"

"I think I have control channel; but if I am wrong, could interrupt control completely, leave Ishiro helpless. What do I do?"

Bennie paused. It was only an instant in reality, but it felt like hours in decision time. "No. We can't interfere now. He did it, he's on his own now." He cut back to the lander loop. "Ishiro, you don't have to do this. You've improved the controls. Let's take that to Mission Control and make a case."

"Commander, you know how that goes. Always the same: Masha takes it upstairs, and they say no. Now please, very busy, I must pay attention to controls."

Bennie couldn't say anything. Ishiro was right, he couldn't afford to be distracted. So Bennie could only watch tensely over Masha's shoulder as Ishiro piloted.

"Look, Benjamin. Look at fine pulses." Bennie nodded silently. Ishiro held the course somewhere between a fall and a controlled glide. Whenever things seemed most precarious, he pulsed the jets just enough to stabilize, using minimum fuel. "He might make it."

But then a new squall blew in unexpectedly. Before Ishiro could respond, the lander flipped completely upside down. His immediate reactions told Bennie that Ishiro was disoriented. His reflexes only made matters worse, pushing his craft lower. "Masha! Take control!"

But it was too late. Ishiro's next pulse threw the lander into an uncontrolled spiral straight at the Martian surface. Masha turned violently away from the displays. Bennie saw a single tear squeeze from the iron maiden's eye and just hang there in free fall. Then he saw the displays from Lander 6 flare up and go dark.

⸸

This incident, of course, could not go unreported; but before Bennie even had a chance—good God, what a mess!—Mission Control was on the command circuit. Director Crane scowled from the screen, Lee Klein standing behind her. "Cooper, what is the meaning of this? We just got this from JAXA. Watch it, Cooper, and get back to us immediately!"

Masha and Bennie sat in Bennie's office, strapped into couches and watching the wall screen. The JAXA logo appeared, followed by a scene of an elderly Japanese administrator that Bennie recognized from mission planning. The man spoke directly to the camera. "I am Natsuo Azuma, liaison to the *Bradbury* Project for the Japan Aerospace Exploration Agency. I am recording this to inform you that Mission Engineer Ishiro Hitara, under my personal orders, has downloaded new programming for a Mars Lander and is currently piloting the lander to the Martian surface. We encoded this new programming in his personal communications, and we incorporated the latest research out of Japan's engine laboratories. I take full responsibility for these decisions on behalf of JAXA. Commander Benjamin Cooper is unaware of these actions and bears no responsibility for the consequences.

"JAXA formally acknowledges that this step violates the protocols of the *Bradbury* Project. We voiced our objections to those protocols during mission planning, and our objections remain unchanged. We believe that exploration and settlement of Mars is vital to mankind's ultimate survival, and JAXA shall not shirk our responsibilities in such an important matter. By the time you see this, Engineer Hitara has either succeeded or failed; but either way, the effort is a *fait accompli.* We hope that this will convince the mission planners to rethink their decisions. We continue to believe the mission protocols are a mistake."

Azuma's image faded, and Crane and Klein once again filled the screen. Klein was fuming. "That hasn't hit the Internet yet, Cooper, but it's only a matter of time before it leaks. Do you know how bad this makes us look? And don't for a second believe that it absolves you from responsibility. I don't care what Azuma says, you're the commander there. You're supposed to know what's going on! Do we have to put Desney in charge?"

Crane waved Klein back from the camera. "Lee, threats aren't helpful here. What's done is done. You being an ass won't help Cooper to get things under control.

"But Commander Cooper, this is the worst black eye this office has had in a generation. We're not going to live this one down for a long time. I need your recommendation for how you're going to get control of your crew and make sure there are no more incidents like this. Or we *will* put Desney in charge. We won't have a choice. The administrators have to know that the person in charge is *in charge*. So record your response and get it back to us on your next transmission. And make it soon."

Crane looked down at her desk. "One more thing, Bennie. Hitara recorded a message to be released in the event his landing... fails. Fatally. I don't know what has happened there. Maybe he's safe. Maybe somehow you stopped him. But maybe... Maybe you should see this, too."

Crane touched a button, and Ishiro's face filled the screen. Bennie swallowed; but the lump in his throat wouldn't go down, especially once the dead youth's image spoke. "This is Mission Engineer Ishiro Hitara. With orders from Administrator Azuma and under my sole initiative, I have chosen to refit a lander with new pulse micro-jet programming and pilot it down to Mars. If you are watching this, then my flight has failed, and I am deceased. I take full responsibility for this decision. Commander Benjamin Cooper, First Officer Masha Desney, and JAXA team leader Nichie Machida were all unaware of this plan, and they bear no responsibility for my death. It was an honor serving with all of you. If my mother is right, I go now to join the spirits of my ancestors, though it may take long to find my way from Mars. To my nephew, my little namesake: please know that your uncle loves you, wherever you go and whatever you do."

Nothing replaced Ishiro's image, and the screen faded to black. Bennie turned to Masha, then turned away. For the second time, he caught her crying, and he didn't think she would appreciate that. He also didn't want her to see his own eyes.

Finally Bennie spoke, still looking at the screen. "So what do we tell them?"

Masha was silent for almost a minute. When she finally spoke, she sidestepped the question. "I could have stopped him."

Bennie unstrapped and turned to face Masha directly. "Masha, don't torture yourself like that. Ishiro and JAXA worked hard to conceal this. You caught and defused plenty of wild schemes. Don't beat yourself up over the one you missed."

Masha didn't look at Bennie, and she continued as if he hadn't spoken. "If I had known... I did not realize how strong his dream. He... He wanted to be first. Like Daniel. Like Grandfather Oleg. They want to explore, and they want to pioneer. You cannot train that out of them."

"I hope you're wrong, Masha, but I don't know." Bennie wasn't sure. If Masha was right... "That's not an answer, Masha. Mission Control wants a response."

"*Is* answer, Benjamin. This will not change. Humans explore, is what we do. Cannot put goal this close and not expect to finish race."

Bennie thought about it. Masha was taking this too hard, and she wasn't even that close to Ishiro. Without Masha's support, Bennie's job would only get harder. He didn't want to admit he was losing control of his crew; but maybe he needed to convey that to Mission Control, or something close to it.

"All right, let's tell them that." Bennie sat straighter in his couch and strapped back in. "Come on, Masha, we need to be unified in this. Sit up. Computer, begin recording message for command priority broadcast to *Bradbury* Project Mission Control."

Masha sat up. The Recording light lit up, and Bennie and Masha faced the camera. "Mission Control, this is Commander Cooper and First Officer Desney. We have conferred, and we have our recommendation. We realize this goes against mission protocol, but we believe it is in the best interests of crew morale.

"We understand your reasons for Tele Orbit Rendezvous. We and our crew have had those reasons drilled into us for forty months. We can make the arguments ourselves. But respectfully... Look, your reasoning is all wet. You don't want to risk a crew, and the landings are risky. But look at our success record with the landers! Sure, we lose some, but the odds are better than the test pilots faced back in the X-1 days. That's safe enough for me. For us. And for our crew. This program has become too risk averse. None of us want to die here. We all... We all miss Ishiro. But none of us want to die without taking a swing at this challenge, either.

"It is our considered opinion as commanders of this mission that TOR is just too much stress for our crew to bear. For *any* crew. We've come so close. Let us finish the mission if you want this project to succeed.

"You asked for our recommendation, and that's it. Please take it under advisement. We await your answer. Computer, end recording."

The Recording light dimmed, and the computer spoke. "Review message before transmitting?"

Bennie looked at Masha, but she shook her head. "Negative. Sign it Commander Cooper and First Officer Desney, and transmit it."

"Transmitting."

They sat in silence. Finally Masha spoke. "You did well, Benjamin. But you know it will not change their minds. Planners have too much invested in TOR."

"Maybe. But we've tried. We'll have an answer in forty minutes or so. Now we need to do something to help this crew deal with their grief and start thinking like a team again."

"And what do you suggest?"

"I don't know. Maybe we'll think of something in forty minutes."

Masha left the office, and Bennie sat in thought.

⚔

Bennie was still thinking in his office, still sitting in semi-darkness, when his console chimed again; and when he heard Karthik's message, Bennie wondered if he was in a recurring nightmare. "Commander, another unauthorized lander launch."

"What?" But Bennie didn't dare believe this was a nightmare. He should be so lucky. "I'm on my way. Call Masha up to the control deck."

"I'm sorry, Commander, but I think Officer Desney is on the lander."

Bennie's head swam. The office spun around him like a nasty bout of spacesickness. Again he wondered if this were a nightmare, a guilty rerun of Ishiro's death. Masha? His last anchor to sanity on this mission? No, he must have heard wrong. "Please repeat, Karthik."

"Commander, I can't find Officer Desney's signal on board. I think she's on the lander."

The nightmare continued inexorably. Bennie would go to the control deck. He would watch Karthik try to communicate with the lander. He would watch him fail. He would watch the lander flip, and tumble, and crash into the red plains; only this time it would be Masha he watched die. And then Bennie would be without his second in command, the one person he had relied on for forty months. No. No.

No. Better to stay strapped down, stay in the darkened office and just... just...

No. That way lay a psych discharge. And before that, Bennie's crew—Bennie's *team*—would suffer and pay because Bennie had failed in the end.

No. Bennie had experienced shocks before. Never quite this many, this large or this close together; but the program had a long tradition: *anything that doesn't kill you instantly, you have a chance to survive.* Bennie wasn't even threatened by this, not physically. It was just shocks in a series. Bennie would tell his crew to bear up under them, and he would help them do it. Now he had to bear up for them.

In Bennie's head, his indecision lasted hours; but an outside observer would've seen Bennie pause momentarily between Karthik's message and Bennie's exit. The moment was over, it was past, and he was on the way to the control deck.

When Bennie reached the control deck, Karthik called from Bay 2: "Officer Desney is on the comm, Commander."

"I'll just bet she is." Bennie jacked into the lander circuit. "Masha, get your ass back up here. Now."

"*Privyet*, Benjamin. Nice day for flight, da?" Masha's words were casual, but Bennie could sense a nervous edge in her voice.

"Masha, this is crazy! Are the Chinese the *only* ones on this crew that *aren't* building landers behind my back?"

Masha laughed. "Who you think I get lander from? When I find their modified lander structure, told them would not turn them in. Told them no need cause trouble. But I must confiscate their modifications, of course. I see their plans, I see *all* plans. Except poor Ishiro's. CSNA has new wing design, better glide configuration. CSNA plan has best chance to succeed, so I take that plan."

"So *everyone* on this mission is bucking Mission Control? *No one* gave a damn about the plan?"

"Your naïveté is touching, Benjamin. We all want Mars. All want to be first. Is national pride, personal pride. If I had moved sooner… Ishiro might be alive."

"Masha, don't be foolish. We'll get there some day. We will. Who cares who's first?"

"*Every* program wants to find way to be first on Mars, Benjamin. Roscosmos, ESA, JAXA, all of us. None of us want to be second. Grandfather Oleg and LOK were second to Moon, and so never went at all. I lie to Daniel: victors go, victors don't wait. Only program foolish enough to actually *believe* in TOR is yours. Rest of us know, without ever discussing: this is our one chance, and you gave it to us with *Bradbury* Project. After this mission, your commercial interests follow. And they will not apply NASA's risk protocols. They take the data we gathered, and they find a way down. So if we want to be first—if we want say in future of humanity on Mars—then we have to do it now. And for Russia, that is what I do. For Grandfather Oleg.

"Now must have quiet. Must concentrate on flying." And with that, Masha turned off her comm.

And then Bennie was immersed in the nightmare once again. He watched the screens in silence as Masha descended. She lacked Ishiro's pulse-micro control, but her better glide configuration seemed to compensate. And Masha was a much better pilot than Ishiro, and the storms were more forgiving. Bennie wasn't sure he could ever forgive Masha for her betrayal, even though he understood what motivated it; but for this moment, none of that mattered. He was a pilot, one of the fraternity of pilots, watching another pilot brave the unknown and praying she would do what no one else had done.

Despite his better judgment, Bennie let himself believe. Thus he was even more stunned when at the last instant, Masha's port wing dipped unexpectedly right at landing. Bennie couldn't see the wing hit; but watching through her camera, he knew that's what must have happened. Suddenly the image spun wildly to port and then shifted madly. Bennie could only imagine the scene on the surface: the lander tumbling, rolling, twisting, and crashing; air spilling out from multiple cracks in whatever pressure cabin Masha had improvised; Masha screaming and dying, either from impact or lack of air.

As the moment dragged on, Bennie feared he would succumb to the nightmare and despair once more. But then Masha's voice from the speakers pulled him away again. "*Bradbury*, Lander 6. Down... on surface. First Officer Desney... injured but... alive."

Bennie breathed out a huge sigh. "Masha, I'm so glad to hear that, I might not put you on report."

Masha breathed into the comm. Her breath came in ragged gulps. "Not care about... report now, Benjamin. Think not... matter for long."

"Masha, I won't put up with talk like that. What would Grandfather Oleg say if he heard you give up? Now give me a status report."

"Da. Lander is... inoperable. Might be repaired, in time. Consumables are in good shape. Air for several hours. Water for... Sufficient water. Spare fuel is... Gauge says spare fuel is leaking, probably too little remains for ascent operations... But lander in no shape for ascent anyway."

"What about you, Masha. How are you?"

"Pilot... injured. Leg broken. Sore, but... meters show no definite internal injuries. Ribs maybe broken, too, but cannot tell for sure."

"That's good news. I thought you were a goner."

"But *am* goner, Commander. CSNA plan was best plan. I am best pilot. Still not good enough. Tell Mission Control… TOR is right. Landing still too risky."

Bennie looked at his command circuit. The incoming message light was blinking. There was an answer from Mission Control. But Bennie had just decided on his own answer. "Nope, too busy."

"What?"

"Nothing. I'm just reprioritizing some mission objectives. You sit tight, Masha."

"*Da*. Sit tight. As long as can. I record my observations."

"Sure. Karthik will keep you company. I have to hold a team meeting." And with that, Bennie switched to the all-ship channel. "All hands to the hangar deck. Emergency priority." He flipped off the comm. "Karthik. Keep her talking. Keep her spirits up."

When Bennie reached the hangar deck, he floated in to a sea of anxious faces. Ishiro's death had shaken them; and already news of Masha's crash had spread throughout the ship. In their own ways, they each depended on her as much as Bennie did. He could see that his nightmare was contagious, and his crew were falling victims to the despair that had almost claimed him.

Bennie had thought this through all the way from the control deck. There were a lot of things he should say as commander of this mission. He should address their ongoing grief over Ishiro and their shock over Masha. He should chew them all out for their insubordination and their private schemes. He should remind them all of their obligations. He should listen to that damned message from Mission Control, play it for them all, and then tell them to get Mars landing out of their damned heads once and for all and start acting like the professionals they were supposed to be.

But here, two-hundred million miles from Earth, there was something more important Bennie had to do. Masha's words came back to him: *But you made us team, and you will keep us team.* That was his task: to make this mob a team again, Mission Control be damned.

But Masha had helped in making them a team, and he needed Masha's help again now. And so all Bennie said when he had their attention was his prepared speech: "Masha's on Mars, and we're going to rescue her. All of you with all of your secret landing plans, put them on the table. Now. Starting this instant, we stop tackling the landing as a bunch of rogues, and we tackle it as a team. We're going to Mars. For Masha."

That was all he said—one of the oldest tricks in the history of team-building—but that was enough. The teams offered up their ideas. Dan synthesized a hybrid design incorporating their best elements: Rick and Linda's redesigned frame, Ishiro's new pulse micro-jet programming, the CSNA glide configuration, and Dan's newest adaptive glide surfaces. It turned out that most of the rogue efforts were well under way, and parts of each could be incorporated directly into Lander 14. Rick and Linda put the mactories into overdrive.

And three hours later, Bennie and his team—*his team*—looked with pride on Lander 14 Prime. It was a spindly-looking thing, but the designs showed a surprising strength and agility. As a finishing touch, someone had painted a name on the nose: *Ishiro Hitara*.

"All right, team." Bennie felt a new warmth all through his body. "We're going to do this. We *are*. But this next part, I have to do alone. I'm flying it down."

Dan raised his hand. "But Commander—"

"Sorry, Dan, it has to be me. I can't order any of you to disobey Mission Control. Besides, if *I* disobey, it sends a message: we're redefining the mission objectives. *We*. The team. So it has to be me."

"Of course, Commander," Dan said. "But you don't fully understand this design. You'll have a copilot, too, via teleoperation."

"There's too much data for one operator," Linda explained. "That's what Ishiro and Masha missed. A teleoperator can watch the big picture, and you can watch the details. And Dan understands the design best."

"Hmmm. I can see that. That could work. Okay, Dan, I want you up in Bay 1. I'm getting my suit."

The lander slid from the hangar deck, pushed out by the launch sled. Once safely away from the *Bradbury*, Bennie experimentally pulsed the jets. The *Ishiro* jumped in response, nimble as a leaping deer. Bennie activated the comm. "*Bradbury*, this is the *Ishiro*. Communications check please."

Dan's voice sounded in Bennie's ear. "*Ishiro, Bradbury*. All comm circuits check. How are the controls, Commander?"

"Very smooth, Dan. My compliments to the team."

"I shall convey them, Commander. May I test teleoperation, sir?"

"Clear to test." Bennie relaxed as Dan put the lander through a series of tests.

Finally Dan and Bennie were both satisfied, and they began the descent. "Okay, Dan, let's plan our landing path. We want to get near Masha, but not so near we risk a collision. We can roll the lander over to her once we're down."

"Agreed, Commander. Karthik has already plotted three options." Dan pushed the options to Bennie's display.

"Hmmm... I like number two. Let's go with that. Any crawlers in that vicinity? Any air stills or fuel stills? Wouldn't hurt to have some spare consumables."

"Karthik's ahead of us there as well. He has crawlers topping off Masha's air now."

"How's she doing?"

"You can ask her yourself. I'll patch her in."

There was an electronic *click* sound, and then Masha's voice. "Benjamin?"

"How are you doing, Masha?"

"Pain down. Meds good." Her words sounded fuzzy, her accent

thicker than usual. Good meds indeed. "But Benjamin, why robots are refilling air? Only... prolong inevitable."

"They didn't tell you?"

Dan cut in. "No one thought to, Commander. We were all too busy. By the time we thought of it... Well, we decided you could tell her."

Bennie grinned. "Sure. Masha, hold on. Keep watching the skies. We're coming down for you."

"What? *Nyet!* Is too dangerous. Cannot risk another in crew."

"Sorry, Masha, we're unanimous. You're outvoted. Your team is rescuing you. I'm on my way down now."

"*Nyet! Nyet, nyet, nyet!* No! Cannot risk commander especially. Complete vio—violation of mission protocols."

"Ha! *You're* telling *me* about mission protocols? After the scheme you pulled right under my nose? You're not one to talk."

"Sorry, Commander... Did what had to do. For Grandfather Oleg..."

"And we're doing what we have to do. Now kindly shut up. Must have quiet, as you said."

The lander had started to buck amid the first faint traces of Martian atmosphere. Bennie's control harness translated the hull readings into tactile feedback all across his body. The tactile feedback freaked out new pilots every time, and some of them never adjusted to it; but those who adjusted soon said it was the only way to fly. With his whole body mapped cybernetically to the skin of the lander, Bennie's full range of senses were dedicated to the task of piloting. It felt as if Bennie flew under his own power, as if the man were flying, not the lander.

And up in Bay 1, Dan felt the same forces buffet his body. But where Bennie saw a lander's eye view of his flight, Dan had a more global view: weather fronts, wind patterns, dust clouds, and other threats that might approach unawares. Bennie clicked back to Dan's circuit. "How's the weather looking, Dan?"

"Not good, Commander. The winds have shifted, and dust is kicking up. I recommend shifting to approach one."

"Approach one, confirmed." Bennie banked to starboard. Approach one ended up in the same area as approach two, but it required him to start sixty kilometers farther south.

As Bennie banked, the wind shifted. The lander dipped too far. Perhaps this was what had happened to Masha, only she had been too close to the ground. Bennie had time to recover. A quick pulse of the jets, and the nose and wing lifted back into the glide path. "Nice move, Commander."

"Thanks, Dan. Where did that wind shear come from?"

"Trying to track that now, Commander. Adjusting the Doppler frequencies. That will shorten the range, but it should give us finer discrimination."

"I think that's a good trade-off. Nice plan."

"All right, you're closing in on approach one, Commander."

"I see that. Lining up now." Bennie veered back to port. "All right, I'm on the approach. Beginning my descent now." Bennie eased forward and down: just a subtle shift of his body, but the lander smoothly matched and amplified his motions.

Soon the lander was in full descent mode. It was part glide, part thruster ride, with the pulse micro-jets chipping in where the atmosphere failed to provide lift. Bennie almost started to enjoy the ride.

And then suddenly the nose dipped dangerously; and just as suddenly, it pitched back up. Bennie felt a sudden instant of nausea, gone almost before he noticed it; and Dan spoke in his ear. "Sorry, Commander. Doppler picked up another shear. There wasn't time to tell you, so I overrode to correct it."

"Good job, Dan, exactly right. Maybe I should just relax and enjoy the ride."

"I am but a co-pilot. My skin isn't on the line, so I can take a relaxed view. But I'm not sure you should."

"All right, co-pilot, I'll pay attention."

Dan and Bennie slowly worked out their collaborative piloting approach; and so the rest of the descent was uneventful. Bennie made mental notes as they went. Over time, they would turn these into new mission protocols. *Manned landing* protocols.

And at last they came to the landing. They actually pulled Karthik into the task, watching the Doppler while Dan watched for wind shears and Bennie watched the ground. There was one final gust, one quick instant of terror, but Dan reacted instantly and just enough. Bennie barely felt the shift as he pulsed the jets into a smooth landing.

"*Bradbury*, *Ishiro* is down. Repeat, *Ishiro* is down safely."

"Good news, Commander." Bennie heard cheers behind Dan. It sounded like half the crew had crowded the control deck.

Bennie switched Masha back into the circuit. "Officer Desney, we are on the ground."

Masha sounded more clear-headed than before. "So you have done it. You landed safely on Mars." There was an edge to her voice. Maybe the meds had faded, and the pain was back?

"Yes, with a lot of help. I'm rolling up to you now." With help from the computer, Bennie spotted Masha's wrecked lander. It lay partly off the landing strip. Its landing gear had snapped or scraped off. Amazingly after the tumble, it had settled right side up; but the entire port wing was gone, rubble spread far across the Martian soil. Scavenger robots were already reclaiming bits of metal.

The *Ishiro* rolled up next to the wreck, its port wing practically touching the fuselage. "I'm here, Masha. How's your suit?"

Masha's response was slow. "Had two… holes I could see. Patched already. Seems to hold pressure."

"So you have your helmet on?"

"Da. Helmet… on…"

"Okay, I'm coming over." Bennie checked his own helmet and suit pressure. All good. Then he opened the lander hatch and set a splint kit out on his port wing. He crawled out onto the wing, picked up the kit, stood, and walked across the wing to Masha's lander. He dropped down onto her remaining wing and opened her hatch. "First Officer Desney."

"Commander." Masha's face didn't show pain, but she was strangely downcast.

"Let's get you out of there. I need to splint that leg and check that suit. Then we'll get you on the *Ishiro*, and Dan can fly you up to the *Bradbury*. I'll wait here until it returns for a pickup."

Masha nodded. "All planned out, *da*. You make it work. Always you make it work."

In Mars's low gravity, it was easy to pull Masha out and set her on the wing. Bennie splinted her leg in the suit, checked the med pack in her belt, and replenished the painkillers.

Finally Bennie realized: Masha wasn't in pain, she was *sullen*. Instead of being glad she was rescued, something was bothering her. Well, he couldn't let that stand. "Okay, Masha, spill."

"What?"

"Explain yourself. What's bothering you?"

"*Nichevo*. You rescue me. Am grateful. Am."

"But?"

Masha sighed. "But is like Grandfather Oleg. In the end, forces beyond his control ended his career. Only in my case is worse. I broke protocols, forced you all to break protocols."

"Forced? Ha! Masha, you should've seen the way they worked. There was no stopping them, once they knew they were working for Masha. You made them a team again."

"For Masha?" Bennie nodded. Masha almost managed to grin. "A team. Feels good. But still... Roscosmos will review mission. Will go down as failure in my record."

Bennie patted the splint. "You survived. That's not a failure. That's our victory."

That time Masha *did* smile. And she only winced a little as Bennie bent down and lifted her in his arms. He walked over to the edge of the wing. "Okay, I have one more question before I put you in that lander and Dan flies you back up. Do you think you can stand on that leg?"

"Da... Can stand in this gravity, I think. But why? You will not carry me up to lander?"

"I just wanted to be sure. You're going on that lander, and you're going up for medical; but we have a new mission objective to complete first. And I would hate for the first words of the first person on Mars to be 'Ouch!' Here we go!"

And with that, Bennie twisted Masha around in the air and lowered her over the edge of the broken lander until her boots touched the ground and took her weight.

Masha bit back her scream. Grandfather Oleg would've been proud.

# RΛCING TO MΛRS

I was thirty-four years old, in what should have been the prime of my medical career; but in fact, I was washed up, a victim of my principles and my temper. My life as a doctor was over—until Nick Aames unexpectedly swept in and threw me a lifeline, asking for me personally to be chief medical officer on the Mars cycler *Aldrin*.

And I hated him for it.

Oh, not right away. I had never met him, so how could I hate him? I was grateful! So as soon as I had dropped my gear in my office, I headed up to the bridge to thank him.

But when I got there, my image of my benefactor was shattered. As soon as the bridge door opened, I heard him berating his crew. "Howarth! Why are those mooring lines not reeled in? Sakaguchi, are those engines ready yet? We boost in two hours, people. Don't waste time. *Move!*"

I peered in through the door. Nick Aames loomed over his bridge, a red-headed, gray-clad vulture looking to swoop down on anyone that drew his ire. The bridge was arranged in the classic "mission control" layout, three rows of desk stations facing a main display, officers in gray uniforms manning each station; and at the rear was the captain's raised aluminum-and-web chair. The curve of the deck and the height of the chair combined to give Aames an elevation of nearly two meters relative to the front row of stations, so that he could look "down" upon each station and see the displays. He glared at everyone and everything around him, a scowl fixed in place. His uniform was immaculate, and his red hair and beard were neatly trimmed; but despite the tone of his voice, his slouch and his attitude made him seem sloppy, just as I had heard from his detractors. But when I saw the glare in his eyes, I decided that he was not sloppy, but rather *dismissive*: he was busy, and he had no time for anything but planning the maneuvers.

Chief Carver was a contrast to the captain: just as neat and trim, but his dark face was alert and warm as he greeted me at the bridge door. I saluted (still not comfortable saluting even after my Academy training), and I introduced myself. "Dr. Constance Baldwin, reporting to Captain Aames."

Carver returned my salute, and he smiled just a bit. He was a charmer. "Welcome aboard, doctor. We're glad to have you. Let me introduce you to the captain."

He walked over to the captain's chair, and I followed, trying to imitate his precision stride and failing utterly in the one-quarter gravity. Carver cleared his throat and announced, "Captain, Dr. Baldwin is reporting for duty."

I saluted again; but before I could say a word, Aames snapped at me without taking his eyes from the stations: "Is anyone sick here, Doctor?"

I was unsure what to do, so I held my salute; and I answered without hesitation: "No, sir."

"Have there been any injuries that I missed? Did someone call you to treat a bout of spacesickness?"

"No, sir."

"Then what the *hell* are you doing here? I do not tolerate spectators on my bridge, particularly during departure maneuvers. Get the hell off the bridge, Doctor, and back to your office where you belong!"

And that was my introduction to Captain Nick Aames. I owed him for my second chance as a doctor. And instinctively, I hated him. I had the urge to knock him out of that chair, but I held my temper. Barely.

I had signed aboard the *Aldrin's* first full cycle to Mars and back. She had been through shakedown cruises in Earth-Luna space before then; but now she would begin a series of boosts and slingshot maneuvers to launch her on a cycler trajectory to Mars. There, another carefully calculated set of slingshot maneuvers would send her back to Earth; and then with skilled piloting she would repeat that cycle, Earth to Mars and back, again and again with minimal fuel costs. All it took was time: five-and-a-half months out, months longer back, and months of slingshot maneuvers on each end. I faced nearly two years under a captain whom I hated. My streak of career bad luck looked to stay unbroken.

I returned to my new office, a small space that smelled like a doctor's office should—disinfectant with a tang of medicine—but looked like the interior of a mud hut. Back then, the *Aldrin* was still owned and managed by Holmes Interplanetary, and they had painted the interior in their corporate colors, a hideous shade of orange-brown. Oh, they called it "ochre"; but in my dark mood, "orange muddy" was all I could see.

"Suck it up, Connie," I said to myself. "You're still a doctor. You have a practice. That's enough."

I opened my old black medical bag and pulled out a clear plastic tube containing a sheet of ivory parchment: my medical diploma from the University of Michigan. I had almost left the tube at home—our mass budget for personal effects was *that* tight—but I couldn't make myself do it. I removed the parchment, unrolled it, and wondered how I was going to hang it. The frame had been too much for my mass budget, but I had no intention of going to space without that parchment.

I had worked too hard to get that diploma—and then fought too hard to keep it. I had reported sanitation violations at my hospital. They sued, and I countersued. The evidence was all with me, and I was vindicated. Eventually I won; but in the process, I lost. I had the court settlement on my side, and a big damage award; but I also had a reputation as a troublemaker. One slimy investigator had pushed me too hard one night, trying to provoke a reaction; and I had lost control, punching him when he had grabbed me in a restaurant. *Smart, Connie, really smart.* Witnesses had testified that I was provoked, so the police never pressed charges, but that became my reputation: the temperamental woman who punches men in bars. The hospital's PR flacks made sure that story was in all the media, and I was marked, a whistleblower with a temper. No one ever used the word "blackballed", but no hospital would grant me admitting privileges. Without those, no practice would accept me. I was locked out of medicine.

At first I was angry. Despite my natural temper, I had kept my calm throughout the court proceedings. (Punching holes in walls at night didn't count.) When I realized how screwed I was, I was angry enough to punch more than a wall, but I was smart enough not to make that mistake twice. Eventually I figured I was still young enough to switch career paths, so I used my settlement to fund my training in space operations and space medicine, and I also became a Reservist in the Space Corps. Then I sent applications to all of the transport companies.

And then I waited. It seemed the blackballing went farther than I had realized. I had good recommendations from my instructors at the Academy, but I received no interview requests. *None.* I still read about shortages of doctors in space, but apparently the shortage wasn't enough to overcome my reputation. My medical career was over, it seemed, and I didn't have a backup plan.

But then out of nowhere, my fortunes completely reversed: instead of an interview request, I received a job offer from Holmes! But I was confused. I had applied there, yes, but I had never heard a word from them—until this offer.

I was torn between celebration and doubt, and doubt won. I didn't want to derail the job offer, but I hate not understanding. So I called their personnel director, and I asked her to confirm. She was very positive: "Yes, it's very unusual, Dr. Baldwin. But your Academy record and your C.V. are exemplary. And your instructors spoke highly of you, Mr. Quintana particularly." Quintana had taught our unit on emergency management. "That was enough for Captain Aames. He insisted we hire you. Our launch schedule is very aggressive, so we didn't have time for the customary rounds of interviews. I hope that's all right with you?"

Absolutely it was all right! And before I knew what was happening, I was on Farport, boarding a rendezvous shuttle, and looking forward to meeting the man who had believed in me.

That bastard, Nick Aames.

After the second *Bradbury* expedition, most people knew Aames by reputation. For a while he was a media hero. And he was also somewhat legendary at the Academy, though a lot of people there were *not* fans. "Difficult," they said. "Sloppy." "Obstinate." "Insolent." "Arrogant." "Smug." And often more: "Arrogant bastard." "Smug asshole." I had written these off as jealousy or petty rivalries. Now I was ready to believe them. And worse.

Oh, well. I had worked for tyrannical bosses, and I had put off hitting them for over two years (until I found out they were compromising patient safety, and then I hit them in the court room). I could put up with Nick Aames for that long. The boss didn't matter, only the patients mattered.

But soon I was as fed up with my patients as well as my boss. Or to be more specific, *a* patient: Anthony Holmes. He first came to my attention when my assistant, Dr. Santana, brought me the ship's medical report, a summary of the condition of the crew and the passengers. When he pushed it to my desktop display, I skimmed over it. I knew Santana's record, so I trusted he had done thorough work. But then I saw that one line was marked **Incomplete**. "Who's this Holmes, Anthony, and why is his record incomplete?"

Santana whistled. "A hundred-twenty passengers and crew on board, and you zoom right in on the one incomplete. You're pretty sharp, doctor." I nodded, acknowledging the compliment. "Anthony Holmes is the sole heir of Anton Holmes, chairman and primary stockholder of Holmes Interplanetary. In other words, he's the boss's son, and he damn well acts like it."

I pulled open Anthony's file and skimmed through it. Twenty years old. Overweight by Corps standards, but reasonably fit for a civilian. Excellent dentition and bone health, the best a billionaire's son could buy. Neurotransmitters all in optimum range, cardiovascular efficiency in the eightieth percentile for civilians of his age range. Therapeutic nanos... "Damn, he's a NoNan."

Santana nodded. "He refused to accept his nano injection. The admitting nurse insisted, and Holmes fired him."

"Fired him? Can he do that?"

"No, doctor. Chief Carver stepped in and explained that you have authority in all medical personnel decisions. But by the time that was settled, we were far behind on our passenger screening. The Chief said we should deal with Holmes later."

I sighed. "And this is 'later'." I tapped the **Contact** button on Anthony's file.

A few seconds later, the channel opened, showing a young blonde man with well-coiffed curls and an expensive smile. His face was on the heavy side of average, and his eyes were bright blue. "Hey, this is Anthony, what's up?" The voice was young, cheery, and didn't sound at all like a troublemaker. I hoped this was all just a misunderstanding.

"Mr. Holmes, this is Dr. Baldwin—"

Anthony interrupted me. I hate being interrupted; and it didn't make me any happier when his cheer was replaced by an edge. "Doctor. I expected this call. I've made my decision, you're wasting your time."

I swore under my breath, remembering my bedside manner for difficult patients. Then I continued. "I respect that, Mr. Holmes, but they pay me to waste my time. Could you please visit my office after boosting, so that we can discuss your treatment options?"

"Treatment?" He laughed, and then he sneered. It turned his pleasant face into something uglier. "I don't *need* that 'treatment', doctor, I've done my research. And I'm busy after boost. We're holding a launch party. You're welcome to join us, but you're not going to change my mind."

I shook my head. "Mr. Holmes, I have to be on duty for any injuries that come up in boost. It would be a lot easier if you could come here."

"Sorry, Doc, I just don't have the time." And he clicked off.

*Damn!* Save me from self-educated "experts" who think they're doctors...

But before I could get any angrier about Anthony, Chief Carver's face came on the ship-wide comm. "Attention, all department heads: departure boost in fifteen minutes. Secure your areas. Departure boost in fifteen minutes. Level One boost alert."

Level One: not even a quarter G, just enough to correct our course and inject us into our cycler orbit to Mars. I had trained all the way to Level Five in the Academy. You would think Level One would be a breeze; but because no one took it seriously, ships usually had *more* injuries at Level One due to loose objects that no one had secured.

But not on the *Aldrin*! When the boost horn sounded, I kept an eye on the med feed on my desk, watching for red lights indicating injuries; but the board stayed green. Aames's crew didn't leave loose ends.

For nine minutes, the big fusion engines burned. Between the spin and the boost, the "gravity" pushed toward the aft curve of the outer wall. Passengers were strapped in, but boost-certified crew could move around as duties required.

At the end of nine minutes, the boost horn sounded again, and Carver returned to the comm as the boost ended. "All hands, we're clear of boost. All personnel are free to move around. Next boost alert will be at Mars!" And he grinned and signed off.

I checked the medical board again: still greens across the desktop. I flipped to my office status view. Everything was fully stocked, we had no patients in the infirmary, and all our paperwork was up-to-date.

I was still steamed, but I had a job to do; and no matter how I searched, I could find no excuse to delay any longer. So I headed to the passenger lounge and to Mr. Holmes's party.

⊥

It was easy to find Anthony in the lounge. The kid was heir to several billions, no matter what currency you measured in; and that much money generates its own gravitational field, drawing in a crowd of sycophants and a ring of nervous corporate bodyguards. I pitied the guards: no one could miss them in those ochre uniforms. I was glad we wore the grays of the Space Corps instead of those awful things. The kid and his crowd were a marked contrast to all of us: they wore a wide range of civilian attire. The kid himself was in a blue silk shirt and darker blue slacks, both designer fashions. That outfit probably cost more than I would make that month.

I had to show my ID for scanning before the guards would let me within sight of Anthony; and they wouldn't let me any closer until they confirmed with him. A guard went over, whispered in his ear, and pointed at me. Anthony nodded and waved me over.

I stood beside him, and he said, "Have a seat, Doc." I looked around his table, but saw no place to sit. A crowd of passengers, young men and women bound for the Mars mission, occupied every seat. I just looked pointedly at them, and Anthony added, "Folks, can you give me a minute to consult with my doctor?" The passengers quickly stood and made room, and I sat down. Anthony gestured to one of the guards, a tall, bald, dark-skinned man with a serious look. "Chuks, get the lady a drink."

The guard scowled—at Anthony, not at me—and I shook my head. "I'm on duty."

Anthony laughed. "Doctor, it's all right. Dad won't mind."

I frowned and narrowed my brows. "I don't answer to your 'Dad', Mr. Holmes. The Corps rules are very clear. Now please, this is not a social call. I'm very concerned. You're at risk for muscle and bone loss, and also for low-level radiation effects. These are easy to avoid, but we really need to set up an appointment for your therapy nanos."

He picked up his glass and took a long drink. The glazed look in those blue eyes told me it wasn't his first. "Sorry to waste your time, Doc. Not gonna happen."

My voice was chill. "My name is Dr. Baldwin." Then I remembered that getting angry would make things worse, so I aimed for a lighter tone. "Let me assure you, the therapy is perfectly safe."

Anthony slammed down his glass, displaying his lack of space reflexes: the drink in the glass lagged behind, then splashed to the bottom and splattered out all over him and the table. "Shit!" Anthony said. From nowhere, another guard appeared with a napkin and started sopping up the mess. Ignoring the guard, Anthony continued. "Safe? I've read the NoNan reports, doctor. Your 'therapy nanos' are associated with higher incidences of rheumatoid arthritis, schizophrenia, insomnia, peripheral neuropathy…" He continued with the usual litany of unconnected symptoms, ticking them off on his fingers. He covered every one I had ever heard of, plus a few new ones.

I knew better than to interrupt a NoNan zealot in mid-zeal; so though I wanted to tell him what an idiot he was, I let him ramble on until he ran out. Then, in my calmest, most reasonable voice, I responded. "Mr. Holmes, those 'reports' are pseudoscience promoted by celebrities trying to stay relevant and entertainment 'doctors' who know more about audience ratings than medical research. The NoNan literature has been discredited by every scientist who has reviewed it. I can assure you that the reputable studies do not show any significant correlation between therapy nanos and any of those symptoms."

Anthony shook his head. "'Studies' funded by the companies that manufacture nanos. What's your cut, Doc? How much do you get for jabbing me?"

He grinned as he said that, but he was pushing my limits. "Mr. Holmes, take your accusations and shove them. If you want a painful death, don't let me stop you."

I stood and started to leave, but he grabbed my arm to stop me. "Doc, relax."

My vision started to go red, and I felt my temple throbbing. I yanked my arm away and raised my voice so the whole room could hear. "Keep your hands to yourself, asshole, if you don't want them broken. Boss's brat or no." Anthony let go, but the dark-skinned bodyguard moved to stop me. He was a head taller than me, and in very good shape; but I fixed him with the glare I had learned to use on hospital lawyers. "Out of my way, or I'll see you in the infirmary." He stepped aside, and I stormed out for my office.

⚓

But I didn't get far down the corridor before I heard a deep voice calling. "Dr. Baldwin."

Still too pissed to stop or turn back, I kept marching. I heard feet hurrying behind me, and I tensed, expecting someone to grab me and try to stop me. *Relax, Connie, you'll take their head off.*

But my pursuer was smarter than that. Faster than I could follow, a flash of ochre swept past me, climbing halfway up the wall. In one smooth motion and without ever touching me, the tall guard had leapt in front of me. Despite his bit of acrobatics, he wasn't even breathing hard. He stood there, full of wiry energy, and that ochre uniform wasn't the least mussed. He *almost* made that color look good. Almost.

The guard held out a hand to stop me. "Doctor, please wait."

"I'm sorry. Mr. Chuks, is it?"

He straightened and smiled. "Major Adika, Chukwunwike Adika. Only my friends call me 'Chuks'." He had a nice smile; but then it fell. "And over-privileged billionaire's sons. I have the... privilege of leading young Mr. Holmes's security detail."

I rolled my eyes. "I'm *really* sorry, Major Adika. You'll notice *he* grabbed *me*. I never laid a finger on him. I lost my temper, but I'm not a threat to Mr. Holmes." *As long as he keeps his hands to himself...*

The major nodded. "We had scanned you for weapons. Our bio-scans had read your heart rate and blood pressure, and our thermal sensors showed no significant increase in activity in your limbic system, so we judged you as non-threatening." And then the Major's smile returned. "But if in your anger you had slapped the young mister, we might not have noticed, officially. Some of us believe that the young mister gets away with too much because people want something from him. And his father, the brilliant businessman, has a blind spot where his son is involved." Then the smile turned to a broad, likable grin. "Should I ever choose to resign in style, I might slap him myself."

I had prepared for another confrontation. My pulse had been racing. But the major's humor relaxed me. There was a lot more to this man than muscle. "Thank you, major. That... helps. Did you follow me just to apologize?"

"It is not right for a professional woman such as yourself to be treated so. An apology was required." His voice had a hint of an accent, and his word choice was rather formal. I suspected English was not his first language. "But no, that was only part of my reason. What you said, doctor... Is Mr. Holmes really at risk?"

I nodded. "You've had your therapy nanos. Were they explained to you?"

"Doctor, I and my team were selected for this detail because we all have space experience. Mr. Holmes senior wants us ready for any risk

127

to his son. We all have been briefed on therapy nanos. But young Mr. Holmes's sources—"

"—are a bunch of quacks and kooks and attention-seekers who might get him killed. They play off the public's lack of science skills to inflame ridiculous fears. Those fears are harmless on Earth; but here and on Mars, therapy nanos are his best defense against a number of general metabolic ailments. I can't guarantee those will be fatal, but the risks are high. Unacceptably high, in my medical opinion. He risks decreased bone density and muscle tissue loss due to the low gravity, and cumulative effects of low-level cosmic radiation in open space. He'll survive, probably, but he risks painful, permanent injuries. And death can't be ruled out. Angry as he made me, I still can't put him through that without a fight."

The major added, "And if he gets injured or sick, you will have to put up with him in your infirmary." I laughed at that, and the last of my tension slipped away. He laughed as well—a good, deep, hearty laugh—and then continued. "Doctor, if you tell me his life is at stake, I will sit on young Mr. Holmes while you give him the injections." The major's grin grew. "I might even enjoy it."

I grinned back. The major should've been a doctor. He had a talent for putting people at ease.

But then I shook my head. "I'm sorry, I wish I could, but regulations and my code of ethics forbid me from performing invasive therapy on an informed, competent patient who refuses it. His behavior aside, Holmes is competent... legally."

His grin turned down, and his face turned solemn, every muscle standing out in frustration. "Then I do not know what to do, doctor. You cannot treat him and I cannot protect him if he refuses to allow it."

By then I had decided how *I* would deal with the problem: I would pass the buck. It was a corporate political problem as much as a medical problem. "Let's let the captain deal with this. Perhaps he can persuade Holmes senior, and then Holmes senior can persuade junior."

The major looked doubtful. "No one has persuaded young Mr. Holmes against his will in years." But I didn't see any other option, so I tapped the captain's icon on my comm.

Captain Aames's face appeared on the comm screen in my sleeve. He still had that casual air, almost—almost *slovenly* in contrast to the alert bearing of Major Adika. But Rank Hath Its Privileges. If the captain wanted to be casual, it was his command.

His tone, however, was just as sharp as I remembered. "Dr. Baldwin, I hear you had an altercation in the passenger lounge. Do I need to rule that off limits to you? Do I have to worry that you'll assault someone again? Or can you behave as a respectable officer of this ship?"

"Captain, I don't know what you've heard, but—"

"What I *don't* need to hear, doctor, are excuses. I have three complaints from Anthony Holmes: two about your behavior and one about his missing security chief. I don't need trouble with the boss right at this moment, nor with his son. Can you skip the excuses and explain yourself?"

So I explained everything that had happened. Occasionally I looked up at Major Adika for confirmation; and each time he was watching me carefully and nodding as I went. His intense stare unnerved me even more than the captain's glare.

I was careful not to gloss over anything, avoiding anything that might sound like an excuse; but when I was done, the captain snapped, "Is that it?"

"Yes, sir."

Then the captain leaned in toward the camera and raised his voice a notch. "And you chose to discuss a patient's private medical matters over *an open comm* in the middle of *a public corridor* where *anyone could overhear*? Do you know how much trouble Anthony could make with a breach of privacy claim? Why didn't you come to me in person?"

I clenched my fists, out of view of the camera, but not of Major Adika. He waved both hands palms down in a calming gesture; and that gave me just enough control to keep going. "Captain, you said you never wanted to see me on your bridge."

Captain Aames looked upward and snorted. "I'm not *on* the bridge, doctor. I'm quite certain my schedule is posted, and it shows me in my office right now. Did you even bother to check my schedule?"

I swallowed my reply, because I knew he had me. "No, captain, I did not."

Then Captain Aames surprised me with his answer. "That's better, doctor. The facts. Don't pretty them up, and damn sure don't cover them up, and things will go much better here."

I was confused: ready to fight, and suddenly the fight was gone. Just like with Major Adika. Was I too defensive? Was I *looking* for trouble?

I would have to think on that later; but right now, I seemed to have calmed the captain, and I wanted to build on that. "Understood, captain. I'll head to your office immediately."

"No," the captain waved that idea away, "it's too late for that. If privacy has been breached, it's done already. No... I think I'll need to clear this up in person, so as not to further antagonize the boss's son. Wait for me outside the lounge, doctor."

⚓

By the time Captain Aames reached the passenger lounge, Major Adika had gone back in. The captain didn't say a word to me, he just nodded and entered the lounge. On the doorstep he looked back at me for a moment and waved his head: *follow me.*

So I followed. The captain strode directly up to Major Adika, held out his badge for scanning, and held his arms away from his side. Again I noted the contrast: the major was coiled energy, watching for trouble and ready to spring, while the captain was casual. Yet the captain was every bit as confident, and his eyes swept the room in the same fashion.

I noticed the major's aide subtly scanning for weapons as the major re-scanned my badge. When the aide nodded, Major Adika let us approach the table. Again all of the chairs were occupied by hangers-on; but Captain Aames cleared his throat and stared down at them, and they couldn't meet his stare. They quickly slipped away, and the captain sat across from Anthony. I joined them, caught uncomfortably between two men each of whom had already pissed me off once that day. I could feel my anxiety mounting, and with it my temper.

Then a subtle movement caught my attention from across the table: Major Adika moved to stand near the table, just outside of the circle of conversation but close by if there was any trouble. He stood poised in the low gravity, as if ready to spring, but with his arms lightly crossed in front of himself. He caught my eye and gave me a barely noticeable smile; and just like that, my anxiety blew away on the wind.

The table now held the remnants of a plate of nachos and soy cheese. The table had damp streaks as if it had been wiped clean at least once, indicating one or more spilled drinks. Anthony had had a few more drinks since I had left, and he was showing the signs. His body mass let him absorb a fair amount of alcohol, but his head was weaving, and his hands were unsteady. He looked at Captain Aames, startled as if he hadn't noticed our arrival. "Nick! Hey, how's things on the bridge, Cap? Chuks, we need more drinks here!"

Major Adika didn't move, and Anthony didn't notice. He didn't have time: Captain Aames took control of the conversation. "Mr. Holmes, I understand there was an unfortunate incident between you and Dr. Baldwin earlier."

Then Anthony finally noticed me. "Oh, hey, Doc... SNo hard feelings, right? Get the Doc a drink, somebody! Look, Nick, it's no big deal." Anthony had a drink in his right hand and waved it around, gesturing with it as if making a point. "The Doc just got a little... you know... hot. She's used to ordering patients around, and I don't take orders."

"I understand, Mr. Holmes. The doctor just didn't realize how

131

strongly you hold to your NoNan views."

I began to get annoyed all over again. What happened to Nick Aames, the Terror of the Spaceways? Here he was, coddling the boss's son just like all of the other ass-kissers. Aames could learn a thing or two from Major Adika!

And Anthony was lapping it up. "That's right, NoNan!" He raised his voice. "NoNan, everybody! Say it with me! No! Nanos!" And just as he commanded, many in the crowd joined in as Anthony stood. "No! Nanos! No! Nanos! NONAN!!!!!" Anthony waved his drink around, spilling it, and I barely dodged the alcohol.

The room broke out in scattered applause, and Anthony bowed and sat. As the applause died down, he waved his empty glass at the captain. "No nanos, Nick. I'm keeping my body pure. And that's final."

The captain nodded and spoke calmly. "I understand. Dr. Baldwin has explained the risks if you decline therapeutic nanos?" I tried to answer, but the captain held up a hand. "Let him answer, please, doctor. For the record."

Anthony stared into space. "She didn't, but… Ummm… That nurse guy, Floyd—"

"Carl Lloyd," the captain corrected.

"Yeah, Lloyd. He read off all the risks, all the usual nano company lies. I've heard them all before."

"So you were informed of the risks, and you're declining treatment. For the record," the captain repeated.

"Yes, and yes."

"So noted." The captain tapped a button on his comm, and Holmes's statement was recorded. That was it? That would get me and him off the hook legally, but it wouldn't do a thing about the risks.

But the captain wasn't done. "And now I think an apology is in order."

My jaw dropped. No! I couldn't swallow that much pride. No way would I apologize to that young punk, even if it meant my job.

Before I could object, Anthony blinked twice and then responded. "It's all right, Nick. The Doc meant well. She doesn't have to apologize. We're good, right, Doc?"

I was ready to shout that we were not at all good; but before I could, Captain Aames raised his voice and said, "You've made a mistake, Mr. Holmes." He looked down at his comm. "It's you who are going to apologize to Dr. Baldwin for manhandling her, a professional and one of *my* officers. You're also going to apologize for your slanderous accusations."

"What?" Anthony leaned over the table. "You forget who you're talking to. You're outa line, Nick."

And before anyone knew what was happening, the captain reached out and swiftly slapped Anthony across the face. "That's 'Captain Aames' to you, kid."

Everything happened at once. The room grew silent at the slap, so everyone heard the captain. The guards moved toward our table; but Major Adika held up one hand, and they stepped back. I noticed a very slight grin on the major's face.

Anthony rubbed his jaw. "What—Nick—" The captain raised his hand again, so Anthony corrected himself. "What do you think you're doing, captain? Who do you think is in charge here?"

The captain checked his comm again, and then he pushed a file to the major's comm. "As of two minutes ago, *I* am. We just passed Earth's gravipause."

Anthony tried to focus. "Earth's what?"

"If you actually *belonged* in space, you would know that the gravipause is that point where the Sun's gravitational pull exceeds Earth's and Luna's combined gravity."

Anthony acted like he understood, but I doubted anything had penetrated all that alcohol. "That... interesting... But it's still no excuse to be insolent!"

"You damn bet it's an excuse! According to my contract with your father's corporation, once the sun's pull takes over, I have plenary power here. I can do whatever I, *in my sole judgment*, decide is necessary for the safety of my passengers and crew, and for the safe completion of our mission. I can dispense orders, regulations, and discipline as I see fit."

Major Adika nodded. "He's correct, Mr. Holmes. This contract is very clear. He can't have you flogged or keelhauled, he can't violate your fundamental rights, but he has practically the powers of an old British sea captain when it comes to the smooth operation of this ship."

Captain Aames glared at Anthony. "And smooth operation requires proper respect for my officers and crew while in performance of their duties. You will apologize to Dr. Baldwin. Now."

Anthony scowled. "I will not!"

As quick as before, Nick reached out and slapped Anthony again. Then he lowered his voice so that only the three of us could hear. "If you make me slap you again, kid, I'll pull your pants down to do it, in front of all your adoring fans. Now: apologize to the doctor. Make sure everybody hears it." Then he sat back and waited.

Anthony stared, a mix of emotions struggling in his face: defiance, fear, anger, and shock. I might've felt sorry for him, if he hadn't pissed me off in the first place. Finally he leaned back in his chair, looked around the room, and raised his voice. "I am... sorry... Dr. Baldwin. It was disrespectful to accuse you of taking money from the nano companies. And I... was wrong to grab you like I did. That was no way to treat an officer of this ship." He paused, looking down at his empty glass. Then, even louder, he added, "What are you all looking at? This is supposed to be a party! Bartender, a round for the house!"

The noise picked back up again, though it sounded bit forced. Under the rattle of glasses and the buzz of conversation, Anthony added, "Happy now, *Captain* Aames?"

The captain ignored the scorn, but he laughed, haltingly. "Kid, your entire fortune couldn't make me *happy*. But for now, I'm satisfied with your apology."

Anthony was surly, and he didn't try to hide it. "I suppose now you're going to force me to take therapy nanos."

Captain Aames shook his head. "No, that would be a clear violation of your fundamental rights. I can't force you to accept invasive therapy against your will. But I can take other measures for your own protection. Dr. Baldwin!"

I sat up straighter. "Yes, captain."

"Doctor, what was the preventive therapy for musculoskeletal loss and incidental radiation exposure *before* we perfected therapy nanos?"

"Captain, it involved tripling the recommended exercise regimen. That provides sufficient muscle growth and bone development to counter the losses; and a good, healthy, active metabolism can repair most low-level radiation damage. Assuming he stays healthy otherwise."

"I see. And has the kid even started the standard regimen?"

I checked Anthony's chart. "Not yet, captain. Of course, it's still early in the day."

"Nonsense, doctor. Never too early for exercise." The captain stood. "On your feet, kid!"

"Fuck off!" Anthony tapped his comm, but then he looked puzzled. He stabbed with his finger, but still nothing happened. "Hey! Why can't I call Dad?"

The captain replied, "I cut off your outbound communications."

"You can't do that! You can't violate my rights!"

"I can't *violate* them; but in the interests of ship operations, I can regulate and restrict them. We only have so much communications bandwidth, so I have to meter it. You will get *one* fifteen-minute call, once per day. Your slot is *after* your workout. Now *on your feet*." And with that, Captain Aames reached down, grabbed that expensive blue shirt, twisted it into a knot, and easily lifted Anthony in the low gravity.

He set the young man down on his feet, looked him over, and sneered. "Drunk. Flabby. Out of shape. We'll have to do something about that. Kid, the running track is one ring up, but you can start running *now*. Get up there and give me some laps!"

Anthony looked indignant. "I'll be your boss some day!"

"Only if I can keep you alive that long. Now move!" The captain raised his hand again, and Anthony flinched. Then he stumbled through the crowd. Major Adika moved ahead of him, clearing a path, and Anthony ran to the door.

"That's a start," the captain called after him. "But faster!" He turned to me. "Doctor, shouldn't you be supervising his therapy?"

"Yes, captain." I didn't see why I needed to watch the kid run, but I wasn't ready to cross Captain Aames. I got up and headed to the door just in time to see Anthony bolt antispinward, toward his cabin; but the major grabbed his arm, spun him around, and shoved him spinward toward the ramp to the upper ring. Adika grinned as they passed me.

I started jogging as well; but I had gone only a few meters when a bit of gray appeared in my peripheral vision. Turning my head slightly, I saw Captain Aames jogging beside me. "Best you can do?" he asked.

And then he pulled ahead of me, rushing to pass the major and catch Anthony. He prodded the kid all the way up the ramp and onto the big running track. The track was a third of a kilometer, completely circling the upper ring. By the time I reached the top of the ramp, the captain and Anthony were out of sight around the curve; but I could still see Major Adika, so I rushed to catch up with him. Then we both picked up speed until we were up with the captain and the kid. The captain had thrown off his uniform jacket somewhere, and his shirt showed sweat stains. I decided he was smart, so I threw off mine as well.

The captain set a reasonable pace, especially in one-quarter G, but Anthony soon showed signs of fatigue. That only made Captain Aames more persistent. "Slacker! Are you *that* soft, kid?" He cajoled and taunted to keep Anthony moving.

Sometimes the captain moved ahead and jogged backwards, keeping right in the kid's face as he tossed out casual insults. "Your problem is you can't pay someone to run for you. Do you ever do *anything* on your own?" *That* spurred the kid onward, though he didn't have breath to respond.

After fifteen loops, I slowed down. I was in okay shape, but I didn't run much. The major dropped back with me, though I'm sure that was just courtesy: he didn't show any signs of strain. Anthony attempted to slow down as well; but instead the captain pushed him even harder. Soon they were out of sight again, and I enjoyed my leisurely run with Adika.

Not long after that, the captain and Anthony passed us. A little later, they passed us again, moving faster this time. The kid was looking pale, and I raised my hand for the captain's attention; but he pointedly ignored me. It gave me some comfort to see that the captain's shirt was drenched with sweat. He wasn't a machine after all.

Halfway around the ring, we had to dodge around a mess on the track. I smelled stomach acid, and I saw bits of undigested soy cheese in the mess.

The next time around, the captain and Anthony had finally stopped. Aames stood and supervised as Anthony, shirtless, sopped up the vomit with an expensive blue silk rag. The captain called "Halt!" and Adika and I came to a stop. Anthony looked up from his work, panting, and glared at Aames. The captain returned the glare and then turned to me. "Doctor."

I recognized the command in his tone, so I dropped to my knees, grabbed Anthony's wrist, and felt for a pulse: 180, high but not dangerously so for his age and health. His respiration was labored, but already it was slowing. I leaned my ear to his chest. His heart sounded busy, but good. I didn't have my bag, so I couldn't check BP or electrolyte balance, hardly any of my routine checks; but I had enough data to give a preliminary answer. "He's fine, captain. He'll feel it tomorrow, but he's fine."

"You bet he'll feel it." The captain paused for breath. "Major Adika?"

The major snapped to attention, his broad chest rising and falling steadily in that damp ochre shirt. "Yes, captain."

"Major, this has been fun, but I can't spare this much time day after day, even for the health of the kid. He needs three runs per day, doctor?" I nodded. "Since he's such an *important* kid, I can take time to run with him third watch every day. Major, can you handle first watch?"

Major Adika nodded. "Yes, captain."

The captain turned back to me. "Doctor, this is therapy, so we need medical supervision. I need you to take the second watch run."

"Yes, captain. I'll need to trade watches with Dr. Santana."

"Don't bother me with details, doctor, just do your job." He held down a hand to Anthony, but the kid ignored it. The captain snapped his fingers twice, and finally Anthony got the message. He took the hand, and the captain pulled him to his feet. "So, kid, that'll be your routine from here to Mars: a half hour run, once each watch. Except fourth watch, we'll let you sleep through that one. You'll need it. Doctor, should that be a sufficient substitute for therapy nanos?"

I smiled and nodded. "It should, captain."

The captain continued, again looking at Anthony. "Three top officers watching out for your health. That's how important you are. Does that sound good, kid? Or would you like to get those injections now?"

Anthony couldn't stand straight, but he lifted his head enough to glare at the captain. "No, *captain*." And without another word, he staggered down the ramp to the main ring. Major Adika ambled after him. Aside from the sweaty shirt, you might never have known that the major had had a workout.

I waited until they were out of sight down the ramp, and then I spoke up. "Captain, you know he's going to call his father immediately."

The captain turned and stared at me. "Did I ask for observations, doctor?"

"No, captain."

"Good!" My eyes widened. "Don't look so shocked, doctor. I expect you to bring things to my attention when you think they're important. You can expect me to chew you out when I think you're wasting my time. And I expect you to push back because you know you're right. I expect you to fight me until we know what the facts are. I don't need a bunch of yes-men for officers, I need the whistleblower who gave up her career because she knew she was right. That's who I hired, is that who I got?"

"Yes, captain."

"That sounds rather timid to me, doctor. Are you ready to fight me when I'm wrong?"

"YES, CAPTAIN!"

"That's better." And then the captain surprised me: for just a fraction of a second, he smiled. "You're right, doctor, he'll call Anton Holmes. Not immediately, he's too exhausted. But eventually. And then Anton will call me. And then... I don't think the kid will like the outcome."

"Understood, captain. But might I ask one favor?"

"Spit it out, doctor."

"Captain, I would dearly like to listen in on that call from Anton Holmes."

Again just the hint of a smile. "Doctor, it would be my pleasure. Besides, I may need the kid's physician to back me up."

⚓

When the time came, I wasn't the only one waiting for the call. Major

Adika joined us. The captain's office was decorated all in tasteful dark shades: black walls, big black desk with a touch-display surface, dark gray carpet, and brushed metal accents. The navy blue chair provided a spot of color that drew attention to its occupant. It was such a relief from the ochre throughout the ship, I felt the urge to hide there through my entire tour. But that would've meant hiding out with Captain Aames; and despite our new détente, I wasn't ready for that. He still struck me as volatile and demanding, and I didn't need that kind of stress all day long. I didn't know how Chief Carver could handle it.

Behind the captain, a massive window showed Earth and Luna slowly spinning past, over six light-seconds away. I stared at the dwindling planets, and I thought about escape: all my past mistakes, all the wreckage that had been my career, it was all just a microscopic point on that little blue dot in the distance. I might make all new mistakes here on the *Aldrin*; but this really was a second chance for me. I was determined to make this work.

My thoughts were interrupted by a chime from the desk. A beat-up old ereader sat in the middle of the desk. Captain Aames slid it to the side, and then he waved us to stand behind him. He tapped the surface, and a woman's face appeared in a window in the center of the glass. She said, "Incoming call from Anton Holmes, captain."

Aames nodded at the desk. "Put him through, Miles." The woman's window moved aside, and another window appeared, showing an older man who was recognizably a relative of Anthony Holmes. The hair was the same dark blonde, but short and bushy and with many gray bristles. The face was thinner, harder, and more serious; but the bone structure was the same, and he had the same intense blue eyes. Those eyes were narrowed at the screen, though he probably couldn't see us yet.

"Mr. Anton Holmes," Miles said, "Captain Aames can speak to you now. Please remember that the light-speed delay is six seconds one way, twelve seconds round trip. Mr. Holmes, please begin." Experienced interplanetary hands can speak in parallel, each person making points while listening to older points as they arrived; but for most people, it was simpler to wait for each statement, and for one party to control the discussion until passing control to the other. Miles had just given Anton Holmes control, so we had a twelve-second wait for him to begin.

The woman disappeared, replaced with the view from the captain's camera, a narrow focus that showed only him, not the major and me. After a pause, Holmes spoke. "So, Nick, I understand you had a problem with my son."

The captain responded. "Your son was drunk before we reached the gravipause. He grabbed my doctor. He's lucky she didn't belt him! She has a history, you know." He looked up at me, eyebrows raised as if daring me to protest.

Twelve seconds later, Holmes rolled his eyes. "I think you're making a big deal out of nothing. Can't we just start over, pretend this never happened?"

Aames nodded. "We can start over... with a new captain, and with you fulfilling the cancellation clause in our contract. That would be five years' salary, payable immediately, plus a commission on each trip for that period. Would you like to invoke that clause?" He paused, but not long enough for Holmes to take control. "But wait... There's no qualified captain aboard, and we can't turn back now. That would be a mess, wouldn't it?"

Twelve seconds later, Holmes was exasperated. "You can't be serious! You would quit over such a small matter as this?"

"No, but unless you fire me, I'm going to run this ship my way. And it's not a small matter. Do you still insist on sending Anthony to Mars?"

"Damn straight I do. This is a *Holmes* mission to Mars, and there's going to be a Holmes leading it!"

The captain sighed. "You forget, Anton, I've been to Mars. I know Mars. He's not ready to go there, and he's damn sure not ready to lead any mission."

"Oh, I know that." Holmes leaned into the camera and lowered his voice. "It's just symbolic for the media, and a notch for his resumé. He won't do anything but give speeches. It'll just be a quick down-and-back on a drop shuttle as you swing around for your slingshot. You can pick him up on your way back. Adika will keep an eye on him the whole way, and there won't be time for him to get into trouble. I may be too busy to go myself, but by damn, there's going to be Holmes footprints on Mars. That will be worth a lot of points on the stock market, and also in boardroom battles."

"I still think it's a stupid idea, but it's out of my hands once we reach the Mars gravipause. My only responsibility is to get him there safe and healthy. That's not going to happen if he suffers bone and muscle loss and radiation symptoms. Since he's being a stubborn ass about his therapy nanos, hyper-exercise is what my doctor prescribes. Isn't that right, doctor?" And he widened the frame to show me and the major standing behind him.

"Yes, captain," I answered. "This is the recommended non-nano therapy for a space traveler of his age and health."

Aames turned to the major. "And is young Mr. Holmes in any physical danger?"

Adika shook his head. "Mr. Holmes, I agree with Captain Aames: your son has no business on Mars, and our security team will be very busy keeping him alive. But here on the *Aldrin* with this exercise program, he is perfectly safe."

Aames continued. "So in the best expert opinion on site, this is in Anthony's own best interests. May I proceed? Or should I clean out my office?"

In the twelve seconds it took to respond, Holmes's glare intensified as he listened. Finally, he sighed, but he had a look of determination. Billionaires are accustomed to doing things their way. "All right, I'll talk to him. Are you satisfied, *captain*?"

Aames smiled at the camera, but it wasn't a warm smile. It was almost predatory. "Quite satisfied, *boss*. Now is there anything else? Or can I go back to running my ship?"

"No, nothing else. Get to it." And just like that, the image cut out.

"He's a busy man," the captain said, swiveling his chair to face the major and me. "That conversation probably cost fifty-thousand dollars of his time, plus bandwidth charges. We should feel privileged. Do you feel privileged?" Before we could answer, he continued. "So, doctor, major, we proceed according to plan." Then Aames grinned at the major, showing real warmth for the first time that I had seen. "Just like Luna, eh, Chuks?"

Major Adika grinned back. "Just like Luna, Nick, except this time we are on the other end of the stick. I believe Sergeant Fontes would laugh to see us now."

"No, thank you," the captain answered, "I heard enough of his laughter in basic." For a moment he stared out the window, back at Earth and Luna. Then he turned back to his desk. "Let's hope our 'recruit' is no more difficult than we were, eh?"

Adika shook his head. "He is not difficult, but he will never be ready for a dangerous place like Mars."

The captain nodded. "That's why he has you watching over him. He couldn't be safer. But enough of this. I have work to do, and so do both of you. If you don't, I'll find some. Get out of here."

So we left his office, returning to the world of awful ochre in Carver's office, the gateway to the captain's sanctuary. Chief Carver was on the bridge, so we were alone; but I waited until we were safely out of Carver's outer office and in the corridor before I turned to Major Adika. "You said only friends call you 'Chuks'. I take it you know Captain Aames?"

Major Adika smiled again. I could get used to that smile. "Doctor, we have a saying: 'Space is vast, but the Space Corps is not.' If you stay in the Corps long enough, you will be amazed at how many people you will meet. You could not possibly remember them all; but one does not forget Nick Aames. Though many would like to." And he laughed.

I could get used to that, too.

The next day, when it was time for my run with Anthony, I tracked him down in the lounge again. I expected the bodyguards to let me pass, since they had already screened me twice the day before, but they were more professional than that. They were cordial and courteous— and the major even gave me one of those big smiles—but they scanned me as thoroughly as they had the first time. Then they let me through.

Anthony was sitting at the same table, but alone this time. A few passengers waved at him as they passed by, but none sat down. As they walked past me, I heard muted giggles and comments under their breath, including the word "brat".

I sat down at the table. Anthony stared down at a glass of what looked like tomato juice. Without asking, I picked it up. "Hey!" he objected, reaching for the glass.

But I pulled the glass away. "Doctor's orders. I need to know what you're drinking." I took a sip. It *was* tomato juice, reconstituted, without any hint of vodka. I set the glass back down. "Good choice."

Anthony took the glass and stared into it again, slumping in his chair. I sat down next to him, took his wrist, and started checking his vitals. He was silent and sullen as I worked. He had some pallor, nothing bad, but he looked like he had been kicked around. I guess he had, in a way. Despite myself, I started to feel almost sorry for him. Sorry enough to fudge the truth a bit. "It seems your pulse is a little erratic, Mr. Holmes. I'll sign a doctor's slip excusing you from this afternoon's run, if you'd like."

Anthony shook his head. "No." And then I saw something of his father in him, the same steel behind the blue eyes. He drank the rest of the tomato juice, set down his glass, and rose. "Let's go." He led the way to upper ring, and a guard trailed us, taking a position at the top of the ramp. We started running; and as we ran, I saw another guard at the top of each of the four ramps. We had the ring to ourselves.

Anthony took off at a very fast pace, much too fast to maintain for a half hour even in our gravity. I rushed to catch up with him; but when I did, he put on more speed. I had to run all out to catch him again.

Anthony kept going as fast as he could for as long as he could, barreling forward as if Captain Aames were still chasing him—or something worse. I could see he was getting tired and sloppy, and I worried he might hurt himself.

Eventually he slowed down. I was relieved, because I couldn't keep up that pace much longer. But though he slowed, he remained at a running pace, not a jog. Whatever reserves he had wouldn't last long.

When I saw Anthony's face getting red, I called out, "Enough." And I halted, but he kept going. "Stop!" I shouted. This time he stopped, and I walked forward to check him over, a guard running up as I did. The guard, a tall Asian woman, paid no attention to me. Like me, she was worried about Anthony.

His heart rate, respiration, and temperature were all dangerously high. "That's enough, Mr. Holmes. Don't make me get rough. You've got to pace yourself, or you're going to make yourself ill, maybe injure yourself."

Anthony leaned against a wall, head resting on his arms. The guard put a hand on his shoulder, but he shook it off. "Leave me alone…" he panted. "I… can do this…"

"You can't do anything if you keep this up. Don't argue with your doctor."

But Anthony shook his head. "He… thinks… I can't do this…"

"Captain Aames?" I looked around as if the captain might be listening. "That man's a closed one, Mr. Holmes. Don't assume you know what he's thinking. He's manipulative, that might be exactly what he wants. If you try to out-think him, you'll only hurt your head."

"No… Not Aames…"

"What, those people in the lounge? Is that what they were laughing about?"

Anthony glared at me. "Laughing… Billionaire's son… getting

what's coming to him..." His breathing was becoming more regular. "Phonies... But not the first. Always want something from me, but I see through them."

"Then why do you care what they think?"

Anthony straightened and snarled. "Not them, my Dad! He thinks... I can't do this. He thinks... I don't have to." His breathing was even, but now he hesitated for a different reason, choking back his emotions. "He thinks Aames is just... punishing me for... grabbing you." He swallowed. "Doctor, I'm so sorry. I was drunk, and I was completely out of line. It won't happen again."

"Damn straight it won't, next time I'll punch you for sure." But I smiled as I said it. "We can pretend it never happened, Mr. Holmes, if that will help with your father."

"Please, call me 'Anthony'. When people call me 'Mr. Holmes', it usually means they want something."

"All right, Anthony. Call me—"

Anthony held up a hand. "I'll call you 'Doctor'. The captain wants me to respect his officers." He tried to smile, but it faded, and he shook his head again. "But it won't help with Dad, he just wants this over. He thinks I should just put up a show for a while, and Aames will get bored. He says... not even a week, just a few days. He says... He says, 'Put in a minimum for a few days, satisfy Aames. Even you can do that.' *Even you.*"

I turned away, and so did the guard. It looked like Anthony was about to cry, and we didn't want to make things worse for him. Looking toward the wall, I replied, "Anthony, you *can't* do this if you keep pushing this hard. You're on the edge of exhaustion. But you can, you *will* do this if you just build up. At your age and in your condition, you can keep this up all day, once you work up to it. But if you go trying to prove something to your dad, you're going to prove him right. If you want to prove him wrong, you're going to have to work smarter. Can you do that?"

"Yes, doctor."

He sounded more in control, so I turned back to him. "We'll finish this half hour walking. You've already overexerted yourself this watch. Then I'll set up a pace schedule for you, building up gradually as you go; and you will stick to that pace no matter who tries to push you harder. Tell them it's doctor's orders. Understood?"

Anthony managed to smile at that. "Even Captain Aames?"

"You let me handle Captain Aames. Just concentrate on your workout plan, and you'll show him. And your dad."

"Yes, doctor." And we started walking. And talking. And despite myself, I found myself coming to like him. Anthony drunk was obnoxious, but Anthony sober was a pretty nice kid.

Not that I would call Anthony a kid to his face, not like the captain did. I could see his pride was mostly a defense, and it could be easily battered. But he *was* a kid. Not chronologically—I had known twenty-year-old soldiers and EMTs and astronauts who were by no means kids—but in terms of experience. Poor Anthony at twenty had never had to do anything, not anything hard. Oh, he had been places, symbolic trips to half the world. He had been on aid missions as a front man for the Holmes Trust, and he had done symbolic spade work for the cameras; but it was never real, never anything he *had to* do because the job had to be done and he was the only one to do it. It was all just tourism masquerading as effort. And this Mars expedition was more of the same: Anton wanted to "expose" him to the world, but Anthony never even had to finish a job. As soon as the media attention drifted, Anton would whisk him back home while other people did the hard work. This one little thing, this ninety minutes of running every day, may have been the most sustained effort Anthony had ever put forth.

⚓

I had just dropped off to sleep that night when my comm chimed. I lay in bed, eyes closed, and called out. "Comm, answer. This is Dr. Baldwin, is anything wrong?"

Captain Aames's voice came through the comm, and my eyes snapped open in the darkness. "Baldwin, what the hell's up with changing my orders for Anthony Holmes?"

I was glad my comm camera was off so the captain couldn't see my face. "I changed *my* orders, captain, because in *my* judgment he can't handle the way he was pushing himself. He's out of shape, he needs to work up to that pace. Otherwise he'll break down before he ever gets to Mars."

"Good! If that keeps him off Mars, that's better for everyone."

"What? I thought you were doing this to get him ready for Mars."

"Doctor, I'm not interested in getting him ready. I just want to test him and find his limits. And if those limits keep him off Mars, so be it. Let me test him!"

"Captain, he can do this. Give him a chance."

"You can give him a chance if you want, doctor. Not my concern."

"But his health is my concern. This little game of yours isn't. My order stands. Comm off."

I pulled my covers over my head. It took nearly an hour for me to calm down enough to fall asleep.

⸸

Monitoring Anthony's progress was most of how I passed my time at first. Our work in the infirmary was light: periodic screenings, treatment of minor injuries, monitoring of health and nutrition, and lots of paperwork to send back to Earth. We were staffed to cover unexpected emergencies, which meant we had plenty of time to cover normal operations.

We were a week out from the gravipause when I came into the infirmary and found Dr. Santana with a patient: Major Adika. The major sat on an exam table, shirtless, as Santana ran a scanner over his shoulder. I couldn't help staring: Adika's muscles were even more impressive without the shirt; but more impressive yet were the scars.

Then I noticed the major smiling at me, and I realized that I was staring. "Excuse me, I have work to do." My face felt warm as I ducked into my office.

I found myself reading the same page of the same routine report for the third time and still not noticing what I read, when Dr. Santana came into my office. There was an odd smile on his face. "Dr. Baldwin, I think you should see this patient."

"What? Push me his chart. Is there something wrong?"

Santana's smile grew. "No, doctor. I think *you* should see *him*. He asked for you. Personally."

I flushed again. "Oh. Thank you." I stood, felt my hair to see if it was out of place, and walked back into the infirmary.

Major Adika still sat on the exam table, still shirtless. I fought, but I kept my eyes on his face so as not to get flustered. "So, major, what's the problem today?"

Then he smiled, and I got flustered despite my plan. "I think I have pulled a muscle in my shoulder."

*Those muscles? I can't believe that!* But I resisted saying that out loud. "How did this happen?"

"Oh, it was a foolish thing. I was sparring with the captain in the gymnasium, and he got the better of me with one of his *capoeira* moves. He sent me tumbling, and I grabbed a grip to stop myself; but I failed to account for the ship's spin, and I felt a pull. Or possibly a tear."

"I see. Well, Dr. Santana has already examined you, but let me take a look." I pulled out my scanner and ran it over his shoulder. As I did, I got a close-up look at those scars. One ran from his right clavicle almost to his spleen. Another crossed his left bicep like a tattoo. There were smaller scars all over his torso, including one circular red tear in his right deltoid that I was sure was from a bullet. "This isn't your first injury by any means, major. You've lived a dangerous life."

"Mine is a dangerous profession, doctor."

149

"Are there a lot of attacks on Mr. Holmes?"

"No, but I have been a bodyguard only for a few years. Before that, I was in Initiative Security, Rapid Response Team. This job is a vacation after that."

"Uh-huh." I lowered the scanner. "Well, major, you're correct: it's a muscle pull, nothing torn. I prescribe a few sessions of massage and some analgesic cream." I looked back in his face. "But I'm not sure why Dr. Santana couldn't have prescribed that."

Adika put his shirt back on, and the big grin came back. "But then I would be asking Dr. Santana if he is free for dinner tonight, not you. He is a very nice gentleman, but I would prefer your company, doctor."

Again my face felt warm, but I kept my voice steady as I answered, "I would like that, major."

"Please, call me 'Chuks'."

After that, Chuks and I spent a lot of time together, as our duties allowed. I learned to appreciate his quiet humor, his enthusiasm for space, his dedication to duty, and his gentle strength. He was a good man, and comfortable to be with. He was proud of his homeland, Nigeria, and proud of his warrior heritage. Although he was powerful and skilled and capable of great violence, he saw restraint as the mark of the true warrior: violence was a tool he used to protect the weak and defend what he believed in, not an end in itself and not something that drove him. Knowing how hard it was to restrain my own temper sometimes, I was impressed with how well he had mastered his own. He could be passionate in his mission, but he was always in control.

I learned that incredible body of his, including that roadmap of scars that hinted at the violence in his past. These fascinated me from a clinical perspective: how had he suffered that cut in that spot? How had he survived a deep trauma like the long scar across his chest? Who had shot him in the back, and why? But he refused to talk about these past missions, preferring to leave his past buried. The only scar he commented on was in his calf: a nearly perfect impression of human teeth, both upper and lower jaws. When I asked about that, he laughed and said, "It was a performance review that got out of hand." But when I asked for details, he refused to say more.

But I didn't mind. I had secrets—I never explained how I had landed on the *Aldrin*—so I could hardly fault him for his own. These secrets only intrigued me more. The only real disagreement we had regarded Anthony: I was getting to like the kid and see potential in him; but Chuks kept cautioning me. "His enthusiasm never lasts, Constance." Normally, "Constance" bothered me. It was such a formal name, and it didn't feel right to me. I was just "Connie". But when Chuks said it, he imbued the name with a softness, a quality that made me feel special.

We sat in an observation room, curled together on a couch and staring out at the stars as they spun by. "You've known him longer, Chuks, but I just... I just see something there. I think he's changing." I didn't tell Chuks about Anthony's conversation and his determination to show his dad he could do this. That was private, not my secret to share. But after that, I believed in Anthony, and I wanted to support him. "And I don't think Captain Aames would push him like this if he didn't believe Anthony could do it."

Chuks shook his head. "You do not understand Nick Aames yet, Constance. He tests people, tests them to the breaking point. If they pass the test, he raises the bar. If they break, then he is satisfied, because he knows their limits."

I looked into his eyes. "I thought the captain was your friend."

"He is. But it is difficult being Nick's friend. He tests his friends, too. It is just what he does."

"Some friend." I frowned. "Well, maybe he doesn't believe in Anthony, but I do."

Chuks wrapped his arms tighter. "You are a good woman, Constance. Despite your temper." I glared at him; but then he smiled, and I did, too. "I just don't want you to be hurt when Mr. Holmes returns to form."

Over the next few weeks of running, my faith in Anthony grew as he shaped up well. Thanks to the exercise and a carefully selected diet, he quickly dropped his excess weight, and that made the running easier. Soon I was able to lift my limits and let him set his own pace. I was glad that *I* was getting a good workout, too: it was the only way I could keep up with him.

As his body shaped up, so did his mood, and not just because he had more stamina. The passengers who had laughed at him soon forgot his embarrassment, but they didn't forget his power and influence. They began trying to curry favor again; but with his new confidence, Anthony also became more discerning. He was quick to cut out the obvious toadies and focus on the ones who were willing to treat him as just one of the crowd. And one way he selected his companions was by inviting them to run with him. The sycophants soon gave up on that, while those who stuck with it grew closer as they challenged each other to faster paces and longer runs. It wasn't long before I gave up on keeping up and concentrated on my own pace. Soon we had six regulars who joined us each day, four scientists and two bodyguards. We ran for a full hour, followed by dinner in the lounge; and they were *friends* to Anthony, perhaps the first true friends he had ever had.

And sometimes we had another companion: at least once a week, Captain Aames joined us even though it wasn't his watch to run. *Then* I *completely* gave up on the race, and I just hung back and watched. The captain still pushed and still taunted, but Anthony found it easier and easier to keep up. The captain still won every race, but their times got faster every week.

On the days when the captain joined us, he also dined with us, and he even put dinner on his tab. I won't say he let his hair down, but he showed a shrewd appreciation for morale and unit cohesion. He sat with us, inquired as to experiments and preparations, and listened to jokes and stories; and then every week he stood and said, "Ladies and gentlemen, ship's duties call, and I must go. Let the real party begin." And after that, just as he said, the celebration started and the drinks were ordered. But Anthony never again drank like he had that first day, and he would stop if I commented, or even just gave him an odd glance. He was determined not to lose control again.

In the tenth week of racing, however, Captain Aames broke the routine. He stayed at the table long past his usual departure; and he signaled the waiter for a round of drinks. Anthony ordered his usual, the house beer, and slowly sipped it. The captain watched him, not judging, just watching. Finally he asked, "So kid, are you ready for those therapy nanos yet?"

Anthony almost spewed his beer. The captain had sucker-punched him there. Then he took a long drink. I suspected that was to give him time to think of his answer. Finally he set down the half-empty glass. "No, captain. I'm still not interested. I think Dr. Baldwin is doing a fine job of keeping me healthy *without* polluting my body with unnatural machines."

The captain almost smiled at that. "'Unnatural machines.' Ah, yes... Doctor, I completely forgot we had an expert on nanomachines here."

Anthony tightened his grip on his glass, but he kept control. "Not an expert, captain, I've just done my research."

"Yes, yes, your research. I forgot. Don't be so modest, kid, it sounds like expertise to me. So tell me: what is the activation frequency of a salt-ion scavenger nano?"

Anthony hesitated a second. "I'm not sure, captain. The... ummm... sound frequency—"

"*Light* frequency, kid," the captain interrupted. "Modern nanos are generally activated by specific spectral signatures. Try this one: what's the orbital period of Phobos?"

"Oh, I know this one!" Anthony was so eager to answer, he ignored the fact that this wasn't a nanotechnology question. "Approximately 7.7 hours."

"Approximately will get you dead in space, kid. Okay, back to nanos: how many generations of sintering nanos can you get out of a typical batch before they start to degrade?"

"I don't know, captain. We have specialists on the mission to deal with that sort of issue."

"Specialists, yes," the captain nodded, "and what is your specialty, kid?" He let the question hang in the air for almost three seconds before turning to the rest of the runners. "Oh, that's unimportant right now, we have all of these experts with us. Isn't it fantastic that we have all these experts on this mission, doctor? Savoy, what's your specialty?"

Laurence Savoy, a tall, shy Frenchman with dark, curly hair, blinked. He wasn't used to the captain's attention. Finally he stammered, "Atmospheric chemistry, captain."

Aames nodded. "And you, Meadors?"

Minnie Meadors, a tall blonde from Boston, was quicker with her answer. "Astronomy, captain. Seven hours, thirty-nine minutes, fourteen seconds."

"What? Oh, yes, Phobos. You must love the viewing from here."

"It's phenomenal, sir. A dream come true."

"Enjoy it, Meadors. It only gets better as we approach Mars. This is a chance most astronomers will never get. And you, Krause?"

Katherine Krause, a short, sturdy German woman, replied eagerly. "Geology, captain. I'm counting the days to my first field survey."

"I look forward to your reports. And Martinez?"

Jerry Martinez, a medium-height, muscular Hispanic male, answered with a big smile. "Software Engineering, captain." He pointed a finger around the table. "As soon as we land, they're all going to think up new requirements for their systems, things they never thought of before. Somebody has to reprogram all their gear to meet those new requirements."

"Excellent! You should talk to Chief Carver. He pulled out some software wizardry on our Mars mission." He paused. "Of course, a big factor in our survival was cross-training. Did I tell you about that, doctor?"

I wondered where Aames was going with this, but I played along. "No, you didn't, captain."

The captain nodded. "We lost some good personnel, but we had the essentials covered, thanks to cross-training. Say, does your mission have a cross-training plan?"

Meadors shook her head. "No, captain, but that's an excellent idea. I'll bring it up with the mission planners."

Aames shook his head. "Don't bother. I already suggested it, fourteen months ago, but they rejected it. They said that was 'Old Space thinking', and they have a New Space mission plan. But now... It seems like your people have a lot of leisure time." He slapped his leg. "That's it, I'm making an executive decision. You'll all start cross-training seminars for your team. And for my crew as well, since many of them hope for a Mars mission someday."

The runners stared at him, open-mouthed. Finally Martinez spoke up. "You're serious."

"Deadly serious, Martinez. Deadly. These will be seminar format, but with the sessions recorded so crew on other shifts can follow along. I'll expect each of you to organize the seminars for your field and to present me syllabi and progress reports to review. Martinez, you can start with software engineering on Mondays. Everyone should know more about programming and how to communicate with programmers. Meadors, you'll do astronomy on Tuesdays, Krause and geology on Wednesdays, and Savoy and atmospheric chemistry on Thursdays. I'm sure I can talk Major Adika into teaching Martian survival on Saturdays, and we can all take a break on Sundays."

Anthony looked at the captain and swallowed. "And Fridays?" But I was sure he already knew the answer.

Aames stared right back at him, but those blue eyes didn't flinch. "On Fridays, you're going to teach us everything there is to know about nanotechnology. And when we have questions, you'll find the answers and teach us those. And repeat, and repeat, until we're all as expert in the subject as you are." And then he leaned in, almost into Anthony's face. "Unless you think you can't do it, kid?"

Anthony held the captain's gaze, and he kept his voice low and level. "I can do it. Captain."

"Good! That's what I like to hear! Doctor, if the kid needs any help, see to it that he has supplemental reading. Oh, and kid, I expect you to be an active participant in *all* of these seminars. Can you do that?"

This time there was steel in Anthony's voice. "Yes. Sir."

Aames leaned back. "Good, good!" He looked around the table. "That goes for all of you. If this is going to work, I need you to set examples for the rest of your team." At last his gaze returned to Anthony. "I expect you to be *leaders*, not spectators. For the good of the mission." Then he placed his palms on the table and stood; and just like any other week, he said, "Ladies and gentlemen, ship's duties call, and I must go. Let the real party begin." And he left.

As soon as the captain was gone, Anthony drained the rest of his beer. Then he stood to leave as well.

I was worried. The captain was pushing too hard, and this was completely out of nowhere. I was afraid all the work we had done might be lost in this one blundering move by that—by that tyrant, Nick Aames.

I looked across the lounge. Chuks stood in a corner with a good vantage on the room. He had his earpiece in, so I was sure he had heard the conversation. He looked at me, frowned, and shook his head. I had learned to read his face and body language: *I am sorry. The bar has been raised.*

But I wasn't ready to give up hope. I ran after Anthony, and I caught up to him in the hall. "Anthony, wait." He kept walking toward his cabin, so I ran to catch up. "Anthony, stop. Let's talk." But he kept walking, so I kept pace. "Anthony, you've come so far, you're doing so well. Don't let—" I looked around to see who might be listening. A guard stood a discreet distance away, so I lowered my voice. "Don't let the captain's pig-headedness undo everything you've done here."

Anthony just kept walking, not looking at me, but at least he answered. "I'm not, doctor. He can't break me that easily."

"But then where are you going? What are you going to do?"

"To my room. To study. I have a seminar to prepare, doctor." And then he did turn and look at me. "I look forward to your supplemental reading list."

That stopped me in my tracks, but he kept going, back stiff and straight and walking with an easy stride. For the first time, I really saw his father in him.

<hr/>

But as determined as Anthony was, he still needed a lot of help for this challenge. I ended up spending my spare time tutoring him, not just recommending reading. He was bright—his father's genes ran true there—and he had the benefit of a very expensive education and private tutors; but he had never had to work at learning. Material that came easy to him, he blew through. When a topic proved too tough for him, though, he just turned to something else. No one had ever expected him to have the discipline to see his way through a hard part, and no one had taught him the analysis and study skills to master a subject. Now suddenly he was "enrolled" in five graduate-level studies, plus *teaching* one, and Captain Aames expected him to sink or swim.

And he wasn't sinking, but only because he spent all of his non-exercise time studying. He even stopped showing up for dinner after workouts, until I put a halt to that.

"Doctor!" he protested.

But I answered with a phrase he was learning to hate: "Doctor's orders. You need some down time, or you're going to have a breakdown." He accepted my order, grudgingly, but the dinner conversations became more like an extension of the seminars. He kept probing his friends for answers, desperately trying to keep up with their work. His alcohol consumption dropped almost to zero, but I made a point to buy him a glass a night just to relax him. When he refused the first glass, I threatened to write out a prescription.

Anthony's determination was infectious. If Aames wanted to break him, then I was determined to keep him whole. But that had a cost: our tutoring time meant less time with Chuks; and though Chuks was a good man and tried not to show it, he resented it. "Constance, you will only be disappointed," he said one night; but I read disappointment in his own face. "You waste our time; and in the end, Mr. Holmes will lose interest, and you will have accomplished nothing."

*Our time*: I bristled at that. "It's *my* time. If I want to spend it tutoring, I will. You don't own me."

"I don't want to own you, Constance, I want to protect you."

"You're not paid to protect me, you're paid to protect Anthony. Is my tutoring a danger to him?" Before Chuks could answer, I stormed out of the observation room. I was tired and frustrated, but that only made me more stubborn: if I had anything to say about it, Anthony would master his studies.

Eventually Anthony's hard work and my tutoring paid off. He started asking smart questions in the seminars. When it was his turn to lead a discussion, he was always prepared, though I noticed he had a trick of delegating the more technical parts to the experts in the room, then synthesizing their responses into new insights.

In Chuks's Martian survival seminar, Anthony was often the first one with the right answer to any challenge. It turned out the one topic that really did interest him was Mars itself. He had to know everything about it; and in every other seminar, he managed to turn the topic back to "How will this help a team to survive and succeed on Mars?" Chuks was harsher with Anthony than with the other students, always dissecting his answers and pointing out weaknesses and mistakes; but Anthony just studied harder, and soon there were no weaknesses for Chuks to find.

And in his own seminar, Anthony quickly grasped how limited his "research" had been. He devoured my supplemental reading, until I had to call up more from Earth. He kept challenging the scientific consensus on nanotechnology, but his arrogance and confidence were gone. He now demanded that each precept be challenged and defended. He worked with the discussion leaders to explore nanos from the ground up. He asked Lt. Copeland, supervisor of the *Aldrin*'s nano labs, for permission to observe the labs; and after Captain Aames intervened, she approved him. Several weeks later, he asked for permission to run some experimental batches. That approval took longer, and the captain demanded stringent oversight; but in the end, Anthony was approved to test a new design for waste reclamation nanos. His first two batches made an unholy stink, but Lt. Copeland said they showed promise. His third batch produced no odors, and his fourth batch improved on the efficiency of our stock nanos. Copeland agreed to put them through further testing.

We were about four weeks out from the Martian gravipause at that point. The next Friday, when I showed up for Anthony's seminar, I was surprised to find the classroom almost empty. There were usually a dozen students, plus another dozen watching via comms. This time, the only people in the room were Captain Aames, Lt. Copeland, Chief Carver, and Chuks. I didn't look at Chuks. My temper had passed since our last argument, but something else was wrong, and I wasn't sure what. As Anthony grew more capable, Chuks became more distant, but he didn't explain why. I wondered if he resented being wrong. Then I refused to believe that such a good man could be so petty. Then I grew angry at myself: did I really know Chuks was a good man after only four months?

Captain Aames was not big on saluting except when on station, so I wasn't surprised when he spoke before I could salute. "Just in time, doctor. Have a seat. Mr. Holmes should be here any minute."

I sat in the seat that he indicated, making me the last person in a semi-circle around the podium. Aames gave me no instructions, so I sat quietly.

When Anthony came in the door, I could tell he was as surprised as I had been; but he had practiced being unflappable in front of the captain, so he just walked up to the podium. The lights automatically lowered around us, and a big ceiling spot came on, pinning him in its beam. In the spotlight I could see just how much the exercise regimen had done for him. He was leaner, he stood straighter, and he carried himself with confidence. He looked every inch his father's son, only more at ease.

Anthony wore a forced smile as he said, "Well... It looks like my lesson notes won't be needed today, so instead let's get right to it. Are there any questions?"

The captain never looked up from his desk as he asked from the shadows, "Mr. Holmes, what is the activation frequency of a salt-ion scavenger nano?"

Without missing a beat, Anthony answered, "There are many variants, captain. The prime variant on this Mars mission has a primary activation spike in the Ultraviolet C range at 210 nanometers, and a secondary spike at half power in the visible spectrum at 560 nanometers. We also have a variant with three spikes at 240, 500, and 614 nanometers. We have designs for other variants, but none in production. I can look those up if you'd like."

The captain looked at Lt. Copeland, and she nodded. Then he answered, "Unnecessary. How many generations of sintering nanos can you get out of a typical batch before they start to degrade?"

Again Anthony's response was immediate. "It's a trick question, sir. Sintering nanos are almost always destroyed in use, sacrificing their own component atoms to fabricate some new part or tool. So looked at that way, the answer is one. And sintering nanos are not self-replicating, so the answer is also one from that perspective. But if you look at the seed nanos that construct the sintering nanos, those are typically good for at least fifteen generations. In a pinch, you can push them to twenty, but the reliability of the sintering drops to the high risk range above fifteen." Copeland nodded, and Anthony added, "And the orbital period of Phobos is seven hours, thirty-nine minutes, thirteen-point-eight-four seconds. Dr. Meadors rounded to the nearest second. During the course of the *Aldrin*'s rendezvous with Mars, that error will add up to almost forty-seven seconds. If you had had a discrepancy like that on the second *Bradbury* expedition, you and the other survivors would be dead right now."

This time the captain did look up, straight at Anthony. His eyes gleamed in the reflected light. "You think you're pretty smart, huh, kid?"

"Try me." Anthony smiled. "Captain."

"Okay, kid, tell me about your waste reclamation nanos."

"What about them, sir?"

"Everything. From concept to production to testing. Convince me that we should risk this Mars mission on some billionaire's son's hare-brained scheme."

And Anthony set out to do just that. He started explaining the history of reclamation nanos, the nanochemistry behind them, and the current state of the art. He was just summarizing the articles that inspired his new approach when Chuks interrupted him. "Mr. Holmes, you are stranded on Mars in the Elysium quadrant during a meteorological survey. It is early spring in that region. Your shuttle is incapacitated. Where is your best place to scavenge water, and why?"

That brought Anthony to a halt. He was deep in the middle of nanotechnology, and suddenly he was fielding a question on Martian survival. I was sure he was stalling when he asked, "How long do I expect to wait before rescue, major?"

But Chuks smiled, and I knew Anthony had done well. "Two days,

Mr. Holmes. Possibly less, depending on weather conditions."

Anthony didn't smile, but I saw confidence in his eyes. "For two days, major, I wouldn't even try to scavenge subsurface water, though there's probably some in the area. For such a short trip, I would scavenge from the shuttle's cooling system. It would be easier to scavenge from the meteorology station, but we might need that station functioning at optimum in order to do local weather forecasts and bring my rescue shuttle in. If my landing shuttle was damaged so as to lose all cooling water, *then* I would scavenge just the minimum fluid from the station. I wouldn't even try to set up subsurface reclamation in only two days. I brought enough water with me for that period."

Chuks nodded. "Very good, Mr. Holmes." And he looked at me with a strange sadness on his face. "Please continue enlightening us about nanos."

And that was how it went. Anthony presented an informal paper on his reclamation nanos, answering questions, particularly from Lt. Copeland; and every so often, someone would pepper him with questions on other subjects. Chuks tested him on Martian survival. Chief Carver probed him on software requirements and verification. The captain questioned him on chemistry, astronomy, mathematics, and geology. And I questioned him on just about anything we had studied.

After an hour of this, Anthony was sweating, but still going strong. I ducked out and found him some water, and he just kept going.

After three hours, Anthony had thoroughly covered the planning, design, generation, and testing of his waste recycling nanos; and he had also answered practical questions from across the range of Mars mission disciplines. He looked tired enough that I was ready to open my medical bag, but he was smiling as he asked, "Any more questions?"

The captain looked around the semicircle, and we all shook our heads. He shook his as well. "No, Mr. Holmes. Lights!" The room lights came on. Aames stood, walked to the podium, and looked at the rest of us. "Ladies, gentlemen, I have one question for you: has Mr. Anthony Holmes mastered the material presented in his seminar courses?"

As one, we answered, "Yes, captain."

"Very well." He turned to Anthony. "Mr. Holmes, congratulations." He took Anthony's hand and shook it. "While it has no force outside this ship—and not here, while we're inside the gravipauses—in the judgment of this review board you have earned a Doctorate of Areology with a Specialization in Nanotechnology. We would be honored to attest as much should you wish to apply to any graduate or post-graduate program back on Earth. And who knows, maybe someday we'll have an *Aldrin* University, and you'll be our first doctorate recipient, retroactive." They shook hands again. "You've exceeded my highest expectations, Mr. Holmes. That doesn't happen often."

They stood at the podium like that until finally Captain Aames pulled his hand away. "So do you have anything to say for yourself?"

Anthony nodded. "Yes sir, captain." He turned to me. "Dr. Baldwin, I'd like to set up an appointment to get my therapy nanos as soon as possible."

The captain raised an eyebrow, and then he turned around and sank into his seat. "I suppose I'm going to start losing our races now."

Anthony blinked. "Sir?"

"Think, man, you're half my age! And in better shape than me, at least now. The only reason I've been winning is you have a handicap: you don't have half a million little machines constantly rebuilding bone and muscle damage. Your musculoskeletal damage has been slowed by exercise, whereas mine has been reversed by the nanos. Without that edge, I wouldn't stand a chance against you! I would've been eating your dust for at least the last month. With all your studies of nanotechnology, you hadn't figured that out?"

"No, captain. I just... figured you were that good." Anthony hesitated, but finally he blurted out, "You cheated, captain?"

"*No one* is that good, Mr. Holmes. It's not cheating to know your subject, do your homework, and use your resources. It's smart; and if you're half as smart as you think you are, you'll learn to do it as second nature. When you have an edge out here, you take it. Your mission and your survival may depend upon it."

"Yes, captain."

"When you take the nanos, it will be a relief. I can stop trying so hard, because I know I'll lose in the end. Aside from Major Adika, you may be the healthiest person on this ship."

"Thank you, captain."

Aames turned to me. "Doctor, you should be able to accommodate Mr. Holmes immediately, shouldn't you?"

I picked up my bag and stood. "Yes, captain. Right away." I started for the door.

But Anthony just stood at the podium, staring at Captain Aames, a big grin on his face. The captain stared back and asked, "Is there anything else, Mr. Holmes?"

Anthony nodded. "You called me 'man', sir."

The captain's eyes widened. "I did?"

"Yes, captain. 'Think, man, you're half my age!' You didn't call me 'kid', you called me 'man'."

Captain Aames smiled. "So I did. Was I wrong?"

"No, captain." Anthony saluted, turned, and left for the infirmary.

⚲

After I gave Anthony his injections, I traced down Chuks in his cabin. He let me in, and I threw my arms around him without saying a word. He kissed me, and we stood like that for a while. I just wanted things to be right between us, whatever that would take.

But when I pulled away, I saw sadness in his eyes. "Chuks, what's wrong? He did it! Are you that sorry to be wrong?"

He shook his head. "It is nothing, Constance. Life changes, that is all, and change always brings good and bad."

"What could be bad here? We should be proud!"

"I am proud. Do not worry, I am just being foolish. Tomorrow will bring what it brings. Tonight we are together. We should celebrate."

And we did, and it was very good, and eventually his fantastic smile returned. But I couldn't forget his sad expression, and I couldn't stop worrying what might have caused it.

Three weeks later, the review board and Anthony met in the classroom again. We were joined by Savoy, Meadors, Krause, Martinez, and a number of other senior mission personnel; and the rest of the mission watched on the comms. Captain Aames directed a revised briefing on the mission plan, with each department head going through a grilling much like Anthony had. It wasn't Aames's mission, and he wouldn't be going down to Mars; but as the commander of the second *Bradbury* expedition, he was the local expert on Mars *and* he had plenary powers between the gravipauses. If he wanted to be briefed, he would get briefed.

At last all of the departments had reported to the captain's satisfaction, and he reclaimed the podium. He looked around the room. "Ladies and gentlemen, this looks like a very professional mission plan, and you've got answers to every question we can imagine. Now for the bad news: when you get down there, Mars is going to raise questions you *can't* imagine. Nothing in our evolution or experience can prepare us for Mars. Until you're there, you won't understand that. But if any team is ready for Mars... you are."

At this rare bit of praise from Captain Aames, Chief Carver and I and other ship's officers rose and applauded. This team had earned that.

When the applause faded and we all sat down again, the captain continued. "But you're not ready. Remember that, keep your wits about you, and you'll survive until the *Collins* arrives to pick you up. Never forget: Mars is going to surprise you. Now, are there any last questions?" Anthony raised a hand. "Yes, Mr. Holmes?"

"Captain, I've been thinking."

"It's about damn time," the captain said. Everyone laughed, including Anthony.

He continued. "Captain, I don't think I want to do a down-and-back on the drop shuttle. I respectfully request to be reassigned as permanent staff for the mission."

The captain looked around at the mission heads, and they all nodded slowly. "Are you sure? There's no turning back on this one. It will be fourteen months before the *Collins* arrives."

Anthony smiled. "I'd like to put this new degree to good use. Fourteen months is a good start on that."

Aames turned to me. "Doctor, is he in physical condition for the mission?"

I rose to attention. "He is, captain."

The captain turned to Adika. "This would mean your team has to stay through as well. Are you all right with that?"

And suddenly I understood why Chuks had been so sad: he had known this was coming. He knew Anthony, and he knew how much Mars meant to him; and he knew that once Anthony qualified for the mission, he would insist on going.

I had looked forward to the long voyage home and a lot more time with Chuks. Selfishly I hoped he would say "no", and then we could still be together in the coming months. But then I got angry with myself. Anthony had earned this, he deserved this, and it was the natural outcome of all our efforts. So despite my anger, I was proud when Chuks stood as well and answered. "Captain, my team would enjoy the chance to spend more time on Mars; but the mission plan does not allow enough spare rations for that many. I believe there's enough buffer to safely cover myself and Mr. Holmes."

I would miss Chuks, but his plan made sense. I looked at him, and I smiled: *I understand. I'm proud of you.* He smiled back, and it was a perfect blend of his sad look and his big smile.

The captain stared at Chuks. "Major, that would do a lot to lower the risks in this mission." He turned his stare on Anthony. "Mr. Holmes!"

"Yes, captain!"

"You would have to understand one thing: if you do this, you're not Anthony Holmes, the boss's son. You're bottom of the totem pole. You will do what you're told when you're told by whomever tells you. These people have been training for this mission for three years, some of them for longer. Their whole lives, even. You've had four months of cramming. That's not the same. You're not an expert, you're a nobody who *might* become an expert if you come out of this alive. The way to do that is to follow orders. Can you do that?"

"I wouldn't have it any other way, captain. I'd *like* to come out of this alive."

Captain Aames looked at his comm. "All right, under those terms, I think you'll make a hell of a Mars explorer. I support you in this decision."

Anthony shook his head. "You 'support' me? So am I authorized to go or not?"

The captain shook his head. "I *can't* authorize it, Mr. Holmes. As of three minutes ago, we passed the Martian gravipause. I'm not in charge any more. You're the boss's son. If you want to go, who am I to tell you no?"

# SNACK BREAK

Becky looked around at the Martian desert, and she wondered what she was going to do now. They had been expecting a food cache at this spot on their trip, and there wasn't one. This was supposed to be a simple survival school training exercise, not an actual real survival challenge. But she didn't want to panic and scare the kids.

The first thing she did was check her comp. Yes, these were the proper coordinates. The next thing that common sense said she should do was call back to the headquarters and ask who the hell screwed up the food delivery. But that idea went against an ingrained habit of survival school: giving up meant you failed the exercise. Even if you're the instructor. You don't give up, unless you actually find that the lives of your students are at risk. And today, she wasn't ready to admit that.

Yet.

So the other possibility, if no one had screwed up, was that bastard Michaels was testing her. What was she supposed to do in this situation? Obviously, the most important thing she was supposed to do was keep the kids alive. If she went out with five kids and she came back with four, she failed. So first she counted, and made sure she still

168

had five. "Everybody gather around me," she said. The children gathered in a half-circle with her at the center.

Next she had to think about what they would do in this situation if there were no backup. If there were no survival school headquarters that she could call on for help. "First, let's pool our rations. Let's see what's in your backpacks." The kids pulled off their backpacks – difficult to do in suits, but kids are limber – and they started to unzip them. Becky said, "Wait. What are we forgetting?"

Finally Tonya Holmes, the smallest of the children, said. "We should set down a dropcloth."

"Bingo," Becky said. "Points for Tonya. You remembered that stuff gets lost in the Martian dust. All right, let's set out the dropcloth." Becky pulled the lightweight ground cover from her own pack, and the kids spread it out. Then they each dumped the contents of their backpack onto the cloth. Tonya was the only one of the bunch smart enough to arrange her contents in a neat pile. The rest of them just poured their backpacks out. So Becky had to tell each of them to straighten up. She shouldn't be surprised that Tonya, so young, was so on top of her studies. Her parents were some of the original settlers of Maxwell City.

Becky examined the stacks. Each kid had two days worth of ration bars. Those were safe. They tasted so bad, you didn't have to worry about the kids breaking into them early. Each kid had the in a vacuum sealed box lunch they'd been provided, along with their required two liters of water. Two of them had bags of snacks. This was enough food that they could easily survive two or three days out here if they had to.

But she wasn't going to put up with that. She might let them go through a night on Mars, and then she would chew Michaels out for sure. They weren't ready for that. But she could get them through it. Longer than that, though, and she would have to call for help.

"All right," Becky said, "we have food. What's our problem?"

One of the older boys, Wolf, timidly raised his hand. "How do we get the food inside our suits?"

"Very good, Wolf. That's exactly the problem. We have to somehow get food from outside, inside. Does anyone have any suggestions?"

Wolf raised his hand again. "We can use the food port?"

Becky shook her head. "That's an intake for liquids and gels. Who brought gel rations? Anybody?" No one raised their hands on that. "Of course not. And that's not your fault. We would've told you if that was essential on this exercise." Internally, of course, she had no idea was essential on this exercise. Everything was taking a turn south. But the kids had to be confident in her leadership. Someday, they could explore Mars on their own. Today they had to trust in their leader.

Now if only she could do the same.

Becky thought. Was this a test? Was it a screwup? She didn't like it, but it was time to find out. She tapped her comm. "Okay, Michaels, tell me what I'm missing."

"Missing?" Michaels came over the com. "I don't know what you're talking about."

"I'm at the ration depot, and there's no drone here. Are we supposed to search?"

"What the hell?"

"Nothing here, Michaels. I give. If this is a test, I failed. Now help me feed these kids."

"Beck…" Michaels said. "I don't know what's going, on but we had a drone land the package there: standard survival tent for six, plus rations, plus water. If it's not there, we have to pull the plug."

Becky thought. It was all well and good as an Explorer herself to be stubborn and try to work the problem out. Maybe, if this had been adults, she would've stuck it out. But if they lost kids, they would lose their insurance carrier for sure, and the entire survival school would be shut down. "All right, Michael's, send us a pickup. Meanwhile, I'm going to teach them how to police the area."

Becky had a crew. They were young, but they were brighter and more responsible than the average Mars settler of their age, or they wouldn't have qualified for this program. She might as well educate them while they were waiting.

"All right," Becky said over the local circuit, "we have a change in our exercise today. There's food here, somewhere, and there's a survival tent we can eat it in. We have..." She looked down at her comm. "...seventy-five minutes before a pickup shuttle can get out here. So here's today's new game: if we find the food before the shuttle gets here, everybody gets a commendation." The kids got up and started to look around. "Hold it! You do things systematically on Mars or you might die."

If Becky had been teaching in a classroom in Maxwell City, she might've phrased that a little more gently. She could be diplomatic in the city, where there was relative safety and civilization. But out here, any kid who qualified for surface exploration had to learn quickly: Mars was trying to kill you, and you had to be smarter than it to survive. If their parents didn't want them knowing that lesson, they shouldn't have signed them up for this course.

"Let's think," Becky said. "Let's assume that we had good artificial intelligence piloting our supply drone. It couldn't have missed the target by more than... say, one-hundred meters. Look around... Anyone see anything within one-hundred meters?"

The children paused and looked around. Finally, Tonya answered, "Lots of sand?"

"And not much else," Becky agreed. "If the food is here, it's buried. So we have to search the sand to find where it could be hidden. There are no obvious humps anywhere; so if something is buried, it's buried below the level, not above. We need to set up a grid and police it." She looked at the size of the kids. One was an adolescent, growing rapidly in the Martian conditions, nearly 1.8 meters. The rest were closer to a meter. Low sightlines. They would have to work in a close grid. "All right, everyone space out at five meter intervals, centered on me."

Wolf raised his hand. "How do we center an odd number of students on one person?"

Becky nodded. "Good point. All right, three to my left, two to my right." She watched as they spaced themselves out at precisely five meters according to GPS.

"This next part is boring," Becky continued. "But remember: you have to be excellent observers to explore. You're going to walk forward, everyone stepping on my count, just looking at the ground. If you see anything that looks like more than just sand, call stop. Everyone freezes on stop, while I go over and check to see what you found. After that, if we haven't found anything, we continue. Does everyone understand?"

"Yes," they all said.

Becky looked at the oldest girl. "All right, Lauren, tell me what I just said."

"Ummm…"

"Are you ummming because I put you on the spot? Or because you said you understood even though you weren't listening?"

This time Lauren didn't hesitate. "On the spot. You said we all walk forward on your count, and we stop when anyone says they see anything."

"Next time," Lauren said, "have confidence in what you know. Hesitation can get you killed out here, too."

"Okay."

Becky understood. When you're new, you doubt everything. A little skepticism was healthy, but she was here to teach them confidence in their skills, not just the skills.

"All right, on the count… One… Two… Three… Four…"

At the 70 count, Lauren called, "Halt." Everyone stopped as instructed. Becky looked down, made sure she had boot prints to come back to, and went over to look.

"What do you see, Lauren?"

Lauren pointed down. "That odd color there in the sand. It's darker."

Becky crouched down, and with her gloved hands she scraped aside some sand. Underneath she found darker rock. "That's not food," she said, "but it's interesting..." She scraped farther and found a large, flat piece of rock. With further effort, she traced its outline, an irregular shape nearly a quarter meter across. Then she dug it out, and she went from child to child so they could see it. "Does anyone recognize it?"

Finally Tonya raised her hand. "Is it hydrophilic?"

"Indeed, hydrophilic. It had water flowing through it. There might still be some bound inside. If we were on a proper overnight expedition, complete with a still, we could try to boil some out of this. For now, Lauren, put this in your backpack. When we get home, write up a paper on where you found it and what it is, and I'll see that it's published in the Maxwell City Chronicle. It's not food, but that's a good find."

Even through the helmet visor, Becky could see Lauren's face light up. Becky recognized that feeling: An explorer is born.

She went back to her spot. "Annnnnd... 71... 72... 73... 74..." Again they continued walking and eventually they had marched four-hundred paces – well beyond where Becky had expected to find the food cache. "All right," she said, "everybody turn around to the right and we'll continue back." She gave them points in her head because no one complained out loud. She heard some sighs, and she noticed some feet starting to shuffle, but no one voiced any boredom.

And then she had to chide herself. She was so busy watching them and being proud of them that she wasn't watching where she was going. About two-hundred paces back, she was completely distracted.

That's when she decided they needed to stop, not for a discovery, just to stave off exhaustion and boredom that would make them miss something. "Halt," she said, "let's take a break. But before we do, does everybody remember how to start back up where we left off?"

They all shouted, "From our boot prints!"

"Yes, from our boot prints. So walk carefully backward from where you are, and then relax. Drink some water. Shake off your boredom.

173

Look around and enjoy the fact that you might very well be the first people who have ever been in this exact spot. I know none of you chose this life. Your parents brought you here or gave birth to you here. So you didn't choose Mars, but you did choose to be out here. You're explorers by nature. Once in a while explorers should get to enjoy the fact that they're someplace new. We'll get back to the march in five minutes."

So the kids drank, they wandered around, they chased each other a bit. That was not something Becky was used to dealing with: when she taught adult survival school, the students didn't play games. But these kids did.

And maybe there was a method to that madness. Suddenly Becky heard Wolf call out, "Help!" She turned and looked, and he was half buried in the Martian sands. "Lauren," she shouted, "help here!" Becky ran over and grabbed Wolf's hand. "Hold on," Lauren ran up and grabbed Wolf's other hand, and they pulled him from the sand.

When Wolf was safely back on the surface, Becky asked, "Wolf, what did you just fine?"

Wolf stared out at the depression where he had been trapped. "A sinkhole?"

"A sinkhole," Becky said. "That's descriptive, but what does that usually mean?"

Wolf paused. "A hole where you sink?"

Becky laughed. "I'll give you a break on this one, because none of you grew up on Earth. You've never heard of sinkholes like this, I'll bet. But on Earth a sinkhole like this is usually a place where water has eroded the ground underneath. Somewhere under that sand is a hole that may be show signs of prehistoric erosion. And if it's big enough to swallow Wolf, it might be big enough to swallow a drone."

The kids sounded awed in their helmets, though Becky could not read their expressions through their faceplates.

Then Becky thought she could turn this into another exercise. "Who has an idea of how we could search this hole?"

174

The kids were silent for a while before Tonya said, "Just like we searched the main area, with a smaller grid."

"Not bad," Becky said, "but we need some precautions. We know this ground is unsafe. We know that you can fall in."

Lauren raised her hand. "So we should tie to each other so that if one slips, the others can stop them, right?"

"Excellent! Everyone hook your safety line to the person to your left. This time we'll march one meter apart. But first... First, this is important! If you feel uneven ground, immediately call stop. The first thing we're going to do is map the perimeter of this sinkhole."

And so they did. Each of the children identified spots where they suddenly felt the ground under the sand starting to give away below them. Eventually they traced out the boundaries of a sinkhole nearly eight meters across – unheard of in Martian exploration so far. Becky checked her comp, and the sinkhole was well within the error range of the drone. "Kids," she said, "I think we know where dinner is."

Now she had to decide: did they wait for pickup, or did they continue to explore? She knew what Michaels would say. He was all about safety. And that wasn't wrong! In no way did she want to risk the kids. But damn it, they had discovered this! They had earned the right to have their names tied to it. If they waited for pickup and then an exploratory team came out, it would be all tied to the names of Michael's and whoever he brought out with him – because damn sure you knew he'd lead that one – and these kids deserved recognition for what they'd done.

"We're going to try another approach," Becky said, "forward instead of side-by-side. We're going to take our smallest – that would be you, Tonya – and put you at the front of the line. And next Lauren, and then Bob and Mikhail and Wolf, and finally me. That way our heaviest and strongest are towards the back. If anything goes wrong, we can pull you out. Let's set the safety lines at five meters, and then Tonya... Start walking out."

If Becky could've bitten her fingernails through her helmet, she would have. It was all per safety protocol, it was all standard procedure... and they were all thirteen years old and under.

Tonya started walking forward, and soon her boots disappeared beneath the sand. A few steps more, and the sand was up to her ankles. Then her knees. she was not quite a meter tall, so that put it at a quarter meter.

Suddenly she stopped. "I think it's getting steeper here."

"All right," Becky said. "Now Lauren, you walk out to her so we can make sure that the edge can take the extra weight." When Lauren reached the point where Tonya had stopped, Becky continued, "Now Tonya, come back. When she's back here, Bob, you go out."

And thus, with one child at the time, Becky tested the weight that rim would support. Finally she stood five meters back as Wolf walked up to Mikhail. The rim still hadn't collapsed, so she said, "OK, Mikhail, Wolf, both of you come back, and I'll go out." She estimated that the combined mass of the two boys was eighty percent of her own. If they were safe out there, Becky should be safe.

She hoped.

Becky walked out. When the sand was almost up to her mid-calves, she found that indeed the slope grew steeper there. She tested carefully with her boots, and she found that it was slippery. Maybe a basalt? Or maybe...

She stepped back two steps, sat down, and lifted her boot. She swabbed it with her gloved finger.

And the fingertip was wet.

"All right, everyone, slowly back up to our safe spot."

Everyone backed up. Becky climbed carefully to her feet, and she joined them. "We're stopped now," she said. That was met with a chorus of Awwwwws, but she continued over them "You've found water. A whole new set of protocols have just kicked in. As explorers, you have to learn that there are protocols you can't break. They've been decided by people who thought about this for decades. These protocols are what they are for reasons that you do not question."

Then she turned and looked at each of them. "Unless your life depends on it. That's a whole different matter. But we have plenty of water right now. We don't have to scavenge that water, but we definitely have to report it. Mark out the boundaries and avoid contaminating it any more than we can help. Because where there's water, there could be life."

Wolf's eyes grew wide. "Life?"

"Don't get ahead of yourself," Becky said. "It's a possibility, not a discovery. Yet. But the water... Now that's a discovery. Lauren, your rock just became part of a much bigger report. Hydrophilic rock in an area where we found water... This whole area could be porous. So we're going to wait for our pickup to come along, and then every one of you is going back to your parents with a special permission slip. Because there's going to be an expedition to explore this spot, probably for months; and I want every one of you to be part of that if you want. You earned this chance to be real Mars explorers, and I'm going to make sure you get it."

# PART III: THE POURNELLE SETTLEMENTS

Stories from the colonization of Jupiter space.

# UNREFINED

If this had been a vid, there would've been a computer voice over the comms: "Thirty minutes to containment collapse." At least I hoped like hell that I had thirty minutes left. I might need every one of them.

But when you're facing a cascade failure across your computer network, there are no automated warnings, no countdown. I just had to move as fast as I damn well could, and hope I could get to Wilson and get us out before the fusion reactor blew out the end of Refinery Station.

As Leeanne brought the flitter in toward The Tube—the half-klick tunnel of girders that connected Habitat Module to the Reactor and Refinery Module—I hung from its frame and peered ahead, looking for the airlocks into Habitat's Control Deck. If Wilson wasn't there, I wouldn't know where to look for him. There were nearly three million cubic meters in Habitat. And in R&R . . . but I stopped that thought. I'd rather not get that close to a failing fusion reactor.

Refinery Station was the first of Wilson Gray's megastructures, massive artifacts in space that were half constructed, half grown by Von Neumann constructor bots. At one end hung the Habitat Module, still mostly unfinished. At the other end of The Tube was the giant fusion ring.

The reactor provided power for Habitat, but the real reasons Wilson had built the station were the two structures on the far side of the reactor: a giant refinery utilizing the reactor's raw heat for metallurgy, and the two-and-a-half kilometer mass driver that would launch refined metals from the Jovian system back toward Earth. Wilson had invested his entire fortune into the station, and he had convinced a number of other entrepreneurs to sign up as well. Now all those investments were poised to fail, all due to an unexplained computer crash.

Finally we got close enough that I could make out the airlock hatches between the girders. I was glad one of the best pilots in the Pournelle Settlements was flying. As Leeanne neared the closest approach point, the retros fired, bringing us almost motionless relative to Habitat. She had timed it perfectly—less than five meters, Leanne was *good*—so I leaped.

For a moment I floated in empty space. Jupiter hung off to my right, half in shadow. The sunward side showed the giant cream-and-brown stripes, as well as an excellent view of the famous Red Spot. Closer to me but still dwarfed by its primary was Ganymede, our closest orbital neighbor. Its dark, reddish-gray surface was dotted with ancient impact craters, evidence that the Jovian system was a treasure trove of valuable rocks. Under other circumstances I would've enjoyed the sight, but I couldn't waste time sightseeing. I paid close attention to the task at hand, and I grabbed for a girder.

*Contact!* My gloved fingers wrapped easily around the girder, a synthetic carbon crystal rod five centimeters across. I grabbed another and arrested my flight. The girders sparkled in my suit light. Their lattice tied the two modules together even in the face of the minimal tidal force we experienced at this distance from Ganymede. The VN bots had spent over a month assembling this giant structure out of carbon that had cost Willy a small fortune to collect; and now at any moment it could all be shattered by the explosion.

"I'm on, Leanne."

"Don't waste words, Sam! Go get Willy. Please!"

Wilson was Leeanne's husband. Nerves of steel were another trait that made Leeanne a top pilot, but hers were strained near their limit. "I'll get him. You just be ready to pick us up."

Leeanne and I had been hauling batteries from the magnetosphere generators back to Gray City (the collection of ships and small habitats that housed Wilson's team as we built Refinery Station). Until the fusion reactor gets up to full output, the generators were the most reliable source of electrical power in Jovian space, converting the radiation in Jupiter's magnetosphere into electricity and then storing it in batteries. These were one of our most successful products: half the towns in the Pournelle Settlements and a good number of the independent miners bought their power from Gray Interplanetary. But the generator output was too variable, and hauling massive batteries around used too much fuel. With the reactor, Wilson hoped to get a more steady power source for the refinery and the mass driver.

In another organization we could both have pulled rank to get out of such routine work: the boss's wife and partner and the boss's Executive Officer drawing a routine transport run? Ridiculous! But not when Wilson Gray was the boss: "Everybody gets their hands dirty" was one of his top rules to keep us in touch with our crew.

And this particular run . . . Well, it was my fault, really. I had had another fight with Mari Brasco, Chief of Eco Management. It was the same dumb argument that had cropped up since we started dating: her claiming I ran our relationship like I ran a project, me trying to explain myself, and her saying I was proving her point. But this one had been bigger. Maybe she was stressed from all her contract work, I don't know, but we really blew up. She had told me to choose: boss or boyfriend? Before I could answer, she had stormed out. So Wilson had sent me on the battery run to get me away from the station and give me time to cool off. I suspect he had sent Leeanne because she's a good listener and he had hoped she could talk me through my troubles.

When we'd heard the news of the computer failure on Refinery Station, though, my dating woes went out the hatch. We'd dumped our cargo in a stable orbit, and Leeanne had grinned and uttered her favorite words: "Hang on, Sam!" We blew most of our reaction mass getting back to Gray City to render aid if it was needed.

The work crews had evacuated before environmental systems could fail completely. It had fallen to Kim Stone to break the bad news to Leeanne: Wilson had refused to leave, trying to get the system under control and save the station.

At that news, I glanced over at Leeanne. I was sure she was thinking the same thing I was: *If only we had been there . . .* And *I* was the reason we were gone, me and my stupid fight with Mari. If I blamed myself, surely Leeanne would blame me, and I expected an angry glare. But she wasn't looking at me at all. She stared straight ahead out the view port, her normally dark face turned ashen with worry. Flying normally put a broad grin across her round, friendly face; but the grin was gone, replaced by a grim line that turned downward as Kim continued.

The computer failures had spread, so comms to the station were out. Wilson was still on board, and no one wanted to get trapped in there looking for him. But I wasn't leaving my best friend, and Leanne wasn't leaving her husband. Her face had turned steely, and she had flown us to the station at a reckless speed and then had pulled four gees as she brought us to a halt.

The girders were spaced to allow a suited person to climb between them. I did so, pushed toward the airlock, and grabbed the hatch ring to stop myself. The computer display on the hatch was useless: letters and numbers scrolling by too fast to read, occasionally interrupted by a complete screen wipe or random pixilation.

I ignored the screen and opened the lid to the manual controls. I twisted the lever, and the *Cycling* light lit up.

When the lock was in vacuum, I lifted the lever. The hatch opened and I pulled myself in and closed it behind me before cycling the far hatch. My audio pickups gave me the sound of air whistling in. I popped into the Control Deck annex.

I had been inside Habitat enough during construction, so that I knew my way around pretty well. The annex was right off the main cabin of the Control Deck: a bowl shape, thirty-meters radius by ten deep, filled with a triple ring of monitor stations along the surface of the bowl so a supervisor could survey all stations from the center.

I pushed to the door and opened it. Immediately my senses were overloaded, light flashing through my visor and sound overloading my audio. Every computer at every station flashed data, buzzed alarms, called out gibberish warnings, and strobed bright and dark.

I blinked and looked away. "Wilson!" I shouted over the din, but with no hope that I could hear a response even if he made one.

"He's not here." Leeanne watched through my comms. Another person might have sounded frantic, but her control didn't waver. "The motion sensor's flaking out from all the signal noise, but there's no firm signal."

"We can't be sure. Let me get a better view." I pushed off to the supervisor harness, a set of straps in the center of the bowl, and I looked around.

I didn't want to make Leeanne anxious, but I was sure she was right: Wilson wasn't there. Unless he was jammed behind a workstation where I couldn't see, he was nowhere on the Control Deck. That didn't make sense. Where else would he be?

"Sam!" Leeanne called on the comm. "The power monitor station. The panel's open!"

Sure enough, an open panel led into the guts of the workstation. I dove over. Wilson had to have opened it to trace a data feed. I could tell because he had left his network analyzer there, still tied into the juncture box. But the readout on the analyzer made me sweat: *Fusion Deck.*

Leeanne's whisper on the comm lacked her usual steely control. "S-Sam. Don't do it."

"What?"

"You know where he went, Sam. We're gonna lose him. We can't afford to lose you, too."

But it wasn't until she said that that I realized: Wilson had followed the signal to the Fusion Deck. He was less than fifty meters from a glowing ring of fusing hydrogen plasma that was just waiting for containment to fail so it could escape.

Fusion reactions are so difficult to sustain that they can't go critical like a fission reactor. When something goes wrong, the reaction just collapses, destroying the reactor but not posing a threat outside the immediate area. The station was designed so that Habitat Module would be safe in the event of a collapse—but the Fusion Deck and the refinery would surely be destroyed.

So despite Leeanne's warning, I was going after Wilson. "We're not losing him."

"Sam!"

"We are *not* losing your husband, Leeanne! Don't waste time arguing. Just get your ass over to the far end and wait for us."

I went back out through the airlock and into The Tube. There were elevators between the modules, but I crossed the distance faster on my jets.

My rad meters didn't change appreciably as I settled to a halt at the far airlock. The radiation from the reactor was contained by shielding except where it was used in the refinery, and what escaped the shielding was barely above background radiation from Jupiter itself.

I had selected a lock near the control center. At least I hoped so. I was so used to the computer answering questions like that, but I feared to trust my suit comp. It hadn't been compromised yet, but if I tied it into station information, it might be. I didn't need my suit failing me now!

When I got inside, I wished I had trusted the computer. I wasn't in the control center, I was in a darkened room. Flickering lights through a thick window in the far wall showed part of a giant torus, fifteen meters on the short radius and ninety on the long. The fusion reactor! I had entered in a service room off the main reactor chamber, and that room was *hot!* I checked my meters: not hot in the radiation sense, or at least not dangerously so, but the temperature was over $30^C$. Any warmer and it would start to tax my cooling system. I could hear the cooling fans whirring up already.

I looked around the darkened room. The flickering showed no light switches, just a bank of storage cabinets, a row of work pods, and a wall of monitors–malfunctioning, of course. Once my eyes adjusted to the flicker, I picked out two hatches. One led into the reactor chamber. I pulled open the other, exited the service room, and sealed the hatch behind me. Immediately my cooling fans grew quiet, and my temperature began to drop.

I still sweated, though. It wasn't from the heat.

At least I knew where I was going now. I floated in a large transit corridor; and in this part of R&R, all corridors led to the control center. The corridor was in darkness, but my suit light showed a hatch about forty-five meters away. That was my destination.

I checked my comp timer. Despite moving as fast as I could, it had been more than ten minutes since our approach to the station, and thirty minutes had been just a best guess. How long did we have? I broke several safety regulations by using my jets to race through the corridor.

When I got to the control center, I entered a room designed almost as a mirror to Control Deck: a giant bowl with three rings of screens. And just as in Control Deck, most of the screens displayed gibberish. The one main difference from Control Deck was my target: the suited man working inside the panel of one of the stations.

"Wilson!" Suit comms couldn't penetrate station shielding, but they worked fine in the same room.

Without pulling his head out of the panel, Wilson answered, "Sam? Good! Hey, buddy, gimme a hand. Need you to jettison the mass driver, and once that's done, cut us loose from The Tube."

"Boss!"

"We're gonna lose the reactor, Sam. No hope, I can tell. Refinery too. We just have to salvage as much of the station as we can."

Typical Wilson, worrying about assets and losses while his dream disintegrated around him. He could be passionate when he sold an idea; but when it came to implementation, he was a cold-blooded numbers guy.

And as usual, he made sense. There were months and fortunes tied up in the station. If any of it could be saved, we had to save it.

I flew over to the superstructure controls. These weren't part of the main computer network, so maybe they weren't corrupted. Maybe.

If they were, our ploy was already doomed.

But if this was so important to Wilson . . . "Boss, what are you after in there?"

Wilson answered tersely, "Evidence." He went back to work, cursing as he did. When he started swearing, I knew better than to interrupt until he'd solved the problem.

I studied the superstructure controls. They were clean, or at least not flashing gibberish like all of the others. These were part of the construction network, not the station operations network; and when the time had come to hook all the systems together, Wilson and the network guys had debated whether it made sense to tie construction in. I'd never paid attention to the outcome, but it looked as if Wilson had decided to isolate the system.

I'm not a computer guy, but I'm a competent engineer and physicist. I understood the basics of the controls, but it was designed to make it difficult to accidentally cut the station into pieces—like I was trying to do.

I worked through the layers of safeguards and confirmations while also figuring out the process. There were rocket engines on the mass driver and the R&R Module. Explosive bolts would cut the mass driver loose, and the rockets would burn on a preset trajectory. Then I could do the same for R&R.

But first I had to choose the trajectories, feed them to the rockets, double check everything, and confirm everything one more time, all while trying to learn an unfamiliar interface.

I knew that I was taking too long. My suit timer showed twenty-two minutes when I finally felt the station tremble. If it had been the reactor, it would've been a lot more than a tremble, so that must've been the first explosive bolts.

I watched on the screen and confirmed that the mass driver was drifting away from the station, picking up speed as the rockets began to burn. Over ten minutes to figure out the controls.

I hoped I would move faster on the second set.

But I didn't have to. Wilson nudged me aside and handed me a clear bag containing a computer board. "Sam, I've got this. Get that board out of here."

I looked at Wilson through his suit visor. His face, darker than Leeanne's, nearly always bore a smile. It wasn't from humor—though Wilson had a great sense of humor—it was friendliness and confidence. Wilson Gray was happiest when we had a challenge to tackle. So when I saw that his smile was gone, I grew even more worried. "Boss, I'm not—"

"Now, Sam! This wasn't an accident, and the evidence is on that board. Get it off this station!" And Wilson turned to the superstructure controls, hands moving twice as fast as mine.

Despite Wilson's orders, I hesitated. He pushed me away, and I tumbled through the air. Wilson didn't need my help and he wouldn't be dragged away, and arguing would only distract him. Whatever that board held was important to him, so I had to get it out, like he had ordered. I cycled through the nearest airlock and hoped that he would not be too far behind me.

Just as I pulled myself out of the lock, I felt the whole station shudder. Somewhere inside the big disk-shaped module, the magnetic fields had passed a critical point of imbalance. The laws of physics took over from there: on the one hand, the delicate fusion reaction snuffed itself out harmlessly in the first microsecond; but on the other hand, the cooling system failed and the high-pressure coolants escaped and damaged the ring structure.

In a chain reaction, the massive magnetic coils that had taken person-years to assemble and fit into place suddenly broke free from their blocks and ripped themselves to shreds—giant, fast shreds that tore through shielding, tore through bulkheads . . .

And tore through the hull!

I fired my jets at max throttle, getting me away as far and as fast as possible. I barely escaped the flying shards of tin and aluminum and carbon compound.

Wilson hadn't cut the modules apart. The shudder propagated up the girder tunnel, causing it to twist and flex dangerously.

Some girders nearest the R&R Module snapped entirely, something I'd never seen carbon girders do. The lattice structure absorbed the shock, but I had to fly over a hundred meters before I felt it was safe to cross between the rods.

And then I just hung outside the girders, looking back at the wreckage that had been R&R. My best friend's greatest dream, and now his destruction. I floated silently and waited for his widow to pick me up.

Life in the Settlements didn't give us a lot of spare time, not even to grieve.

I assembled a crew, and we went into the shattered husk of R&R to retrieve Wilson's body.

I remembered his last words: *This wasn't an accident. . . .*

I still didn't know what he meant, so I recorded everything for . . . well, for evidence, I guess. The scene was horrific, his corpse filleted by the fast-moving shrapnel. I locked down my recordings. No way would Leeanne see these if I could help it.

Then I had to get ready for the funeral. It took me a while to find my cabin in Habitat, since I still wasn't familiar with the new station. I had only visited my quarters before long enough to stow a small kit bag with clothes and essentials. When I found my hatch, I went inside and sealed myself in.

And then, for a few scarce minutes alone, I cried. Wilson Gray was dead, and people needed me to carry on, but I needed . . . I needed Wilson. If only I had been here sooner . . . But that thought led me to a dark vortex I might never escape, so I wrenched myself out of it.

I had to find something to do, some activity to anchor myself. So I opened my kit bag, unzipped the toiletries pouch, and pulled out my razor. I set it for a short trim, just enough to even out my goatee and mustache. As the blades spun and the vacuum sucked away the bristles, I stared at my eyes in the mirror. They were red against pale skin that bagged around them. I wished I had some water to rinse them, but Habitat didn't yet have water to the residence decks. I would have to live with the red. And with the patches of white in my beard and scalp. When had those appeared? When had my hairline receded so far? This project had made me old, but that day I felt the impact all at once.

I combed my hair, put on a fresh pair of coveralls, and pushed out of my cabin and into the half-completed corridor. Many of the wall panels were missing, exposing conduit and tubes and electronics. There were no signs and no obvious way to navigate, but I didn't need them. I just followed the other stunned, red-eyed faces as they floated their way to the recycler.

As per his will, we gave Wilson a small ceremony—I spoke, and Kim did, as did a few others as Leeanne floated in tearful silence—and then we fed him to the organic recycler. New crew from Earth had trouble with this concept, but the recycler is our version of the natural order of life and renewal. New recruits understand this on an intellectual level, but it still creeps them out. After you've been through a few funerals in the Settlements, though, you start to feel it: Wilson Gray was gone, but his essence would be with us forever.

Most of Gray City attended the service in person or by televisit. The only ones who couldn't attend were the crew I had assigned to stabilize Habitat. We also had visitors and televisitors from across the Pournelle Settlements, the collection of independent towns and stations inspired by an early aerospace pioneer who was the first to describe the energy efficiencies of mining colonies in the Jupiter system. The Settlements were loosely affiliated in trade and support alliances, but most of them prized their independence. It had taken all of Wilson's incredible charm and diplomatic skills to unite them in the Refinery Station project. Some had openly called it Wilson's Folly. They had the good taste not to mention it on that day, but the phrase would soon come back, I felt sure.

By chain of command, Leeanne should've directed the ceremonies and the aftermath; but my steely-eyed pilot had finally given in to her human side. She had watched her husband and her future all shredded in an instant. She had made my pick-up like a pro; but after that she had just stared at the wreckage, her eyes sunk in her suddenly hollow face. She had barely mustered the energy to answer simple questions since. I had had to take the ship's controls, and since then everyone just turned to me as if I were in charge of the entire city. Maybe I was.

*I never signed up for this, Wilson.* I wasn't the decision maker. I was the guy who carried out the decisions. That was my part in our triad: Wilson had the wild dreams and sold them to the world, Leeanne was the practical one who told him when his dreams were *too* wild, and ol' Sam Pike led the grunt work to make the dreams come true.

Now I had to hope that I could remember the lessons Wilson had taught me as I stepped into his role. That included something that always came natural to him, something I could never be comfortable with: leading meetings.

Immediately after Wilson's service, as Kim led Leeanne back to her cabin, I called an emergency meeting. Even limiting it to department heads, there were still thirty people gathered in the Atrium of Habitat, and six more by televisit. That was too many for an effective meeting, but I couldn't guess which department might have a handy miracle or two. We needed every miracle we could scrape up.

The hubbub in the Atrium was more uneasy than I'd ever heard it. Even in the darkest can-we-do-this hours of station design and construction, the department heads had all been on board, drawn in by Wilson's enthusiasm and quick answer to any problem.

Now I saw them clumping into worried groups, bobbing in the air as they talked among themselves. The faces I saw . . . Some looked almost as haunted as Leeanne's. I needed to get them all on task—whatever the task would be.

I pushed off to the chairman's harness in the center of the atrium, but I didn't strap in. It just felt too soon for that, and I was still kicking myself for not being at the station when Wilson needed me. So I strapped into my harness next to his.

Then I raised my voice, but not so much as to echo off the walls. "All right, people. Come to order." Somehow it was easier there in *my* harness. I could pretend that Wilson was just "away," and I was running things in his stead as I had done many times before. So I followed our usual routine. "Status reports, people."

I looked at Hank Zinn from structural engineering, but he hesitated, staring at his hands. Before Hank could answer, the tumult broke out again. This time I did echo: "*People!*"

They dropped silent again. "Okay, we can't pretend we're not shook up. When you get out of here, you all have my permission to panic for an hour. But Wilson Gray hired *professionals*, goddamn it, and I expect you to start acting like it! Or none of us are gonna last long out here."

More tumult. Mari's voice broke over the rest. "We're not going to last anyway!" There were shouts of agreement.

I looked at Mari: a petite woman with golden skin, red-brown curls, and usually a confident attitude that fascinated me. Even now, stressed and grieving, confidence in tatters, she still appealed to me. She was still the fireball I had fallen for. We had dated for several months before our latest fight, and I really hoped we weren't over. So I hated to turn on her, but I had to put this down *now*. I tried to sound cold. "If you believe that, Mari, there's the hatch. I need a united team. If you're giving up on us, hitch a ride to Walkerville or Callisto One or Earth, for all I care. I'll comp the transit costs in your last check. Is that what you want?"

Mari glared at me, and I was coldly sure that our last date had been our *last* date. But she shook her head and bit her lip. I gave her a second in case she wanted to add something, then I continued. "If we're going to come out the other side of this, it will be by following Wilson's troubleshooting protocol: tally our assets and status; define the problem; refine it into a solution; assign tasks to our assets; and design the process and build whatever new assets we need. So it's tally time, people. Hank?"

Hank turned to me. His voice was steady and calm. Maybe I had handled that right. "We're in bad shape. Not fatal, but bad. Habitat still has a slight wobble." We could see that just by looking around. The walls occasionally flexed as a slow standing wave passed through the structure. "We'll have that under control in a couple hours. But The Tube took serious damage at the reactor end. We can salvage the material, but it's going to take a month. R&R is worse. The debris is orbiting with us in a cloud, but some of the material is not recoverable at any reasonable cost. The mass driver is safe, but its orbit is unstable in the long run. We have maybe three months to boost it to a stable orbit before it draws too close to Ganymede and tidal force pulls it apart. We can do that, if you're willing to spend the fuel."

I nodded. Wilson had given his life in part for the driver. We wouldn't give it up now. I turned to Mari. "Eco?"

Mari's voice was bitter. "As I tried to tell you, we're screwed in the long term. We have consumables enough for now. We can scavenge some, and we can barter with other settlements. There's still demand for our batteries, right?" She looked at Sissi Sneve from power management, and Sissi nodded. "But our loads from Earth . . . Well, we've got twenty months in the pipeline. And that may be it. My buyers back on Earth say it was already difficult to get credit before. Sellers doubted Mr. Gray's plan. Now that the news is out, that credit is drying up. We'll see gaps in the pipeline twenty months down; and four or five months after that, the pipeline will *stop*."

I tried to sound conciliatory. "And can we conserve enough to make the difference?"

"Maybe . . ." But her expression didn't look convincing, a combination of a glare at me and a trembling frown.

Discussions broke out again; and for the first meeting in over a year, I resorted to the air horn.

The shriek echoed off the walls, and some put their hands over their ears. When the echoes died, I continued as if nothing had happened.

"Then we'll find another answer, like always. Power?"

Sissi summarized the generator status and the power market—the two bright spots of the meeting—and I moved on to the next topic. By the time most of the departments had reported, I noticed a flash of short platinum hair at the nearest hatch. Kim had returned to the meeting. Her face was even paler than usual, and her delicate face showed—no, not sadness, fury! *Oh, shit, what now?*

Kim gently squeezed through the crowd to join me, sliding up to my side while trying not to draw attention. She handed me the computer board from the reactor, and she pushed a report to my comp. While I listened to the status reports, I checked Kim's data.

*Oh, shit,* I thought again. This was bad. It might be the last straw. Wilson had been right, it hadn't been an accident. This could break our spirits.

Or maybe . . . As the last status report completed, I surveyed the room. "Thank you. That's what I expect from you all: your best effort as professionals. And we need that." I held out the computer board. "I thought we were dealing with an accident. But it turns out we have a whole different problem: sabotage." Immediately the room broke into shouts, and I had to use the air horn again. "I'm pushing Kim's report to you all. It won't stay secret, so I won't try. This circuit board that arrived from Earth six months ago has a very clever, invasive virus hard-coded into its core. Ladies and gentlemen, somebody tried to stop us. Maybe kill us."

This time I let the shouts play out. I *wanted* them shouting. I wanted them *angry*. And amid the shouts, I heard two words more than any other: "Initiative" and "Magnus." Magnus Metals ran an Earth orbit refinery that sapped much of our profits in refining fees; and the System Initiative were the bureaucrats who thought *they* ran space from cushy offices in Rio de Janeiro. Between their regulations and more fees and fines, they sapped much of the rest of our profits.

Refinery Station had been Wilson's giant middle finger to both of them: we would do our own refining, and the Initiative were welcome to fly out to Jupiter to try to enforce their regulations where the laws of physics were the only real authority. Either might be our saboteurs, maybe even both. I didn't need to work out who, yet. It was enough to know that the two things Settlers hated most were the government squeeze and the corporate squeeze. This news had unified the department heads more than anything I could have said.

But Wilson had taught me: some messages are more effective from "the troops" than from the boss. So just as Wilson had often done to me, I tapped out a message and pushed it to Kim. When her comp buzzed, she looked at it. Then she nodded and gently pushed out until she was in among the others, shouting and talking like the others. And as a lull hit, she shouted over the rest. "They tried to kill us!"

The echoes were louder than the air horn. "*Yeah!*"

"Are we gonna let them stop us?"

This had been one of Wilson's simplest motivating questions; and the answer this time shook the walls worse than the standing wave. "*Hell, No!*"

Right then, I knew: I had my team again. We would survive.

Now I just had to figure out how.

⟂

That's what I *thought* I would do; but I had no idea how my time would actually be spent. I had never appreciated what Wilson had done all day. More meetings. More soothing of frayed nerves. More reviews of plans and schedules. More calls back to Earth, pleading with creditors and suppliers not to cut us off until we regrouped.

More calls to our business agents, too, to try to track down the source of the virus. Yeah, like that was ever gonna happen. Whoever did it had covered their tracks too well.

There was so much to do, and every day the list grew faster than I could whittle it down. I started sleeping in my office, when I found time to sleep at all. No matter how hard I tried, the work piled up. Maybe Mari was right: maybe Gray Interplanetary was dead like Wilson, and

195

we were just waiting for it to stop breathing.

And Leeanne . . . Leeanne might've been walking dead herself. For the first week, she didn't come out of her cabin, and she barely ate the food that Kim brought her. Then she started coming out for a few hours at a time, but she spoke little. Her eyes were still wide and red, her face muscles slack and expressionless. One look told you she was still in shock. People tried to engage her, but the conversations always trailed off into uncomfortable silence. Over time she started wandering into the middle of work areas, sometimes talking but mostly watching. People complained to me. They couldn't say it, since legally she was now the top boss, but they wanted me to keep her out of their hair. As if I didn't have enough problems. I added that to my list, but not near the top.

Three weeks after the funeral, though, Leeanne pushed herself to the top of the list, floating into my office as I went over power management reports late at night.

She waited for the hatch to close; then for the first time in weeks she found real energy to speak—and she threw it all at me. "Samuel Pike, what the hell are you doing to my company?"

My mind froze. I don't back down from a fight. Normally a challenge like that would have me shouting back, or worse. But this woman was my boss now, and my best friend's grieving widow. With Wilson gone, she was the closest friend I had. I felt grateful to see her engaged in *something*, even if it was chewing me out.

I muttered, "Leeanne . . . We're trying . . . to put something together here."

"Bullshit!" She waved an arm to gesture at the station, giving her a slight spin until she hit a wall and arrested her movement. "*They* are trying, but they need direction from you. *You* are floundering!"

Despite my concerns, my hackles rose. "Damn it, Leeanne! I'm doing the best I know how! You—" I caught myself before I could spit out an accusation. "You have any ideas for what I can do better, I'm all ears."

Leeanne's tone calmed, but she didn't fall back into her depression.

"What you can do, Sam, is stop driving yourself so hard. You're looking worse than me, and I'm the one who lost my husband! You're going to kill yourself, and kill Wilson's dream with you. What you have to do is what Willy would do: prioritize and delegate."

I sighed. "I know, I'm trying."

Again she said, "Bullshit!" And again she gestured at the station. "I've been all over Gray City, Sam. Everywhere I see the same thing: people are holding onto hope because you and Kim charged them up; but they're slowly losing it because your decisions take so long that the situation changes before they hear from you. Everyone's going through the motions, but there's no plan in effect. And the more you look like a zombie, the more they lose faith."

I breathed out slowly. "You're right, Leeanne. I've tried to hold things together for you. Now if you're ready, boss, I'm happy to take your orders—as soon as I get some sleep."

"Uh-uh!" Leeanne shook her head, bobbing against her handhold. "I never wanted to be the boss. Wilson knew that: I'm a counselor, not an executive. You haven't had time to check Willy's final orders yet, but they name you as his second in command, subject to approval of the Board. And with his shares plus mine, I have controlling interest on the Board, so you're approved."

"But Leeanne, I'm doing a miserable job! You said so yourself!"

"That's because you're trying to solve *all* of the problems instead of just the big ones. You think you're delegating, but your people tell me you're not. You're delegating tasks, not decisions. That's why you have no time to sleep! Any time you've got a problem where your department heads can decide, let them! Let Mari deal with the suppliers on Earth. She always did for Wilson."

"Mari and I . . ." I swallowed. "We're not getting along."

"That's a luxury you can't afford right now. Treat her like a trusted professional, not an ex-girlfriend. Mari'll do her job if you let her."

"Well . . ."

"Samuel Pike, if you let your wounded pride put an end to Gray City,

I'll launch you straight into Jupiter! Mari's a grown up, now you be one!

"And speaking of launching . . . Hank is waiting for you to get off your ass and order him to salvage the mass driver. He has a plan, but it'll take a lot of fuel. He can't authorize that without orders from you. Every minute you wait, the driver gets closer to Ganymede, and the salvage costs grow higher."

"We have over two months . . ."

"And if you'd acted immediately, we would've had three months. By now the fuel costs have more than doubled. You give that order *now* Sam, or so help me I'll steal a tug and start hauling the driver back myself."

At that I smiled. She would, too. I pulled open a channel to Hank. "Hank? Yeah, it's Sam . . . Hey, sorry I've gotten buried here . . . No, you're right and I'm wrong, so I'm doing the apologies here. You're authorized for fuel charges and overtime budgets to go get that driver . . . Yeah, the plan you submitted—Damn, was that four days ago already? Okay, revise the plan as needed, and I'll approve it . . . No, don't wait for final approval, I trust you . . . Thanks, Hank! I look forward to your reports."

I disconnected and looked at Leeanne. "How'd I do, boss?"

"Enough of that 'boss' business. You did okay. Now you make a call like that to all your department heads, and maybe we'll get things under control here. Start with Mari." I frowned at that. "Mari. Now."

I spread my hands up, pleading. "But Leeanne . . . That fight . . ." I couldn't find words. They brought back the pain.

Leeanne's expression softened. Suddenly I saw my friend, Wilson's wife. My pain grew as she asked, "What about it, Sam? You two have fought before. You're a hard-nosed engineer, she's a fiery Cuban, that's no surprise. You've always gotten past it before."

I tried to speak, but I had a catch in my throat. I coughed and said, "But this fight . . . This is why we weren't at the station. This is why—"

"Hush!" Leeanne shouted as she pushed herself across the office to me, stopping herself by wrapping her arms around me and pulling my head down to her shoulder. She buried her face in my own shoulder and said, "Stop it, Sam! Don't say that. Do *not* say that. I never want to hear that again."

I tried to hold back, but I found myself sobbing. "If I had been here—"

"No, Sam. You wouldn't have been here. You would've been with the prospecting fleet. Or negotiating with the other Settlements. Or on any of a hundred other errands for Wilson, just like every other day of this project."

"But—"

"No buts! So this is what it's all about? Sam, someday I'll find who killed Willy, and I'll make them pay. But it wasn't you, and it wasn't me! We're survivors, we're not to blame."

Then I really cut loose with the tears, and Leeanne joined in. More than I had needed sleep, I had needed tears, and someone to share them with.

Eventually, though, I remembered that I had work to do. "Okay, boss—Leeanne," I corrected. I pulled away and wiped my eyes. "Do I look ready for more calls?"

Leeanne smiled at me. It was weak, but it was a smile. She had needed the tears, too. "Stop worrying about looking strong." She pushed back to the hatch, out of the comm pickup. "Call Mari."

I nodded, my body bobbing in response, and I called Mari. As soon as her face appeared on my comm, she started in on me. "Sam Pike, do you *like* making my job impossible?" I shook my head, but she continued before I could answer. "I just answered a call from Bader Farms. I had them, Sam. I had them! I had them convinced that we were stabilizing our situation, and you had a plan to meet our contracts. Then *you* called them, and you ruined the whole thing! They said you didn't strike them as confident, so why should they be? They're ready to cancel our future pipeline loads, maybe even sell some of the in-transit loads to Walkerville."

She paused to breathe, and I finally snuck in a response. "I'm sorry, Mari."

Mari continued. "And furthermore—" Then she shook her head. Red-brown curls became a shimmering cloud. "What did you say?"

"I'm sorry. I screwed up, and I was wrong. If I stay out of the middle, can you fix this?"

Mari's jaw dropped open, and it took a few seconds before she answered. "Maybe. But I'll have to offer points."

I nodded. "Take them out of my account. It's my mistake, so Gray City shouldn't pay for it."

Mari cocked an eyebrow. "And you'll stay out of it?"

I nodded again. "It's your department. Wilson trusted you, and Leeanne and I trust you. I'm sorry if I gave you any reason to doubt that. If you need me, tell me. Otherwise, it's hands-off."

Mari almost smiled then. "Okay, I need to work on repairing this. And . . . Thanks, Sam."

I disconnected the call and started placing more. As I did, department heads pulled tasks from my task list, and some tasks immediately switched from *Backlog* to *In Progress*. A couple even switched to *Complete*. When I finished, I looked at the full list. Those forty-some calls had done more to clear the list than I had accomplished in three weeks.

I held up my hands in surrender. "Okay, Leeanne, you were right. I'm still learning on the job here. What's next?"

"Next we hold an Executive Committee meeting, just like the old days: the Chairman, the Counselor, and your Executive Officer."

"But I'm—All right, I used to be XO. Now I'm Chairman, so who's the Executive Officer?"

"Kim Stone, of course. She's already doing every task you'll let her. I've promoted her and made the pay retroactive—assuming we have anything left to pay anyone with. She's outside waiting for us to have it out. Are we good?"

I thought long before answering. I had so much to learn about being in the top seat; but with Leeanne's help, it had already gotten easier. And now with Kim's help as well, maybe I could handle it.

I smiled and nodded. "We're good. Hell, we're great! Bring on the next challenge!"

Leeanne knocked on the hatch, and it opened. Kim floated in and closed it behind her. The two women floated there, one large and dark, the other a pale blonde pixie; but both were strong, especially inside, and I was going to need that.

"You straighten him out, boss lady?" Kim asked.

Leeanne raised her free hand. "Ah-ah-ah! None of that. Sam's the boss, so let's get in the proper habit."

Kim nodded and turned to me. "Right. Okay, boss, I think we need to get the mass driver ASAP. Tidal force won't be large enough to damage it for a couple weeks, but the strain is mounting. It won't take much strain to misalign the rings."

I tried to answer, but Leeanne jumped in. "You're right, but Sam has that handled already." Yeah, I was the boss all right, except when Leeanne wanted to be in charge. But I could work that way. It was comforting to have somebody watching my back.

Still, I had to keep up appearances. "Yes, Hank has approval to modify his plan as needed. You keep an eye on it. Don't interfere with him, but make sure we're not blindsided by any unexpected charges."

I felt better. Now what next? Well, I would follow Wilson's protocols. "Okay, let's tally our assets and status. We have almost our full crew. Only a few people have quit. We have Habitat, our prospecting fleet, our construction fleet, and all the smaller stations we built before Habitat. We have the fuel depot and the generator stations. And we have active contracts to sell power here in the Settlements, and we have contracts to deliver raw metals to Earth orbit. We also have twenty months of supplies in the pipeline, and we can get more as long as we don't default on any of those delivery contracts. I've persuaded our suppliers to give us a little more time, since we're technically not in default yet."

Leeanne added, "And we have the mass driver."

"Yes, we have the driver, and power to run it, though that will tax our generating capacity quite a bit. Anything else?" Both women shook their heads. "Okay, that also defines the problem, pretty much: we need to find some way to fulfill those contracts, or somehow generate equivalent income to keep the pipeline open. Our credit is stretched too thin: if it looks like we'll miss a month or more in the pipeline, people will start abandoning us. That'll create a feedback loop, and we'll collapse long before the pipeline runs dry. Other Settlements will lay claim to our assets, and who could blame them?"

Kim broke in. "Boss, I've made a few inquiries with friends in other Settlements. Callisto One is primed to take us over. Almost as if they were ready in advance. And they've been making offers to some of our key staff."

I nodded. "Interesting . . ." Callisto One was the Initiative's official presence in the Pournelle Settlements, and had been a thorn in Wilson's side. We all guessed how they had been "ready in advance"; but I shook my head. "Our people hate the Initiative. If we have *any* hope of getting through this, they won't go to Callisto. Now we just have to find that hope."

And for the first time since that call from Kim three weeks ago, Leeanne smiled. "Oh, I figured that out. While there was no hope, I was happy to let you screw things up. Boss." And her smile actually became a brief grin. "But once I saw an answer, I knew I had to kick your ass into gear so you could make it happen. They won't follow me, but you've got the touch. All you need is some hot pilots—me, and I can name others—who really understand gravity deep in their guts. You've all been worried about tidal force and its danger to the mass driver; but tidal force is still a force, just like any other. And force can be dangerous, but it can also be harnessed."

⚓

It took a month to turn Leeanne's idea into a plan, and then another three to put the plan into effect. It took over two months just to pull the mass driver out of its doomed orbit and into one that we could use.

Mari had persuaded our creditors to give us a little more time.

Maybe they figured they couldn't lose much more than they already would, and they could afford to stretch a little in hopes of a payoff. Maybe they just had a lingering respect for Wilson's legacy. Hell, for all I knew his ghost was out there somewhere still applying that old Wilson charm.

But one thing I do know: it wasn't our plan that sold them, since Mari never told them what it was. We had enemies, but we didn't know exactly who they were nor whom we could trust. So we kept the full plan to just the Executive Committee as long as we could, and doled out details on a need-to-know basis. Once we were sure the plan would work and no one could stop us, *then* we filled in everyone in Gray City. The cheer when they understood almost shattered the walls of Habitat. Mari even smiled at me.

When the day came for us to test out the plan, Leeanne insisted on flying one of the chase ships, and I insisted on flying shotgun with her. She tried to argue me out of it, but I pulled the trump card I'd held back since our first Executive Committee meeting. I looked her straight in the eyes and asked, "Leeanne, am I in charge here or not? You can't have it both ways. If you as the Board say no, I'll sit back and watch you run things; but if you as my Counselor say no . . . then I'm happy to take your advice, but I'll do things my way."

For almost a full minute, I thought I'd been fired. Then Leeanne answered quietly, "We can't afford to lose you, too, Sam."

"Then it's a good thing I'll be flying with the best damn pilot in the Pournelle Settlements." And that settled it. I was in the copilot's harness as Leeanne idled between Jupiter and the driver. We watched the feed from Kim and the team on the far side of Jupiter as relayed by polar comm sats.

I called over the sats. "How's it going, Kim?"

Light speed delayed her response by over a second. "Fantastic, boss. The first load just launched, and we've got three more coming. Take a look."

I switched to Kim's station camera, which showed a large lump of ice, dirt, and valuable metals. If we sent that lump to Earth directly,

Magnus would charge us a huge fee for clearing off the dross (which they *claimed* was useless, but we knew they made a few percentage points from the volatiles); and then *they* would assay the remains.

Somehow their assayers always came up with a value far lower than our estimates. If it were random, the error should have been in our favor once in a while, but it never was.

That was why Wilson wanted to break up the rocks ourselves, ship only the metals (which were easier to mass drive, since the driver was strong enough to grab even paramagnetic minerals), and deliver direct to our customers instead of to Magnus.

Now four such rocks were on a trajectory close to Jupiter, and we would rendezvous on the other side. I got on the chase fleet circuit. "Folks, get your rest. Targets coming your way in about six hours. Sleep while you can."

But we didn't sleep, and I doubt anyone in the chase fleet did.

Like us, most spent the six hours watching on the polar cameras as the first rock dove closer to Jupiter. When the rock passed within the Roche limit and started to break apart, I shouted over the chase circuits: "Yes!" And at least a dozen voices echoed mine.

Jupiter's tidal force pulled the near side of the rock much harder than the far side, and the ice and dross couldn't hold together. The metals that remained wouldn't be as pure as we would've gotten from the refinery, but they would be good enough to meet our contracts. I might have to give back a few points, but we would *meet our contracts.* We would survive.

And someday, we would build another refinery, and Wilson's Folly would become Wilson's triumph.

But that would be in the future.

I got back on the circuit. "Computers will feed target trajectories to you over the next three hours. We'll assign pickups. Plant your bots on the big targets, then look for targets of opportunity."

The drive bots would attach themselves to the metal fragments, calculate a burst plan, and drive the metals to the induct of the mass driver.

There the magnetic fields would grab them and accelerate the metals on their path to Earth. It all took careful computer calculations. That had chewed up much of our planning time: making sure our computers were *clean*.

The effort hadn't been wasted: we found three more virus traps waiting to be sprung. Someday, somebody was going to find out just how angry I was that they had killed my best friend.

But not today. Today we had metal to chase. "Leeanne, you picked our first target yet?"

"Yeah, boss, but it's not on the computer's list."

"Huh?"

She pushed a spectrographic report to me. "That blip there? That's nearly a quarter tonne of platinum. Computer says it's on a bad trajectory, we'll never recover it this time."

"Then leave it! We can get it on another orbit!"

"And let some other Settlement claim it after we did all the work? Hang on, boss!" And instead of waiting for the fragments to approach, Leeanne powered up the engines. She turned us back, and suddenly my view port was filled with brown bands and the Red Spot. I was pushed back into my couch at over three gees as we dove toward Jupiter.

What could I do? "Leeanne, you're fired!" But I said it with a big grin on my face, accentuated by the acceleration.

Leeanne grinned back even bigger. "Take it up with the Board. After we get that platinum!"

She laughed, and we sped deep into Jupiter's well. At a certain carefully calculated point, Leeanne flipped us around and fired the thrusters to slow us. I watched the computer project our course, and I was happy: the old Leeanne was back, at least for now.

"Not to backseat drive, Leeanne, but how do we get this baby on course?"

Leeanne pushed her analysis to my comp. "I think we can do it with three drive bots. Yeah, that's a lot, but this lump is worth more than any three we've picked out."

I nodded and readied the drive bots for firing. When our velocity nearly matched the lumps, I fired off the bots. Then I watched them on the scope.

*One*... The first bot touched down, scrambled for a hold, and finally attached itself firmly. *Two* . . . The second bot attached. *And* . . . "Damn!"

"What is it, boss?"

"Third bot didn't attach. It might make a second pass, but that'll burn a lot of fuel. It might not do the trick. I'll launch another."

"Never mind, boss. I've got a better idea!"

Suddenly I felt the explosive *thump* of the tether launching. "We're gonna haul this sucker to the driver ourselves."

"That'll take a lot of fuel . . ."

"You'll approve it, boss!" Leeanne laughed, and I laughed as well as the tether struck the lump and scrambled for its own attachment.

When the tether controller showed a firm grip, I gave Leeanne a thumbs up. She gunned the engines and between our tether and the drive bots, we started nudging the platinum into a new trajectory. We passed a few other likely targets as we flew, and I launched drive bots at them as well; but Leeanne was right: this lump of platinum was the best possible proof of our plan.

As we approached the driver induct, I knew today would be a very good haul. I pushed the *Release* button on the tether controller, and the platinum was on a free trajectory straight for the induct.

We didn't go after more fragments, not quite yet. We just sat in silence for several minutes as the platinum drifted closer and closer to the mass driver.

When it got close enough, the magnetic field grabbed it, a weak hold on the platinum itself and a stronger hold on the metal web the bots had woven. The lump turned slightly, lining up with the magnetic rings; then it picked up speed. Soon it shot through the rings and out of sight.

We sat there a few minutes more, neither of us speaking.

I could see by the instrument lights that Leeanne was crying. I felt tears welling in my own eyes, a damned nuisance in zero g. But Wilson's dream was worth a few tears.

Then I realized we didn't have a contract for platinum. I pulled open a comm channel. "Mari, I have good news! You can start contract negotiations for a mass of platinum, specs attached." I pushed the specs into the data feed. "That should buy us dinner for a while!"

After the light speed delay, Mari responded, and her grin was a mirror of my own. "I have good news too, Sam. We've already got our dinner orders filled. I forwarded our suppliers a copy of Kim's satellite feed. As soon as they understood your plan, they upgraded our credit rating with all services. We're not back where we were, but we'll get there."

She broadcast the video? But I hadn't authorized that.

Then I saw Leeanne staring at me, and I knew there was only one proper response: "Great work, Mari. Gray City owes you. I owe you, big time."

Mari nodded. "You bet you owe me! Dinner and beer for starters. And I get to choose the place. Someplace expensive, with real meat! I'm sick of soy."

"Real meat, Mari. I promise." I closed the comm channel, and I felt warm inside.

I looked over, and Leeanne was still watching me. No time for that! It was time to get back to work. "Pilot! Next target!"

"Hang on!" Leeanne grinned through the tears as she wheeled the ship around again. I grinned, too. For the first time since the sabotage, in the middle of a three gee turn, I relaxed.

If I could've spared breath against the turn, I might have sung. I could pay people. I could *feed* people.

And finally, the word fit: I was the boss.

# BLΛCK ORBIT

Cynthia Allen floated in the airlock of the Initiative transport, swallowed hard, and leaped into light and darkness.

Behind the transport hung Jupiter. Sunlight reflecting from the giant planet flooded the sky, washing out the stars and even some of the fainter moons. Cynthia felt exposed, like the Red Spot was a giant eye looking for her; but she hoped her *real* hunters, the Initiative officers on the transport, would struggle to see her as Jupiter's glare blinded them, making the shadows of the transport that much deeper.

If Cynthia were lucky, they didn't even know she had left the ship. She had done her best to cover her tracks, especially her theft of the evidence that proved their complicity in numerous crimes in the Pournelle Settlements. They knew *something* was going on, though, and a rumor was spreading: *Internal Affairs has a spy on board.* As one of the newest in the crew, Cynthia Allen (or Patty Murphy, her cover identity) would be a top suspect. That slime, Baker, had already asked her some pretty uncomfortable questions. She expected him to return at any moment, and he had a violent temper when he wanted something.

So she had formulated a plan to escape with her evidence before things got that far. She had stolen a suit from stores, along with a spare air tank and hose. Now she plugged the hose connector into the tank regulator and used her knife to cut the hose from the connector.

Without the connector in place, the regulator's shutoff would engage, and the air would be securely contained in the tank; but with the shutoff defeated, Cynthia opened the stopcock on the regulator, and pressurized air jetted out. She clung to the tank with both hands as her makeshift rocket drove her away from the transport and toward Refinery Station.

After a long burst to set herself on her way, Cynthia closed the stopcock. This plan was a calculated risk. Her investigations had revealed that *someone* at Refinery Station was collaborating with Baker and the corrupt elements in the Initiative, but she still didn't know who. On the other hand, she knew that most residents of the station and the rest of Gray City distrusted the Initiative. There was no safe place for her, but the station had to be safer.

As Cynthia drew closer to the station, though, she doubted her decision. Two Initiative security shuttles were docked at the side of the long cylindrical Habitat module, at the extreme far end from the Refinery module. Two shuttles meant two squads: a show of force. They were hunting for someone, and she was the obvious choice. And Kyle Baker was head of Initiative security in the Jupiter system.

Cynthia didn't panic. Internal Affairs agents operating so far from Earth usually had no help within an AU or more, so they were trained to improvise—to survive if possible, but to complete the mission at all costs. Even if Cynthia didn't make it, if she could get this evidence to Inspector Park, IA would clean out the criminal ring that ran the Initiative's operations in Jupiter space.

*Improvise...* She didn't have much to work with: her computer, the suit, its air, a tool kit, and her improvised rocket. She had two priorities: to get her evidence to Inspector Park, and to let Park know it was coming without Baker learning about it. Surviving would be a nice bonus, but that was looking less likely as time went on.

First things first. Cynthia looked around, and she saw one more asset she could use: the shipping queue for Refinery Station's mass driver. The large cloud of floating metal ingots represented the Jupiter system's primary export, metals mined and refined here in system and then shipped to paying customers in the Earth-Moon system. The shipping queue was actually closer to Cynthia than the station was. She had enough air in her rocket to divert there and still reach Refinery. Maybe.

She aimed the makeshift nozzle, opened the stopcock, and flew toward the cloud. She wished there were an actual queue, but the shippers didn't waste propellant lining up the ingots, they just orbited them near the mass driver. Then drive bots clamped to each ingot would steer it into the driver induct on a precalculated shipping schedule, and the driver's magnetic rings would grab the ingot, accelerate it, and launch it toward Earth. Cynthia needed an ingot that would launch very soon, so there was no chance Baker would find it and intercept it. All she could do was choose one close to the induct and hope.

As she got closer, Cynthia was surprised at the shapes of the ingots. She had never seen them before, but she had assumed they would be spheres. Maybe rectangular. But these... Strange polyhedra were common, pyramids and rhombics and things that reminded her of buckeyballs. There were also smooth, curved shapes, shapes with dents and holes, and shapes with odd fin-like protrusions. They came in a range of sizes, from not much larger than her to the size of a medium transport. Many were also painted with some low-albedo substance that made them practically invisible. There were at least three times as many ingots as she had estimated from a distance. Cynthia floated among them, the only visitor to this remote sculpture park, and searched for a good candidate ingot.

It was an impossible puzzle, with too many variables and too many unknowns. She couldn't know which ingot was going to which customer. She could only guess which ones were launching soonest. She knew that some of the loads followed faster trajectories than others, so she couldn't know how long any given ingot might travel.

Finally she decided to trust in the one constant she had: Park. If anyone could find the evidence, the inspector would, so Cynthia must send a message to her. She saw that the ingots had thin-film shipping labels attached, and she saw one with a shipment number GI12002-

00723. That was her target, a large bagel-like object complete with a hole in the middle. It was nearly eight meters on its long axis. She pulsed the stopcock to push closer to the ingot, aiming for one of the drive bots clamped to its side. She had timed the pulse to not hit the ingot too hard, but she cushioned the impact on her left forearm and held her left hand palm-out in front of her faceplate just in case. She hit, but she had taken harder falls in the *dojo*.

Then the damned ingot tried to toss her off! Her impact, slight as it had been, had jostled the massive metal bagel. *Conservation of momentum wins again,* she thought. In response, a drive bot on the far side fired to correct the ingot's course, and the metal *bucked* towards her. She scrabbled for a grip, barely catching a drive bot's anchor cable—with her *right* hand. In her panic, she had lost hold of the air bottle. Before she had time to think, it bounced from the ingot and tumbled off into space.

*Damn!* Without a means of propulsion, Cynthia's odds of surviving were headed toward zero. More panic set in, and she spent several seconds catching her breath. Finally, grimly, she reminded herself that the odds had been against her since Baker had turned his eye on her. There was nothing she could do except hope for the best and attach her evidence to the ingot. But how would she do that? She couldn't just tape it on and chance that it would fall off under launch stress. Then Cynthia noticed that the drive bot controller was accessible: no locks, no security code. She clung to the bot's anchor cables with her left hand and opened the controller's cover with her right.

*Perfect!* The controller was a common industrial computer, not a custom job, and it took standard memory cards. Most important of all, it had empty card slots!

Cynthia removed her computer from its sleeve and let the sleeve hang in space next to herself. She opened the computer's memory compartment and saw a bank of thirty-two cards. They were indistinguishable from each other, but Cynthia knew which one held her report. She pulled it out, inserted it in an empty slot in the drive bot controller, and closed the controller's lid.

There. If nothing went wrong, if nobody stopped the launch, if nobody intercepted the ingot, and if Inspector Park was smart enough to track it, Cynthia had delivered the evidence. That was the best she could do.

So now she had to do everything she could to ensure that Park knew about the message. She preferred to do that by staying alive and filing a report, of course, but she had to have a contingency plan. Or plans, if possible.

She looked at her computer, its memory compartment still open. For arcane reasons, computer designers still worked in powers of two, and so this bank had two-to-the-fifth slots, or thirty-two. It had been full, but with one card gone there were thirty-one. Or almost thirty... Cynthia removed one more card and then rearranged the rest: seven cards, a gap, and twenty-three cards. Another message to Park, if she could pick up on it.

But how could Cynthia give her that chance? How could she reach the relative safety of Refinery Station? Her jury-rigged rocket was lost. She could try to make another with her own air tank, but that would leave her only the air in her suit. She wouldn't survive long enough with that. Or she could just give up, hang among the ingots until her air ran out and hope that someone trustworthy found her body. But she couldn't be sure who might find her—if anybody—and besides, Inspector Park didn't train her agents to just give up. Cynthia could imagine making a suicidal rush if she saw a way to take Baker and crew with her, but she couldn't imagine just succumbing to death here in this cloud of ingots.

*Ingots... Drive bots...* She looked at the drive bot that she still clung to with one hand. The computer controls were beyond her skill, but there were also manual test controls. If that were true of the other ingots as well...

Cynthia spied a likely candidate, a smaller rock, closer to Refinery Station. To be specific, it was close to the massive refinery at the far end of the station, where it had been refined from raw moonlets and then forged into a long, thin metal tetrahedron with corner fins.

Cynthia calculated an angle, bunching her legs against old 723 as she held onto the anchor cables. Then she let go of the cables and once more leaped into space.

Behind her, 723 once again wobbled. This time the far drive bot made a larger correction, and the rock lurched after her, overcorrecting. Then the drive bot on her side fired to compensate, and a spray of rocket exhaust reached toward her. The plume dwindled as it spread out, but still a mist of hot gas enveloped her legs, and she screamed. The exhaust was gone in an instant, but the pain lasted, and her mind went foggy.

It was several seconds before Cynthia realized that she had survived. That meant her suit had maintained integrity despite the heat; and that was doubly good because her legs were numb, indicating that her suit had diagnosed her burns and injected her with anesthetic. She confirmed that in her heads-up display, but she had trouble reading the data. The anesthetic—or maybe shock—made her light-headed right when she needed to think through this plan.

And right when she needed to catch her ride! The tetrahedral ingot loomed large in her faceplate, and Cynthia barely had time to catch herself. This time she immediately grabbed an anchor cable, and she was ready when the drive bots tried to kick her loose. She held on through the correction. Then she uncoiled a lanyard from her suit and hooked it around the anchor cable. A second lanyard gave her a more secure connection. If the correction was bad, the ride she planned was worse.

Cynthia examined the drive bot. It was a different model from the one on 723, but it was similar enough that she could make it work. The bot was a large, flat disk about two meters across and forty centimeters thick. Much of that space was for the cable mechanism that launched and retracted cables to grab the load. The cables themselves ended in little robotic claws that could grab a load or even "walk" around it for a better purchase. The rest of the bot consisted of computer controls, fuel tanks, the rocket engine, and—yes!—a gimbal mechanism. That would let her steer the rocket ingot without having to rely on multiple bots. On a good day she might manage multiple bots through the controls of this one, but today was not a good day. It was a very bad day, though she didn't feel very anxious about it. In fact, she felt even more numb. The suit must be pumping in more meds.

She switched the drive bot into test mode, and she was happy when testing lights came on for the other bots as well. That way they wouldn't counteract her course corrections. Then she explored the controls, first concentrating on the gimbals. She should be able to steer the ingot. Not well, but she had a pretty large target.

Next she tested the engine, just a puff. The exhaust spit out, and she recoiled in fear, losing her grip on the anchor cable; but she remained clear of the exhaust, and that was the important thing. Hot rocket exhaust scared her, though she had trouble remembering why. She just stared at the engine as the exhaust cut off, and she wondered what that meant.

*Oh, yeah, Refinery Station...* Cynthia remembered now, she wanted to reach the refinery, as far as possible from the Initiative shuttles. She wasn't sure exactly where it was, but she knew it was almost directly behind the ingot from her. And it was a pretty large target.

*Wait? Large target? Didn't I just think that?* It was getting harder to think anything at all. If this was going to work, Cynthia had to get moving while she still could. While she was floating free on her tethers, she peered around the tetrahedron as best she could and estimated an angle. Then she pulled herself back to the drive bot, punched her course into the gimbals, and fired the rocket.

This time she held on better. When she started to get dizzy, she wedged her fingers in between the cable and the metal. That was painful, but it kept her from bouncing into the rocket exhaust when she finally lost consciousness.

*The refinery radars picked up the incoming ingot, and warning lights and sirens sounded all through the area. The supervisors sent a team out to intercept the load, disable the drive bots, and bring it into the work room for inspection. Needless to say, what they found surprised them.*

*The woman identified as Patty Murphy came in and out of painful consciousness a few times before dying of third-degree burns, shock, and hypoxia due to a compromised space suit. The only recognizable words she said before dying were "Park Yerim".*

⊥

Inspector Park Yerim had ignored several calls from Bradley Stewart, the Earthside agent for Gray Interplanetary. Stewart was a regular caller to the Initiative offices, always with some complaint about the Initiative's operations in Jupiter space. Most of the complaints involved Kyle Baker and his security forces. Park had never liked Baker and she didn't trust him, so she suspected Gray City's complaints were legitimate; but without outside collaboration, Baker was the Initiative's chief investigator around Jupiter. So the Admiralty always routed Stewart's complaints back to Baker, and the circle continued.

Now, though, Stewart had called Internal Affairs for three days instead of calling the main office; and he kept asking for Park directly. Park thought that he was just trying to end-run around the system, and so she had ignored his calls—until he mentioned the name Patty Murphy.

"Get Mr. Stewart on the comm," Park said to Ensign Davis. "Tell him I will see him in my office at his earliest convenience."

Stewart's earliest convenience turned out to be ten minutes. Both the Internal Affairs office and Gray Interplanetary's Earthside office were located on Farport Station, just two rings apart. Davis showed Stewart in, brought in a carafe of water and two glasses, and left. Stewart set down his valise and sat in front of the desk, while Park stood behind it.

Park spoke first. "Thank you for showing up so soon, Mr. Stewart. You wanted to speak to me?"

Stewart shook his head. "No, Inspector, I think you want to talk to me." His hair was short and bristly, a mix of black with bits of silver, and his face had lines to match. Park knew from his dossier that he was in his late forties, a little younger than her, but he didn't show it. He clearly kept up on his therapy and exercise. He leaned over and poured some water into a glass, showing the practiced ease of someone who had spent a lot of time in the quarter gravity of the station. Then he took a swallow, smiled, and added, "And you wanted to talk to me as soon as I mentioned Patty Murphy. Who is she?"

Park tried not to show her anxiety. "First I have to know: where is she? Is she all right?"

Stewart shook his head again, but this time slowly, looking down at the floor. "She's... gone, Inspector."

*Cynthia!* Park sank into her chair, her mouth dropping open. "Are... you sure?" But she knew. Undercover work could be deadly.

Stewart looked up and read her expression. "I'm sorry, inspector. She was close to you?" He didn't get an answer, so he continued. "We have a body, and we have matching ID that says she was Patty Murphy. Since we don't know the deceased, we can't say if it's who you're thinking of or not. We do have a televisit set up, but... "

Park stood, her eyes narrowed. "But what? Show me!"

Stewart pushed his chair back. "I'm sorry, inspector. I can see you're hurt, and I don't want to make this worse for you. But you have to see our side of this. I'm here as a representative of Gray Interplanetary, remember, and GI and the Initiative have a number of open disputes with no sign of settlement any time soon. So you see—"

"I see extortion!" Park slammed her fist into the desk. "You're trying to use this—this death as leverage?"

Stewart stood. "No, never!" Despite Park's violence, Stewart seemed neither hostile nor afraid. "I just need you to understand how complicated this is. The Initiative's not very popular at Gray City right now, but I've done my research. I told my employers we can trust you, and... Well, do you understand what we mean when we say ours is a Trust Economy?"

Park nodded. She had studied the theory. It had come up in a number of contract disputes between the Jupiter settlements and Earth. The idea was somewhere between a market theory and a moral code. She couldn't swear she understood it, but she thought she could follow the discussion.

Stewart sat back down and continued. "All right, then understand: I'm adding you into my trust network, conditionally. So since I trust you and they trust *me*, they'll trust you—and I'm responsible if you let them down. So I have power to cooperate with you as I see fit. I'm not asking for anything in return, other than that you not give me a reason to regret this. And when you're ready, I hope you'll trust me as well."

Park sat as well. "I'll... try, Mr. Stewart."

"Then if you have televisit gear...?" Park nodded, and she reached into a desk drawer to pull out the goggles, earphones, and gloves of her TV. Stewart removed his own TV gear, and they both put theirs on. Then he pushed a button to invite her to the televisit, and she joined him in the waiting room, a virtual space where they appeared as images of themselves in a gray lounge with four doors numbered from one. "We have five 'rooms' in this televisit, four plus this waiting room. We prepared these rooms to give you as much information as we could in a single visit. We can record more if you need, but remember it's nearly eighty minutes round trip right now just to transmit and receive. That's not counting recording time, time spent waiting for a channel, and other delays. So let's start with these."

"I understand." Park's avatar nodded.

"And I suppose there's no way to postpone this. I think we should start with the morgue room, so that you can confirm her identity." Before Cynthia could even think about this, his avatar stepped through door two, pulling hers with it.

Beyond was a vivid three-dimensional recreation of a clean white room, with three metal tables and metal drawers set into the wall. If there were tables, there must be gravity, no doubt centripetal gravity. This room must be in the rotating Gravity Module at the far end of Refinery Station. Subtitles at the bottom of her vision read "Refinery Station Morgue".

In her thirty years with Initiative investigations, Park had seen dead bodies. Even dead agents and dead friends. Still she hesitated before walking to the one occupied table and looking down at the face of the body beneath the sheet.

Cynthia's face was still as delicate, still as beautiful as Park remembered, but more pale. Her skin was almost as light as her short blonde hair, and there was a blue tinge. She had lost a lot of blood, and a lot of oxygen. Her eyes were closed, and Park remembered watching her as she slept. But she wasn't sleeping now.

"It's her." Park turned away, but she couldn't leave the room while Stewart was there. Her televisit gear was slaved to his. So she removed her gear and returned to her office. Stewart removed his as well, but then he looked away as she wept.

Finally Park sniffed, removed a tissue from her desk, and dried her eyes. "I'm sorry," she said, her voice unsteady. "Yes, it's her."

Stewart didn't look at her, but he looked up. "Patty Murphy?"

Park hesitated. "Yes." Stewart did look at her then, but he quickly looked away. "I... You said there were three more rooms."

Stewart nodded. "Room 1 is a recreation of Murphy's arrival at the station, her treatment, and her... Well, you can see that if you want, but why don't I just describe it to you?" And so he did, telling everything Gray City knew about "Murphy", from her arrival to her last words. He didn't describe her death. Park was grateful for that small kindness.

She poured herself a glass of water and drank half of it before she felt ready to go on. "So that's why you called specifically for me."

"Uh-huh," Stewart said. "We listened to the recording to be sure what she had said, then we did a search on the name. There are hundreds of Park Yerims in the Solar System, thousands if you include close variations, but you're the most prominent among them. Especially after your handling of the Aldrin affair, which impressed a lot of independent spacers. And now you're in charge of Internal Affairs, trying to root out corruption in the Initiative, a goal we can all get behind. So I took a chance and called. I tried not to use her name until you gave me no other choice. I hope I haven't compromised some... operation?"

Stewart stared pointedly at Park with his last word. She stared back, unblinking. Even in her grief, she could maintain a cover when she had to. "I don't know what you're talking about, Mr. Stewart."

"I see." Stewart reached for his valise. "I'm very sorry for your loss, inspector. I think she was someone very important to you. Gray City extends its condolences." He rose to leave.

"Wait a minute! You mentioned two more rooms."

Stewart shook his head. "I'm sorry, inspector. I extended trust to you, in good faith. Now it appears that someone close to you—close to the head of internal affairs—tried to drive a valuable ingot into our far more valuable refinery. This is a matter of great concern to us, and I suspect it's a matter you might shed some light on. But when given a clear opportunity, you chose not to trust me. Our trust is not reciprocal, so it *must* collapse sooner or later. Better for us both if I end the relationship now, when we have nothing invested in it." He spoke his last lines almost formally, as if reading from a legal document.

Park rushed around the desk to block his path. "I'm sorry, I can't... I don't have the authority to..."

Stewart looked her in the eye. "You're the head of Internal Affairs. If that's not enough authority... Well, I can't help you. You've read my dossier as surely as I've read yours. I don't care about the Initiative, this is just us. Trust has to start with individuals, or it never starts. If you trust me, I may be able to help you. If you don't... then good day, inspector."

But he didn't move to leave, he just kept staring at her. Finally Park said, "I trust you, Mr. Stewart."

"Good!" Stewart sat back in his chair, and all tension slipped away like fog in a strong wind. "Then let's talk about the other two rooms. Room three is the autopsy room. Same as the morgue, but... Well, I'd rather not put you through that unless you think you need to see it."

Park sat down and looked at her desk. "No, I... No. But I have specialists who should see it."

"Sorry, no," Stewart said, prompting her to look up. "I trust you. I don't trust them, not yet. That's not how it works, this is too soon. We have reciprocal trust, conditional, but not a trust network. Not yet. I don't trust them just because you do." Park frowned, so Stewart added, "I can provide you summary reports, though." Park relaxed at that. "And room four is the personal effects room, everything we found with her. I'll let you look at that shortly, but I think you were going to explain your operation?"

Park frowned again. "We have reciprocal trust, but not a network?"

"Not yet."

"So I can trust you with this. And I can trust that you won't share it with anyone, not even your bosses at GI, because I haven't trusted them yet?"

"You're a fast learner." Stewart laughed, and Park even managed a half smile. "All right, trust me: this is only between us until you allow me to share it. You're tying my hands, inspector, but trust is built in small steps."

"Agreed." Park pressed a switch on her desk comp, and her door locked with a loud *click*. At the same time, shields and jammers powered up. All communications into or out of her office were now cut off. She breathed deeply, still uncomfortable sharing this information, but she had to do it. "The person known as Patty Murphy was in fact my agent, Cynthia Allen. Also a close friend." Park didn't say how close. If trust was built in small steps, they weren't to that step yet. "We haven't been blind to your complaints, Mr. Stewart, nor to those from others in the Jupiter system. We were sure that there were real problems there, and that someone on this end was helping to cover them up. So we sent in Allen, one of our top undercover agents, to gather the evidence to put Kyle Baker and his cronies in front of a court martial."

"I see," Stewart said. "And since Baker is still in charge out there, I assume she had no evidence at the time of her death."

Park shook her head. "I think she did. She was close, she said. It was very difficult to get messages back and forth. Besides her having to maintain her cover, you know how difficult it is to arrange private conversations between here and Jupiter." Secrecy was very difficult between Earth and Jupiter. You could encrypt your signal so no one could tap in; but at those distances, even a tight beam signal expanded so much that the entire Jupiter system heard it. Or the entire Earth-Luna system for messages back to Earth. Listeners might not know what you said, but they knew you said *something*.

"So how was she planning to get you the evidence?" Stewart asked.

"Her assignment was complete, and she was coming home. She was just going to bring it back as a memory chip in her personal effects."

Stewart looked up at that. "A memory chip? Maybe we should visit room four. You need to see something."

Park looked at her privacy switch. "We can't yet. I've got the room shielded. I can lift the shields, but I trust you not to mention anything of what you just heard while we're not under shield."

Stewart nodded, and Park turned off the shield. Then they donned their televisit gear, returned to the waiting room, and entered room four: a room much like the morgue, but with smaller tables. On one was spread Cynthia's clothes. Her pants were charred, and Park didn't look too closely at the stains on them.

On another table was an Initiative spacesuit, the legs badly burned. The suit's auto-sealing system had tried to patch the holes, but several cracks in the fused material showed where the seals had failed.

On a third table were scattered tools and spare parts, along with an empty toolbox. And on a fourth was Cynthia's computer. Park didn't recognize it—Cynthia had been too smart to take any of her own gear under cover—but it was the style Cynthia preferred. Instead of a gauntlet comp like Park wore, it was an old-style console unit with a keyboard and a detachable display unit.

Stewart's avatar picked up the virtual computer, flipped it over, and opened the memory compartment. The televisit system followed these commands, showing its virtual representation of the inside of the computer. "Two cards are missing," Stewart said. "I'll bet your—" Stewart paused, looking for a way to continue while the room was unshielded. "—your item of interest was on them."

Park wasn't so sure. The evidence couldn't amount to more than one card, could it? She took the computer, looked it over, and ran her fingers over the cards. Two missing out of thirty-two; but if Cynthia were hiding data on the cards, would she hide it on two adjacent cards? Or did she just lose one? Or were the missing cards a complete red herring?

Ever since she had been a young girl in Korea, Park had counted things: stairs, trees, pebbles, people. Some called this an obsession, but for her it was normal. As her fingers brushed the cards, it was natural for her to count: a group of seven, a gap of two, and a group of twenty-three.

Seven, twenty-three? A message to Park? 7/23 had been the day they had broken up. It wasn't acrimonious, but Cynthia had insisted: as long as they were together, she was sure that Park wouldn't send her on dangerous assignments. So they had cried, and they had parted. And now Park wished for the power to take that all back, to do exactly what Cynthia had feared: to protect Cynthia even though it held back her career.

But seven twenty-three had to be a coincidence. The dark side of always counting was that Park saw patterns and repetitions everywhere, and she had learned not to act on them. But she still saw them.

Stewart's avatar was staring at hers oddly, and Park realized she had been silent for a long time. "You're probably right, Mr. Stewart. Did you find any other cards around?"

"No."

"And these other cards? What's on them?"

"We don't know," Stewart answered. Park looked at him, surprised. "It's another of our customs. The personal effects are property of the deceased, and the deceased can't extend trust. Until their next of kin approves or a court orders it, we don't pry into their personal data. We can look and describe surface contents, but nothing deeper."

Park liked that answer, even if it frustrated her right now. The trust rights of the deceased seemed like a pretty good custom. The dead deserved their privacy.

And speaking of privacy... Park removed her gear and hit the privacy button on her comp. Stewart shook his head as he was abruptly thrust back into reality. "I'll get you that court order, just give me time," Park said. "But for now, let's assume the missing card or cards have our evidence. Where could they be now?"

Stewart removed his gear as well, and they sat in silence for several minutes, thinking. Finally Stewart spoke up. "I think a better question is: Where do we *want* the cards to be right now?" Park stared. "First, they're not on the station. We—well, corporate 'we,' since I'm here on Farport—we searched the station thoroughly, every place she went in the time she was with us. It's not there.

"Second, we don't want them to be on Baker's transport, which is where she must've come from. If they're there, they're lost. Give it up.

"Third is just as bad: open space. 'Needle in a haystack' doesn't begin to describe the odds against our finding them there.

"So that leaves us with one good option. It's either that, or we can give up."

Park asked, "And what is that?"

Stewart responded, but not with a direct answer. "Inspector, I was supposed to wait to ask you this until I was sure I could trust your answer. Your agent—and yes, we assumed that's what she was—approached our station from our shipping queue. Analysis of radar data shows she disturbed at least a couple orbits. So my question to you is: inspector, why was your agent tampering with our shipments to Earth?"

They both knew what the answer was. "But which shipment? Do you know?"

Stewart pulled open a file on his comp. "I have here the shipping records of that day, including the radar data from the shipping queue monitors. I am at liberty to share them with anyone I trust." He paused as Park looked at him. "But this is critical: some of this data isn't ours. It's the property of shippers who contracted with us to deliver loads for them. Some of them may see this data as containing their trade secrets. So if I trust you with this, I'm extending trust that someone else offered me. I can't describe how devastating it would be if you violated this. My reputation would be ruined throughout the settlements. And yours? Well, if you think the Initiative has problems out there now, you have no idea what problems are. So… do you want to see this data? Or would you rather not?"

Park thought carefully. She wanted the data, of course! But the responsibility… She was starting to grasp how complex this Trust Economy was; but more important, she was starting to grasp how much she didn't understand it yet, how easily she might make a simple error and break a trust without meaning to.

But she had another trust: one to her agent, and her former lover. She had to follow through on that. "Show me the data, Mr. Stewart. I won't disappoint you."

Stewart smiled, and he held his hands up, his left index finger pointing up and his right across, forming a T. "Under trust, then." He showed her the data, with special attention on those ingots that had been disturbed. Most of those had been caught in the drive bot exhaust of other ingots, in a giant chain reaction of small correctional bursts. One, though, Stewart was able to identify as most likely the first ingot to deviate from its orbit.

When Park saw the shipping number with its hidden 7/23, she tapped her finger on the screen. "Let's go get it."

⚓

Despite Park's sense of urgency, they couldn't leave immediately. Or anything close to immediately. It took nearly a week for Stewart to persuade her. "It's no good trying to go to the rock. We have to let it come to us."

"But I can authorize the fuel and budget for a trip *now*."

"Not this much." Stewart shook his head. "It's not about fuel and budget, it's about orbital mechanics. To leave now and try to rendezvous with that ingot would require so much delta V that no ship you have could do it. Oh, we could intercept the ingot, but at a relative velocity so high, we'd be two bullets passing in the night. All we could do would be to wave goodbye. That's assuming we could see it."

"Why couldn't we see it?" Stewart made a T with his index fingers, and she added, "Under trust." With Stewart's help, she was slowly learning the "secret handshakes" of the settlements.

Stewart smiled. "It's in black orbit." When she stared at him, he continued. "When you're shipping valuable cargoes of metal with no escort, you're tempting pirates to steal them. Or just customers to pick them up while claiming the loads got lost. So we launch them in orbits that we never register with anyone. Only the shipper knows. And we paint them with a low-albedo coating. Plus our smiths forge them in stealth shapes to minimize radar reflection. That's quite an art form in the settlements."

"So they're practically invisible."

"Uh-huh. And their transponders are locked down. They only wake up when they receive the right coded signal. A load in black orbit could pass right under our nose, and we wouldn't know it was there unless we were shining a light in the right direction at the right time. I recommend we wait for the client to pick it up, meet them, and get the evidence that way."

"We can't do that."

"Why not?" Stewart asked. Park made the T again. "Under trust."

"Under trust: Baker has allies here, and we're not sure who they are. Many in the Initiative, but also in the transport companies. We have to get to that evidence before anyone else does. So that means we have to wait for it to come to us, yes?"

"No, we can meet it en route. But we have to let it get closer first."

⸸

"I don't see anything." Sixteen months later, Park clung to a handhold near the ship's port, floating in the microgravity, and pressed her face to the glass. Her own faint reflection showed there, her dark hair showing a few strands of gray but her face still unlined. Through the reflection she saw a vast field of stars and other points of light. But she saw no sign of Shipment GI12002-00723.

Sixteen months. The pain of Cynthia's death was still there, but now a dull ache, not a sharp stab. Sixteen months of work on other projects and launch prep for this mission had helped her to adjust. She still wanted justice for Cynthia, but the urgent need for immediate vengeance had passed.

And in sixteen months, she had learned to trust Bradley Stewart, and to like him as well. That was good, because this ship was too tiny for people who disliked each other. And it was just the two of them: Stewart had insisted that his trust only extended to her, not to any of her staff. Not yet. Since he had to pilot the ship, she would have to go find the evidence. So she had spent sixteen months brushing up on her long-neglected EVA training.

Stewart had warned her that the ingot of refined nickel would be impossible to spot, but she had long since passed through impatience and into boredom. Looking out the port gave her *something* to do, which was more than she could say for the rest of the voyage. They had spent far too long in this ship with its sweaty air, tasteless pasty meal bars, and microgravity. Park wanted to do *something* besides wait for orbital mechanics to deliver them to their rendezvous.

At least the microgravity no longer made her nauseous. On Park's first trip to space she had learned a very embarrassing lesson in rocketry and conservation of momentum as her own vomit had propelled her across a departure bay. That was nearly three decades past and two AUs from where she floated now, but Park still recalled the taste, still recalled closing her eyes and curling up and wishing she would die and put an end to the torment. None of her space experiences had been as bad as that first one, but she doubted she would ever be comfortable in space.

Unlike her, Stewart moved around the ship with practiced ease. He clung to a strap with one hand, munched a meal bar—he actually *liked* the things!—and studied the radar display. "Nope," he said around a mouthful of soy buds and fake cocoa. "You won't see it. Not yet. But it's a great view, isn't it?"

She liked Stewart, but sometimes his nonchalance infuriated her. Interplanetary transport was a slow, patient business, and he was well-suited to it. She would never be. "So how soon *will* we see it?"

"Not sure."

"Not sure? You launched the thing. That's even a Gray load. You should know the precise orbit!"

Stewart took another bite. "Not precisely. Cynthia perturbed its trajectory, and even tiny perturbations add up over five AUs. Plus the drive bots make minor course corrections. An orbit is like an integral function: there are an infinite number of solutions, but only a handful of right answers. Sometimes only one, or none. We have to scan a range of possible orbits. Then another range if that one doesn't pan out. Then..." He tossed her a meal bar, and she caught it in her left hand. "We have enough air, fuel, and food to let us search for a long time."

Park looked down at the bar. "Food?" But she unwrapped it and took a bite.

⚓

The air was three days more stale, and Park was three days sicker of meal bars, when Stewart shouted, "Thar she blows!" He pointed at his comp screen. A small dot there was labeled Gl12002-00723. "The transponder is awake and signaling."

For the first time in over a year, Park felt a rush of excitement. All the waiting was finally paying off! And Cynthia's death would mean something. "How long to rendezvous?"

Stewart adjusted the ship's controls. "Almost a day," he said. "Don't rush to suit up, but it wouldn't hurt to do another suit check."

⚓

Thirteen hours later, Stewart checked his screen again. "Uh-oh..."

Park looked up from her suit. She had done three pre-checks already, and was working on her fourth. It gave her something to do. "Uh-oh? What uh-oh?"

Stewart pointed at the screen. "The shipment's getting farther away."

"What?" Park let go of the suit and floated over to the pilot station as the suit bounced back into the maintenance pod. "How is that possible?"

Stewart frowned, stared at the screen, and said nothing. Park grabbed a handgrip to stop herself, and then she pulled him to face her. "Hey. This is me." She made a T with her fingers. "Remember?"

Stewart shook his head, his body wobbling in response. "Yeah, but this is..." He let go of his grip and made a T with his whole hands. "This is big. 'Gray Interplanetary trade secret' big. I'm not authorized to share this information with *anyone*."

Park looked him in the eyes. "I understand, but we're not going to get that evidence at this rate. If you want me to help Gray City with their complaints... If you want me to stop Baker and his gang..." She made a whole-hands T. "You're going to have to trust me."

Stewart smiled, a shaky, uncertain upturn at the corners of his mouth. "All right. But remember: trade secret." He took a deep breath. "You know from the shipping code, GI, that that load's not from just any mining operation. It's from us, Gray Interplanetary, and we have the best load security tools in the Solar System. We haven't lost a load in nearly a decade. We pioneered black orbit techniques, and our stealth bodies have the smallest radar profiles around."

He hesitated, so Park said, "And...?"

"And our drive bots might look like standard industrial models, but we've actually found a way to hide an AI in their control units. A small AI, not very bright, but bright enough to steer a load away from any unauthorized vessel that approaches."

"But we're authorized! We have the transponder key."

Stewart nodded. "We have the key. It woke up and responded. But since then the AI must have evaluated and declared us a threat. First it took a station-keeping trajectory, and I didn't realize it wasn't getting closer for a while. Then when I did, I accelerated; and the ingot accelerated more. It's pulling away from us."

"Then let's catch it!" Park said. "Our engines have to be better than drive bots pushing a giant mass of metal, right?"

"If the AI were merely trying to evade us while keeping to its course, yes," Phil said. "But it's not. We've 'scared' it, and it's now heading for its alternate destination."

"Alternate destination?" Stewart Teed his hands, and Park understood. She answered with another T. "All right, trade secret, I know."

This time Stewart hesitated longer. "Gray Interplanetary has a depot station at LaGrange point 4."

Park frowned. "No, that can't be right. The Magnus Metals refinery is at L4."

Stewart smiled. "Not the Earth-Moon L4. Sol-Earth."

"Oh." Then Park thought about that further. "Ohhhh... So that ingot is headed sixty degrees ahead of Earth."

"Uh-huh. There it will match course with a tug, and it will be reprogrammed and routed back to Earth on a new course. It will arrive late, but within the window of the contract. I can have someone at the depot look for the evidence when the load arrives."

"No. Sorry, I trust you, not them. We'll go with that plan only if we have no choice. Can't you catch that ingot?"

"I can try, but it's going to be a rough ride. The AI will try to evade us."

Park thought of another plan. "You must have an override code, right? Just shut the AI down."

Stewart shook his head. "I already tried that before I gave you the news. It was the obvious solution, but it didn't work. The AI rejected the code. Worse, it shut off its radio."

"Why would it do that?"

"Inspector, the one thing I've learned never to ask of an AI is 'Why?' But if I had to guess, I would guess that the AI has detected your evidence chip and assumed it was an effort to tamper with its systems. That would put it into a paranoid security mode where any questionable activity would raise its suspicions. That's probably why it saw us as a threat in the first place."

Park slammed a fist against a panel, and then regretted it as she spun away. Stewart grabbed her arm and stopped her, and she calmed down enough to say, "So we have no choice. We have to catch it."

"Yep. I'm plotting a course now. Strap in!"

"Give me a minute so I can stow my suit."

⬇

Park floated in the airlock of Stewart's transport and looked at GI12002-00723. The large nickel bagel had changed course several times as they had approached, but Stewart had expertly matched it every time. Now it was visibly moving relative to the transport, but not too fast. She activated her comm. "How's our velocity?"

"Delta v is under two meters per second. I doubt we'll get better."

"All right, here I go." Park swallowed hard and leaped into darkness.

Even as she flew, though, the ingot changed course. A burst of exhaust pushed it to port. That exhaust frightened Park. She still remembered Cynthia's blackened spacesuit, but she couldn't let fear stop her now. She fired her maneuvering unit and drew closer to the ingot. The noise from the MU surprised her: space was supposed to be silent, but the hard elements of her suit conducted some of the vibrations straight to her helmet.

Stewart spoke in her ear, shouting to be heard over the MU. "You know what to do, right?"

Park cut off the MU and coasted. Then she nodded, a pointless gesture since Stewart couldn't see inside her helmet. "I remove the foreign memory card, and you give the AI a reset command. Then I wait for you to make pickup. Now quiet, please, so I can concentrate."

The MU radar had trouble reading range and rate from the ingot. Whoever designed that bagel shape had done a great job. Park could see it was closer than the radar thought, so she turned off the radar. She would have to eyeball it from here.

As she looked through the suit controls, though, she noticed a flashing yellow light: EXCESSIVE AIR USAGE. She switched to her environment display, and she felt panic start to rise. Her air pressure was down to 93%. That was way too low. At that rate, she had only forty minutes before she risked hypoxia.

Park got on the comm. "Stewart, does your AI have some way to scramble suit systems?"

"What? No, it's too limited for that. It's a navigation and security unit, but it doesn't have cyber attack capabilities. What's wrong?"

"My air's dropping." Park checked her meter and was relieved that the number hadn't changed. Yet. "I'm trying to figure out why."

"That's crazy. You inspected your suit. I saw you."

"Yes, I—" But then Park remembered that Stewart's bad news had interrupted her last inspection. Had she missed anything? That made sense. "Damn, maybe not. Don't worry, I have twenty minutes at least. That should be plenty, right?"

But as if answering her, the AI picked that moment to try another trick. Two drive units fired this time, neither close enough to make her nervous; but they were on opposite sides of the ingot. Suddenly the metal bagel started to spin on its axis, fast enough to be a danger. And even if she somehow got hold of it, that spin might throw her off.

Park pulsed the MU to slow her approach, but even as she did so, her air meter dropped a percent. If she held off too long, she might as well give up.

As if reading her mind, Stewart came on the comm. "Inspector, come back. It's over."

"No. It's not over, not yet. Stewart, you know what this MU can do. If I can get to the center of the bagel, the centripetal force won't be so bad. I need you to use the ship's radar to time this rotation and tell me when to make a run for it."

"Park, no, I can't—"

Park reflexively Teed her hands. "Stewart, I trust you on this. Do it."

"All right." Stewart looked at his screen. "Ready. Program for maximum thrust on the vector I'm sending now, and switch the MU to voice control. On my mark, MU engage. Annnnnd... Mark!"

At Stewart's command, the MU *leaped* toward the ingot. Park was sure the spinning bagel would smash into her; but the near side spun ahead of her, and the far side was still catching up. She flew straight into the hole and slammed hard against the metal. The impact dazed her, but the thrust from the MU kept her in place long enough for her to grab an anchor. "MU off!" she shouted, and the engine cut off before it could thrust her back into space.

As soon as the engine cut out, Park heard another sound, an alert buzz from her suit controller. She looked at the display: AIR HOSE DISCONNECT.

*Oh, shit!* That was a nasty malfunction, but an easy one to repair under normal circumstances. These circumstances *weren't* normal. With the AI trying to buck her from the ingot, there was no way for her to do emergency repairs. She had only the air in her suit: fifteen minutes in theory, less than ten the way she was exerting herself.

"Park, are you all right? Your suit—"

"Busy!" she shouted. "You may have to pick me up!"

The AI had drive bots, but Park had an advantage of her own: the ingot was almost pure nickel, meaning it was very attractive to magnets. She pulled three electromagnetic clamps from her belt. The first was tethered to her midsection, and she clamped that to the ingot first as an anchor. Then she used the other two, one in each hand, to crawl across the metal: left, right, move the anchor; left, right, anchor;

left, right...

When Park rounded the inner surface of the bagel, she came within view of two drive bots. One of them fired, and the ingot spun faster and more erratically. The bots fired randomly, and eventually Park lost her grip on the clamps; but the anchor clamp caught her. She used one hand to pull herself back on the tether while she scrambled with the other to grab a clamp.

When Park again had a firm grip on the clamps, she resumed her pace: left, right, anchor; left, right, anchor... At last she pulled herself across the spinning ingot and up to a drive bot. The first thing she did was Stewart's idea: she pushed the button to put the bot into test mode. Just like he had promised, lights lit up for the other bots as well as they all went into test mode. She couldn't stop the ingot's spin, but at least the AI couldn't make things any worse.

Park examined the drive bot. This one had no memory bank. It was a slave bot, not the controller bot. She was disappointed, but not surprised: it would take too much luck for her to land right next to the controller, and she wasn't having much luck on this flight.

That made her think of her dwindling air, and that wasn't a good idea. Her head was pounding, and that was an early indicator of hypoxia, but she didn't have time for that. So she shoved the thought back and started crawling to the next bot. Left, right, anchor...

As Park got closer, she saw movement. Was that the hypoxia setting in? No, she blinked and looked again, and there definitely was movement. After staring for several seconds, she realized what it was: one of the anchor claws at the end of an anchor cable was crawling across the ingot to her. She saw a second moving claw as well, and the drive bot was starting to rattle on the ingot. The loss of two anchors was a risky move. Park guessed that meant that this was the controller bot, and the AI was pulling out all the stops.

Park took two deep breaths, air supply be damned. "You want me, bot? One on one, hand to hand? You got it! Come on!"

As if summoned, the first claw skittered toward her from her left; but as she reached to grab it or punch it, it skittered away. And while she was distracted by that one, the other sped in from the right and clawed at her suit before fleeing as well. She heard a brief rush of air, precious air she couldn't afford to lose, before her suit's seals closed the hole.

Now how much air did she have left? Five minutes? Three? Her heart raced, her head was ready to split. She needed to finish this.

"Come on!" Park shouted, wincing as her head throbbed. This time the right claw made the feint, though she was sure the left would soon follow. Instead of the claws, she reached for her magnetic clamps, released them from the ingot, and held them out in front of her. When the right claw drew close, she activated the right clamp, and the claw's efforts to pull away were in vain. The clamp pulled it in and locked it down, and she slammed clamp and claw down to the ingot. The left claw immediately veered away, but Park leaped after it, grabbed it with the clamp, and slammed it down before her anchor tether could stop her.

Park lay against the ingot, panting. *No. Can't afford to pant...* But she couldn't stop, so she had to get moving with a new routine now: grab a cable, move the anchor clamp; grab a cable, move the anchor clamp; grab a cable... And she was up to the drive bot.

Immediately the gimbal spun and the rocket fired. Test mode apparently didn't apply to the controller bot. Park couldn't tell if the AI were trying to shake her off or burn her off, she just needed it to *stop!* She saw the memory compartment and she opened it up, but there was no way she could tell which card was Cynthia's while the ingot bucked and spun beneath her.

*Screw it!* She started pulling cards and sticking them in her pouch. All of them. And at some point the AI was lost with the cards, and the drive shut down. "You're dead, you bastard! Dead! You hear me?"

Those were her last words before hypoxia claimed her.

⚓

Park woke with a massive headache, but at least she woke. On the whole, that was good news, but right now "good" was relative.

She was strapped into her travel couch. IVs fed fluids into her arm, and an oxygen mask covered her face. Intellectually she knew the oxygen was odorless, but she still thought it smelled sweet.

Stewart was across the ship in the pilot station. As Park's headache faded, she wanted to know how things had worked out. She removed the mask and said, "Stewart."

"Ah! Inspector!" Stewart locked down his controls and floated over to her. "It's good to see you."

"What... happened?"

Stewart shook his head. "Too many details. Save it for after you get a good night's sleep. But once you shut down the AI, I picked you up— I was already in my MU nearby—and I used test mode to stabilize the ingot. It's back on its original course, and no one will ever know we were here."

Park smiled at that. "And the evidence?"

Stewart smiled back, reached into his pocket, and pulled out a clear pouch full of cards. "You did it, inspector. Cynthia can rest easy now."

Park reached out for the pouch, but Stewart held back. "But you know, we don't know which card is hers. And the other cards in here are chock full of Gray Interplanetary trade secrets—including a very resourceful AI." Then Stewart Teed his hands and handed the pouch to Park.

She made the T response. "Under trust." And then she fell back asleep.

# PUBLICATION HISTORY

"Scramble" Copyright © 2015 by Martin L. Shoemaker. Originally published by Digital Science Fiction.

"The Night We Flushed the Old Town" Copyright © 2011 by Martin L. Shoemaker. Originally published by Digital Science Fiction.

"Father-Daughter Outing" Copyright © 2011 by Martin L. Shoemaker. Originally published by Digital Science Fiction.

"Not Another Vacuum Story" Copyright © 2012 by Martin L. Shoemaker.

"Sense of Wonder" Copyright © 2012 by Martin L. Shoemaker.

"Not Close Enough" Copyright © 2013 by Martin L. Shoemaker. Originally published in Analog Science Fiction and Fact.

"Racing to Mars" Copyright © 2015 by Martin L. Shoemaker. Originally published in Analog Science Fiction and Fact.

"Snack Break" Copyright © 2017 by Martin L. Shoemaker.

"Unrefined" Copyright © 2015 by Martin L. Shoemaker. Originally published in *L. Ron Hubbard Presents Writers of the Future Volume 31*.

"Black Orbit" Copyright © 2016 by Martin L. Shoemaker. Originally published in Analog Science Fiction and Fact.

Cover design by Luca Oleastri.

Cover image: "Space Station and Shuttle Photo". Copyright © by Luca Oleastri (Innovari). Licensed through Dreamstime.com.

# OTHER FICTION
# BY MARTIN L. SHOEMAKER

*Family Secrets.* A short story collection.

*Lost in the Fog.* A novella.

*A Most Auspicious Star.* A novella.

*Killing Buddy.* A short story.

# NONFICTION
# BY MARTIN L. SHOEMAKER

*Ulterior Motive Lounge: UML, 80s Flicks, and Bunny Slippers.*

# ABOUT MARTIN L. SHOEMAKER

Martin L. Shoemaker is a programmer who writes on the side... or maybe it's the other way around. Programming pays the bills, but his second-place story in the Jim Baen Memorial Writing Contest earned him lunch with Buzz Aldrin. Programming never did that! His Clarkesworld story "Today I Am Paul" received the Washington Science Fiction Society's Small Press Award, and was also nominated for a Nebula. It has been reprinted in *Year's Best Science Fiction: Thirty-third Annual Edition* (edited by Gardner Dozois), *The Best Science Fiction of the Year: Volume One* (edited by Neil Clarke), *The Year's Best Science Fiction and Fantasy 2016* (edited by Rich Horton), and *The Year's Top Ten Tales of Science Fiction 8* (edited by Allan Kaster). It has been translated into French, Hebrew, Czech, Polish, German, Chinese, Italian, and Croatian. It is also the opening to *Today I Am Carey*, a novel coming soon from Baen Books.

Others of Martin's stories have appeared in Analog, Galaxy's Edge, Digital Science Fiction, Forever Magazine, Writers of the Future Volume 31, *The Jim Baen Memorial Award: The First Decade*, and *Year's Best Military and Adventure SF 4*. His novella "Murder on the Aldrin Express" was reprinted in *Year's Best Science Fiction Thirty-First Annual Collection* and in *Year's Top Short SF Novels 4*. His novelette "Racing to Mars" received the Analog Analytical Laboratory Award.

You can learn more about Martin's fiction at *http://Shoemaker.Space*.

Made in the USA
Monee, IL
05 January 2020